THE PALACE GARDEN

THE PALACE GARDEN

Katharine Gordon

This first world edition published in Great Britain 2000 by
SEVERN HOUSE PUBLISHERS LTD of
9–15 High Street, Sutton, Surrey SM1 1DF.
This first world edition published in the USA 2000 by
SEVERN HOUSE PUBLISHERS INC of
595 Madison Avenue, New York, N.Y. 10022.

British Library Cataloguing in Publication Data

Gordon, Katharine
    The palace garden
    1.   Love stories
    I.   Title
    823.9'14 [F]

    ISBN 0-7278-5600-6

Typeset by Palimpsest Book Production Ltd.,
Polmont, Stirlingshire, Scotland.
Printed and bound in Great Britain by
MPG Books Ltd, Bodmin, Cornwall.

THE PALACE GARDEN

Prologue

M id-summer in Chikor. Even up in those high valleys summer days were hot – and very long.

In Chikor, in the old palace, the women of the Zenana were bored. One day after another went by like shadows, with nothing exciting to mark them. When a fortune-teller called, he was made welcome, and taken in to the Zenana. Quickly veiling themselves – for even if he was old, he was a man – the women sat round the fortune-teller demanding to be told of the future.

He told all of them much the same story: happiness, riches, of course, good marriages for the unmarried girls, and many fine sons for the matrons.

He lit a small fire in the earthen dish, on which he dropped a pinch of powder taken from his pouch and then as the acrid smoke rose he fanned it with a fan shaped like a leaf, a fan of peacock feathers. The smoke billowed up and blew across the unveiled face of the Choti Begum Zeena, the spoiled daughter of the ruler, who was sitting amongst the women watching him. She was bright eyed, seven years old and far from interested in fortunes. She was tugging at the arm of her maid Chunia, urging her to come away – it was time to go riding, the horses were waiting. The child's shining eyes

1

caught the gaze of the fortune-teller, and the man suddenly broke off what he was saying. Now he spoke in a different voice, as the smoke rose and coiled across the room.

"I hear music. A love song in a garden. Two hearts that meet – and a rose – a white rose that is a signal. I see a long journey, and a long love, a love that never dies—"

He stopped and the women waited and then began to clamour, "Go on, old man, who has this fortune, tell us—"

"She who accepts this future must be strong of heart. I see sorrow and parting, and a broken trust. Have a care, lady. Turn away from the rose, or the music will turn to mourning. I see a tomb that is not a tomb, and a sorrow that is unending."

The women were silent, the fire had died down, and the old man sat looking at the dead ashes in the dish. Chunia, the Choti Begum's servant took the child out of the room. Zeena was not thinking of the fortune-teller – she had not listened to his words. Roses, love songs and long journeys meant little in her young life. She wanted to go out for her ride.

But Chunia, her young maid, remembered every word the man had said. That night she put a small blue-stoned pendant on a chain around Zeena's neck, and told her she must wear it always. "It will keep the evil eye away—"

Zeena was quite happy to wear this pendant, as all the horses in the ruler's stables had blue beads on their harnesses to keep the evil eye from them.

A week later the rains came to Chikor, and the air grew cooler, and everyone forgot the fortune-teller.

But Chunia did not forget.

One

It was the night of the full moon. The harvest moon, spilling gold over the roofs of the city, paling the oil lamps that outlined every building and shone from every window. This was a night of festivity, the night of the great Durbar in Madore, the last Durbar of the season. The end of summer.

In spite of the clear sky and the moon's golden light, there was a sharp chill in the air. An evening wind that whispered of winter. Soon, the wind whispered, the snows would creep down the shoulders of the mountains to the north. The high passes would be closed – it was time for the visitors, the rulers of the northern hill states, to begin the return to their mountain forts and palaces. Soon the exodus would start, the long journey back across the lower hills and up over the passes. The annual journey home to the hill states, the hidden valleys of Chikor and Pakodi, Lambagh, Panchghar and Jungdah. The town palaces would soon be empty and dark, and the city of Madore would be quiet for another year. But not yet. This was an important night. The last festivity.

The Zenana, the women's quarter of the Chikor Mahal was throbbing with excited voices, high and sweet, like

3

birds calling. The women were preparing for the evening. Although they would not be mingling with the guests in the garden, they would still share in the celebrations, looking down from their screened balconies above the gardens, watching everything. There would be guests up there, too: wives of the rulers who were attending the party and some of the wives of the English guests, such as the Resident, his staff and the officers of the British Regiment stationed in Madore. The wives of these men would come up to the purdah balconies for a time, before going down into the gardens to join their husbands.

This was a night when all the most beautiful *saris* and *gargaras* would be worn – and the most important jewels were brought from the *toshkhana*, the strong rooms. Ropes of pearls and heavily gemmed necklets and earrings would adorn the Begums and ranis.

The two youngest Begums, Zeena, the daughter of Sadik Khan of Chikor, and her cousin, Gulrukh, daughter of Atlar Khan, ruler of Pakodi, were already dressed and bejewelled and had hurried up to the main balcony. They sat close together on heaped cushions, as close to the marble screen as they could be, and peered down through the carvings, to make sure that they had chosen the best viewpoint.

"Ah – this is perfect. From here we can see everything. Oh how I shall miss this when I go home. Only three more weeks, then no parties, no entertainment for months – only the birth of my child, if Allah hears me and sends me a son. There will be celebrations for that of course . . . and then your marriage—"

Gulrukh bit her lip and glanced side-long at Zeena, who

frowned and said, "Speak of the birth of your child, and those celebrations – but please do not speak of the celebrations for my marriage. To me it is as if you speak of the end of my life."

"In the name of Allah the Compassionate, do not ill-wish yourself, Zeena! How can you say such things!"

"Well, it is true. I shall be taken from everything I know and love. I will be living with strangers miles away, a prisoner. I would rather be dead in any case."

"Zeena, marriage is not like that. I am married, and I am happy and contented in my life. I think that my life only began when I entered my marriage."

Zeena shook her head. "It is different for you. You knew your husband, your families were friends . . . Oh let us not speak any more of this. I try not to think of my marriage."

"Well, I wish that you *would* think about it with good sense. Marriage is our destiny . . ."

"Then why can we not choose our husbands? Must there be nothing but money and land, and breeding? We are sold into marriages to suit our families, as if we have no hearts."

"What is this nonsense? You have made something out of nothing – of course there is love, Zeena – and you will love your husband."

"Oh? Is that so? How am I to love a man I do not know? A man I have never seen – a stranger?"

"Love follows after marriage. As you enter your married life, and learn to know your husband and find your place in his life, love comes to you."

"I see. When Tariq Khan approaches my bed and I have nowhere to hide from him, you are telling that then I will

5

find love? For that gorilla? You heard what those two women from Sagpurna said yesterday—"

"Are you going to be so dull-witted that you pay attention to words spoken by two jealous old women who are looking to catch husbands for their unmarried daughters, and are angry that my mother had caught Tariq Khan for you? They are jealous of your good fortune!"

Zeena looked at her cousin disbelievingly. "Gulrukh, when you say things like that I find it hard to trust you. A girl so young, who had to be carried from her marriage bed because she could not walk – her body torn and despoiled—"

"It was not her marriage bed, she was a concubine – and why would those two old hens know what had happened to her? Were they hidden in the bed curtains?"

"A concubine feels as we do, she is a woman too – she bleeds as we do. How can you speak as if what happens to her is unimportant? This girl killed herself in spite of the watch kept on her. She swallowed her earrings and died. Everyone in Jaidkot, and Sagpurna later, is speaking of it – and you say I am fortunate to be given to this man?"

"Zeena-jan, I think you are looking for horrors because you do not wish to marry. I do not understand how you can believe such stories. Do you think your father would give you to such a man? Or that my mother, your loving aunt, would agree to such a marriage? I do not understand you. It is only this year that you have begun to make so much trouble. Before this year you were content with the plans for your marriage – what has happened to make you as you are now?"

Zeena looked away from Gulrukh's searching eyes. "Perhaps I had not heard the tales about my intended lord. Perhaps I am a year older and know what I want. They should have married me off last year when I was only sixteen, and knew nothing. Oh never mind what has changed my mind! Do not let us speak of this any more. Leave it, Gulrukh."

"Very well, I will leave it but you should stop thinking about it too – your marriage is not taking place for another six months. The way you brood about it, anyone would think you were in love with your groom – and I know that is not so! Why do you think about it so much? Marriage and love go together—"

"Marriage and love?" Zeena laughed. It was not a pretty laugh. It sounded too harsh and bitter to come from her beautiful young throat. Her lips curled as she said, "Love? How can I be in love with a man I have never seen? No indeed, you are right – I am not in love. Not with Tariq Khan!"

There had been a hesitation in her voice. Gulrukh noticed it and pounced at once.

"Zeena, are you telling me that you are in love with someone else? Who? How can you be, when did you meet him—"

"I have met dreams, that is all. How can I be in love, how can any one of us know anything about love when we never see a man unless he is a member of the family: a brother, a father, an uncle – or a brother-in-law. Do not worry, Gulrukh-jan, I am not making dove's eyes at your husband!"

"Then who do you think you love?"

"Oh foolish Gulrukh. Do you think I would tell you?"

"You are teasing me, Zeena. There is no one – is there?"

"But of course there is no one – but—"

"But? But what?"

"Well, one's eyes may stray sometimes. Or our hearts

7

may stray in dreams. I am not in love, but I would like to be. I would like to have someone to share my dreams, someone who loves me. Oh, Gulrukh, I would choose someone wonderful – if only I could choose."

"Of course you want someone to love – we all do. Wait, Zeena, I promise you that your dream will come to you – your dream of love. After you marry, you will find – oh do not look like that, Zeena, just listen to me. We marry the men who are carefully chosen for us, matching our background, our way of life. Eventually this suitable marriage brings us children – sons and daughters – and then a full and happy life, with husbands who care for us."

Zeena suddenly shuddered and turned away to look down into the dark garden. Where were the servants with the lamps? She hated the darkness. If there was light, her fears about the future were easier to drive back. Now, in sudden despair she said, "Nothing you have said touches the fears in my heart. I only know that I cannot give myself to a stranger. Not now that I know—"

"Know? Know what?" Gulrukh stared at her with a dawning suspicion. "What is this thing you know?"

Still looking away from Gulrukh, Zeena said, "I know that I cannot enter into marriage with a stranger. I would rather give my soul to hell. I will find a moon plant, a datura in seed, and pound the seeds and swallow them in milk, and die—"

"Be quiet, Zeena. Here is my mother coming out – hush – if she hears what you are saying she will lock you in your room until the day of your marriage."

Zeena looked over her shoulder – here indeed was Zurah, Begum of Pakodi, coming out to join them on the balcony. Wife of one ruler, sister of another, she had an imposing presence. Dressed in a gold-bordered dark blue *sari*, with rubies and pearls at her ears and throat, she sailed out and took her seat on cushions in front of the balcony, looking sternly at the two girls as she passed.

The two cousins were sitting very close to the screen – Zurah hoped that neither girl was going to drop a flower to attract attention, to make a man look up at the balcony, even though he would not be able to see the hidden ladies.

Zeena of course was capable of anything, just to be troublesome, but Gulrukh would stop her. What a good daughter I have, thought Zurah, smiling at Gulrukh. Obedient, willing and cheerful, content in her marriage, and now carrying with ease her first child. Let it be a son, prayed Zurah, sons to strengthen the royal house of Pakodi.

So far, Gulrukh had fulfilled all her mother's wishes – how different she was from her younger cousin Zeena, who seemed to be determined to make as much turmoil in the family as she could. Of course it was Sadik Khan's fault. He had spoiled his daughter from the day of her birth. If only her mother Yasmin had not died during labour, and there could have been other children. Or if Sadik had put away his grief and married again. He *should* have taken another wife, and raised a son for his throne. Now though, on Sadik Khan's death the state of Chikor and all its wealth would join with Pakodi and Atlar Khan, Zurah's husband, would rule both states. Zurah's son, Mirza Khan, would also inherit – but let that time be far in the distance, prayed Zurah Begum, unable to bear the thought of being without her beloved husband Atlar Khan.

Having settled herself on her cushions, she looked across at Zeena again, and sighed. It was not strange that she was so loved by her father. She was the image of her beautiful mother, Yasmin. Perhaps when Zeena was married and out of sight, then Sadik Khan might take another wife. He was still young enough, not yet fifty. There would be no shortage of suitable girls – she could think of at least eight different families who had made enquiries about the possibility of Sadik Khan taking a wife. Her dearly loved brother, she would give much to see him married and happy again, with a young growing family around him – a family with many sons, even if that meant that her own son would have a smaller inheritance.

But how the memory of Yasmin clung to fill Sadik Khan with sorrow – Yasmin, who would never have wished him to mourn so long for her! He could scarcely forget his wife with Zeena bringing Yasmin back to his mind every time he saw her. Yes, the sooner the girl was safely married the better. She had begun to be very difficult, unusually so, ever since the date of her marriage had been arranged.

It would be good marriage, the bringing together of two rich states – and Zeena had no reason to make all the fuss she was making. She would be the man's only wife. His first wife had died, childless, some years before. True, the man was not in his first youth, but that was no matter. Zeena, if she behaved herself, could have a good life, she could be the petted darling of an old man, the mother of sons for his house.

"I wish she would stop staring at me," said Zeena, speaking below her breath, barely moving her lips. "She has the unblinking eyes of a serpent."

Gulrukh, afraid to answer, pinched her cousin smartly as a warning. Her mother could hear a needle drop in snow. Zurah Begum did not remove her piercing stare. She noted that Zeena was wearing the fabulous rope of emeralds that Tariq Khan had sent his betrothed, and smiled to herself. Zeena was wearing the emeralds because had been told by her aunt that if she did not wear them she would not attend the last Durbar. Zeena had flung the beautiful, priceless gems on the ground when she received them. *Impossible girl – and yet she has not always been so rebellious*, Zurah thought.

Zurah Begum had memories of Zeena as a small child, gentle, biddable and quiet. There had to be a reason for Zeena's sudden mutinous behaviour. She saw that the girl was whispering to Gulrukh, and eyeing her surreptitiously a secretive, deceiving look. There was definitely something afoot that she did not understand. Zurah Begum made an immediate decision: the early morning rides that Zeena's father allowed had to be stopped. Never mind that she never went out alone, that old Sakhi Mohammed and her maid Chunia were always with her. Servants could be bribed to silence.

Zurah Begum knew all about bribery. Had she not already bribed Chunia, paying her to bring a detailed account of everything that Zeena did, an account of everyone she spoke to? Now she began to wonder if she could believe the maid when she said that Zeena Begum only rode in two places – either down the river road, or on the old maidan – and that she was never outside the walls of the Pakodi Mahal for longer than one hour. *Could the woman be trusted? The rides must stop.* She would see to it as soon as this Durbar week was over and Sadik Khan was away on one of his Shikar trips with the Resident. Zeena would have no one to run to then.

As things were, Sadik Khan let her do whatever she liked. "She has not many more days of freedom, Zurah Bhen," he

11

had said when she had spoken to him about the early morning rides. "Let her be. There is no wrong in her riding out alone – she will soon be in the care of her husband. I would like her to enjoy these last few months."

It was an order, however gently it was put. There was nothing Zurah Begum could do – though she did insist that Sakhi Mohammed and Chunia went with the girl. *Riding out alone! Sadik was quite mad when it came to his daughter.*

Zurah Begum, having decided to put a stop to Zeena's morning rides, was just about to order the two girls to move further back from the marble screen when she heard the sound of voices in the garden. And seeing the servants running out with lamps, Zurah Begum put the thoughts of Zeena's difficult behaviour and the two whispering girls out of her mind and looked away from her niece and daughter to watch the arrival of guests.

This night there was to be a banquet. The table was set on the dais, where Sadik Khan was already seated. Zurah Begum could see the glitter of silver goblets and the flickering flames of candles making rainbows of the gems that studded Sadik Khan's *achkan*. Sadik Khan of Chikor, one of the premier princes, kept splendid style. Those of the guests that he wished to honour would be called up to sit with him at the table. As Sadik Khan had no wife, Zurah Begum was in charge of his household. She knew that everything was perfect, she had supervised everything.

Looking down, across the garden, she saw that several British men were already seated at the table on the dais. The Resident, Sir Henry Lees, grandson of the famous Sir Richard Lees who had served the rulers of the hill states in the past, was sitting on Sadik Khan's right, talking to the Colonel of the British Regiment, which was stationed in Madore. Beside him was the Commanding Officer of the 14th Dagshai Lancers, newly returned from frontier duties and magnificent in dress uniform.

The wives of these men would soon be brought up to sit with Zurah Begum on the balcony. She checked to make sure that chairs had been brought up for the ladies. Stiff kneed, the British. They did not fold their legs to sit in cushioned ease like the daughters of India. Once down on cushions, they found it difficult to sit with propriety, and hard to rise – and their positions during the process of rising had, in the past, moved the younger women of the court to unkind and unseemly laughter. However, all was well now. The chairs were there. Hearing alien voices on the stairs that led to the balcony, Zurah Begum turned, smiling, to welcome Lady Lees and her two companions.

Gulrukh sighed with relief. "Thanks be to Allah the Compassionate, my mother will be occupied now for some time. We can speak together. Now, tell me what is wrong. You did not make any trouble over arrangements for your marriage and you accepted the news that you would marry Tariq Khan – until last year. What has happened to make you hate the very sound of his name? He is the same man, he has not changed. I think he has been most generous to you. Look at the jewels you are wearing. I cannot believe that you have turned against your marriage because of the tittle-tattle of two jealous old women, so do not make that excuse to me again. Just tell me what has happened to change you – I love you dearly, Zeena-jan. I cannot bear to see you in such turmoil. Let me help you."

If only I could talk to you, thought Zeena, looking into her

13

cousin's kind, worried face. *If only I could ask your advice – no not advice – I know what that would be, I would ask for your help tonight. Tonight.* It was too soon, how could she decide – and she could not talk to Gulrukh, who would rush straight to her mother and Zeena knew what would happen then. There would be an end to all freedom, and marriage at the end of it. Somehow she must find the courage to make her decision, and escape.

Gulrukh was leaning close to her cousin. "Tell me what it is, Zeena – I cannot enjoy this evening if I am worrying about you. I *know* there is something behind all this hatred of marriage. You have someone else?"

This was coming too close to the truth. *How clever Gulrukh was!* Zeena, shocked, tried to laugh. "How could I see someone else? Where would I see him? No Gulrukh, it is not like that. I just cannot bear the thought of that man – unknown, but frightening. Please let us leave it now. I, too, wish to enjoy this evening. Do not worry about me any more. Forget my foolishness. Your mother told me that girls often feel like this before they are married. I want to forget about my marriage – let us think of nothing but the enjoyment of this evening." Gulrukh looked thoughtfully at her cousin. There did not seem to be any point in continuing to unravel this mystery with Zeena. But she would watch her carefully.

She smiled and said, "Of course, what my mother said is quite right. Even I, who had already seen my future husband and liked what I saw, even I wept on my mother's breast before marriage. We will say no more. Look, there is my father and my brother, they must be waiting to greet special friends. Let us watch and see who they greet."

Two

There were no dark shadows in the garden now. It was golden with the light of many oil lamps. Zeena saw her uncle, Atlar Khan, in the full dress uniform of his state force. Gulrukh's brother, Mohammed Khan was with him, holding his month-old son in his arms, his first child. Atlar Khan and his son were of a height, they made a handsome pair.

One of the local petty *zemindars*, with his veiled wife behind him, came in, to be welcomed warmly. The woman took the baby from the arms of Mohammed, and turned towards the balcony stairs. She carried the child up carefully, and Zurah Begum took the baby at once, her face glowing with pride. Unveiled, the woman was revealed as a young girl of great beauty. The *zemindar* was an old man – *surely this must be his daughter*, thought Zeena. The girl had taken a seat behind the other women, she wore no jewellery and, apart from her lovely face, it was her expression of deep sorrow that was most noticeable about her. Atlar Khan and his son, and the old *zemindar* had walked to one of the tables in the garden, where there were other local men sitting.

"Surely that cannot be the wife of that old man," Zeena whispered to her companion. "She is our age, and he is old enough to be her grandfather from the look of him—"

15

"She is his wife. He is one of my husband's men, the *talukdar* of Sangar village. He asked permission to attend. You saw the way his wife took Mohammed's son."

Gulrukh lowered her voice. "She has no child – it is said that if you hold a child close to your bosom, sometimes it brings a child to you. These people believe it anyway. She has tried everything else, and she has not quickened." Gulrukh patted her stomach, only just beginning to curve a little, and nodded at Zeena.

"We are fortunate – Mohammed's son will possibly be the ruler of both Chikor and Pakodi – because your father did not marry again and have a son. It is a serious matter, raising sons for the throne. Your father should have married again. He is a strong man, if he took a young wife he could raise many sons."

"And of course that is the only reason for marriage." Zeena's voice was sharp.

Gulrukh responded quickly, "But of course, when you bear a son, he will be your father's heir – it is interesting to think of our sons ruling after us, is it not?"

"No, not very. I do not believe that babies are catching – that poor girl is married to a man too old and I suppose she is blamed because she has no child. As for my son – as I am not yet married it is difficult to think of him being my father's heir. I am supposed to produce a boy for the *guddee* of Sagpurna. That is of course provided the man chosen to be my husband is not already too old to father a child—"

"You are wrong. A man can go on producing children forever. I am told that there is a man of over one hundred years who is still potent. He can still give his wife a child—"

16

"Provided that she has not already died of old age. Gulrukh I do not wish to discuss this any more."

"But it is very interesting—"

"Gulrukh!"

"Oh very well. Look, there is one of the British officers of the Lancers. How strange he looks in that skirt. He comes from the north of Britain. All men there wear skirts. I think the uniform of our states forces is much better. Also the Dagshai Lancers, their uniform is very fine. Tonight we may see some of the younger Lancer officers – those of them that are not roistering in the House of Many Pleasures. It is said that when they come down from Dera Burra Khan on the frontier, they spend all their time in the street of the harlots, and they are tigers in passion . . . Zeena, you are not listening to me, why do I bother to talk with you – you have gone off in a dream again. What do you dream about, Zeena?"

"I am not dreaming! I heard everything you said. Why should I want to hear about where the Lancers spend their money? In any case, I knew they were back, I saw them arrive yesterday."

"You *saw* them? How?"

"When I was out riding—"

"You saw the Lancers and you said nothing to me?" Gulrukh, hurt and disappointed, was now full of curiosity.

"What was there to say? I was riding on the maidan as usual and they rode past in the road on their way to the lines. That is all." Zeena wished that she had kept her mouth shut. Gulrukh's curiosity, once roused, was tireless. And of course seeing the Lancers ride past had not been all. As they appeared, lances flashing, pennants fluttering, she had looked for *him* and saw him at the very moment when he looked for her. There had been no sign, but she knew that the next morning, she would find him waiting for her when she came to the maidan.

That had been this morning. And now, looking into the lamp-lit garden she was expecting to see him coming in, and she had promised him that she would answer his question – this very night.

They had met every year for three years. The Lancers spent a month in Madore, which was their home cantonment, twice a year. Once a year the families of the rulers of the hill states came into Madore for the yearly Durbars – and the Dagshai Lancers were always there for that month of ceremonies and parties.

Three years earlier, Zeena had ridden out for her morning ride – the same place every day, the only place where she was allowed to ride alone, or as alone as it was possible to be, accompanied by her maid servant, an armed trooper and a syce – all mounted. Every morning Zeena rode out to the old maidan, a two-acre field of sand and struggling grass, surrounded by thorn trees, scrubby bushes, and one big, old Banyan tree. Here she could gallop alone, her entourage sitting holding their horses while they talked and pulled acrid smoke from bidies, rolled dried leaves filled with black tobacco.

Chunia, the maid servant, was a woman from the passes beyond Leh, she could ride like a man, and she adored Zeena. She had looked after Zeena from the moment the motherless baby had been placed in her arms. The trooper was old Sakhi Mohammed, a man from the Lambaghi hills, a retired *sowar* from the state forces. The syce was called Raza, and was a man of the Rann. He had come up to Chikor years before with a consignment of wild-eyed ponies, to be used instead of pack mules. He had stayed on, and was now in charge of the ruler's daughter's horses.

These truly faithful people sat and watched their mistress, and any one of them would have given his or her life for Zeena. They sat observing her, patient and admiring, until her allotted hour was over. She was only allowed one hour, and then they rode back to the Chikor Mahal.

Zeena knew, though, that if she decided to ride anywhere else, or if she wished to stay out longer, or do any of the things forbidden by Zurah Begum, these three people would cover for her, protect her from Zurah's anger in any way necessary, risking their own employment – or even their lives, depending on the seriousness of whatever forbidden thing she did. But Zeena never put them at risk, obeying to the letter Zurah Begum's fiats.

Until three years ago, when she rode as usual to the maidan and found that someone else was there before her.

Up at the far end of the field a man was training a pony – or rather exercising it. It was a polo pony, already well trained, making tight turns, swinging and slowing and turning again, it was like watching a dance. She rode closer, admiring both man and horse. *Who could this man be?* The animal was magnificent, and well used to its rider – they must have performed these manoeuvres many times. Zeena rode forward and heard Chunia hiss a warning.

"Your veil has fallen, Khanum." She pulled her veil up over her head and face, leaving only her eyes uncovered. She was close enough now to see that the risen sun shone gold on his head. *Like the sun itself*, she thought, astonished by the colour of his hair. She had never been so close to a strange

19

man before – and an British man! He looked towards her, in the direction of the sun, and she saw that his eyes were blue – as blue as the bead that Chunia had insisted she wore set into an amulet to keep the evil eye away.

To the man, blinded by the sun, she was just a dark figure on a horse. He smiled and called out, "Salaam, Jiwan! Come, let us practise together. Are you one who is playing in the match this afternoon?" He had taken her for a youth – she was riding astride, her hair tied back and covered, he could not see her veil. He could have been forgiven for such a mistake. She laughed and told him that she would enjoy a turn with him. "But not today – alas, I must go home now."

He realised that this was not a youth. She was a lightly veiled young girl, riding a beautiful mare. A girl of good family, she had a retinue with her, he saw, coming up behind her – a man in uniform, a serving maid and a syce. They were all mounted on horses of distinction. He was fascinated by this encounter. "Will you return tomorrow?" he asked.

"I hope so. I ride here every morning when I am in Madore. It will be entertaining to see how my mare will train, to turn as your animal did on an eight-anna piece. That is what they say a good polo pony will do, is it not?"

Her voice was clear, the English a little stilted and heavily accented but to him this seemed part of its charm. He watched her ride away, wondering who she could be.

He recounted the story of his morning meeting to a friend, one of his brother officers but was strongly advised to avoid going anywhere near the girl again.

"I think that she must have been the daughter of the Chikor ruler – Sadik Khan. His palace is near the old maidan. I doubt if he would be happy that his daughter has been talking to one of us. No, my dear fellow, put that episode out of your mind. You are playing with dragons if you get within two steps of the daughters of these princely houses."

"But she was only a child – and as a matter of fact, I know one of the princes well, Mohammed Khan, the heir to Pakodi state. He was at Sandhurst with me—"

"That will not help you if you start playing about with one of these girls. Believe me. Only a child, you say – what sort of age would you guess at?"

"I should think about fifteen at the most, perhaps less, but it was difficult to say, even if her veil was very light, it still hid the lower part of her face. I could only see her eyes. Beautiful eyes," said the officer who Zeena had met that morning. "Really incredible eyes – very pale grey – or perhaps green – most unusual."

"Alan, I have to tell you that if she was veiled, she was certainly into the danger zone as far as you are concerned. These girls can be married at fifteen. Hands off, Alan. You will have to wait for the next consignment of the fishing fleet and their hopeful mammas—"

Alan Lyall was twenty-two. He had been in India for two years, and with the Dagshai Lancers for one of those years. Most of his time had been spent up in the inhospitable and dangerous areas round Baluchistan and Afghanistan. He felt he knew as much about the habits and customs of India as his friend did, and had no intention of taking his advice. The girl of the maidan had become a figure of curiosity. He looked forward to seeing her again, and discovering more about her.

He rode out before dawn the next morning. The night mist was still lying over the old maidan, coiling and hanging like

smoke in the thorn trees and over the ground. The sky was
growing light when she came, riding through the mist, her
mounted retinue behind her. Her mare and robes, were silver
in that half-light, she seemed as insubstantial as a dream, or a
visitation from another age. He watched her ride towards him,
silent and enchanted. He was no longer curious about her. He
did not need to know anything more. From this moment on,
she had entered a place in his mind, and in his heart, a place
that had so long been empty, and all else was forgotten.

For a month they met nearly every day. There were of
course days when he was unable to meet her, but she went
every day just after dawn, and waited – though she never
waited longer than the stipulated hour. It was more important
than ever now that her morning ride was not forbidden.

That month passed quickly. When they met they would
ride round the maidan, then duty done, they would fill the
rest of the time with conversation, questions and answers,
ensuring their knowledge of each other grew and grew. But
the knowledge that he began to long for, the knowledge of
touch, simply couldn't be fulfilled. She remained veiled, only
her eyes showed. The veil was very light, a shadow of chiffon.
It did not hide her face, it only blurred it a little, but to Alan
it was intrusive. Her veil, her enveloping robes, teased and
provoked him because of what they stood for – a barrier
between them. He asked her one day if the veil worried her.
She shook her head.

"No – it is part of my life – like the closed doors of the
Zenana. You English talk of harems – we call it Zenana,
the women's quarter. But there is an old word for it, an
Arabic word. *Harram*. That is the real meaning of harem.
Forbidden. A woman's life is hidden behind that word." She

sighed, but he could see her lips curve into a smile behind the veil.

He said angrily, "I think the veil is very silly. It hides nothing. It is just a pretence—"

She laughed, and shook her head at him. "This is not the way I usually wear a veil when I am outside the Zenana. This is what you called it – a pretence of a veil. Tomorrow I will wear the proper veil and you will see – or rather, you will not see."

The following day she came wearing a *burkah*, covered from head to feet in a hideous cotton garment. He could no longer see her eyes – he begged her to take it off, but she refused. "No, I cannot do that. But tomorrow I will wear the pretence. I do not care for this either, it is very hot, and not a good dress for riding."

It was what it stood for that distressed Alan. It underlined the fact that she was forbidden fruit. And of course, he told himself, *this is why she has begun to fill my every thought. I am being foolish – this is a child.* Zeena Begum. He had her name, and she had told him her age. *What am I doing dreaming about a child of fifteen! In England she would still be in the school room, in the care of a governess.*

But this was not England. Here a hotter sun brought fruit to a sudden ripeness, tightly closed buds burst into full flowering from one moment to the next. With every meeting the dream girl of the maidan was becoming a woman of flesh and blood, untouchable but desired.

The month ended, and for him it was almost a relief – he would have time in the inhospitable mountains and passes of Baluchistan and Afghanistan to recover from this sweet but trying infatuation. He was sure that that was all it was.

Zeena had not realised that he would be going away. When he told her he saw her close her eyes as if to avoid a blow. When she opened her eyes they were full of tears. At the sight of her tears he felt as if his heart had altered its beat. Breathless he said "Don't weep, Zeena Begum – I shall return. Will you remember me?"

"Are you going away for a long time?"

"Why do you ask that? Do you mean to tell me that if I go for a long time you will forget me?"

She looked away from him saying, "As to remembering you, time will not let me forget you. I only ask how long you will be gone, so that I know when we will meet again. That is all."

"I shall be gone for nine months – is that too long for memory?"

She said quietly, "It is very long. But I shall be here nine months and one day from now."

A surge of feelings welled up in him, feelings that he did not know how to deal with. Any other girl would have been in his arms by now – but this one, he did not even know how to leave her. She made it easier for him by lifting a hand in farewell and riding away before he had thought of a way of saying goodbye. He felt that he had carelessly lost something very valuable. He would have followed her, said something more – but there was nothing that he could think of saying except "Don't go, stay with me." Words that couldn't be said. He turned his horse and rode back to the lines.

Three

Safely away and living his regimental life among the bare mountains of Afghanistan, it was not as easy as he had thought to forget about her. In quiet moments she suddenly invaded his thoughts, he saw her in his dreams, heard her voice saying his name. He did not dream of her as a child, it was a woman who spoke his name. He decided that his friend had been right. He had to stay away from her. He *would* stay away from her. He would not ride again to the maidan when the regiment went back to Madore.

Nine months, nine busy months, full of excitement and peril, passed quickly. The regiment returned to Madore, moved into their familiar quarters.

The following day he awoke at dawn, and without hesitation rose, and called for his horse to be brought round. As the sun was rising he rode to the old maidan.

Hidden from view, with her servants, behind the tangled scrub and the big tree, she saw him arrive. She watched him look around for her, and then she rode out from behind the thicket of scrub and thorn, away from the shelter of the big tree, and went towards him.

He saw her coming and waited. In that moment he saw the future clearly and felt no misgivings. This was how things

25

were to be. Here riding out to him was all he wished for. This is mine, he said to himself, my life and my happiness. He dismounted and stood watching her come.

She rode to his side, silent, her breath uneven, her heart shaking her. Alan could not see her face, the sun was behind her, edging her outline with gold. He thought she looked like an icon, her presence even more than the golden glare that dazzled him. When she came close to him he saw that she was more heavily veiled than he had ever seen her, veiled and robed. All he could see of her that was flesh and blood was her hand holding the reins. Neither of them spoke – then without knowing what he was going to do, he stretched up and laid his hand on hers. To both of them this was a moment of lost breath, unforgettable, heart stopping. The silence between them drew out, a thread of incredulous amazement at the extreme strength of their feelings. Lost, she slipped from her saddle into his arms.

It was Chunia's frantic whisper that warned them, reminded them that they could be seen from the road. Two people were riding by on the far side, a man and a woman. Both were looking over towards the embracing couple and the horses now without riders. Alan released her and stepped back, keeping one hand on her arm. "Unfortunate and unwise of me, but how was I supposed to think when I have not seen you for so long? Do not worry about those two – Edward and his wife, they are friends of mine, they will say nothing – except no doubt to me. Do not be afraid, my dearest love."

All the joy that she had felt, the ecstasy she had found in his arms, had left her. He was convinced that behind the veil she was weeping. He was right. Her voice was broken. "Only a whisper is needed – if it reaches the ears of anyone in the

Chikor Mahal I am lost. Zurah Begum will lock me up until the day of my marriage." He let go of her arm, and stared at her. "Your *marriage*—"

She looked away from him.

"That is what I came for – I have risked my servants' lives to get to you before you heard from someone outside. The invitations for a big feast will go out soon – I had to see you first. I did not come for anything else, I have already been warned that my main and only freedom will be taken from me soon – but I had to see you."

"We both came with bad news – I came to tell you that I am being sent to Mhow for this month. I cannot refuse, it is an order. So this is a lost month – but I did not know of this other danger that threatens. When are you supposed to marry?"

"It will be in March next year – if I do not kill myself first—" She was sobbing, and he could not stand to hear her crying. He took her arm and led her over to the big tree, under its sheltering branches. Her servants were sitting there, but they had their backs turned and with perfect courtesy behaved as if they were alone, completely ignoring their mistress and her companion.

"Listen to me, Zeena. Please do not weep, you are not going to marry anyone but me – that was the other thing I wanted to tell you. But there is so little time. Let us go back now, and you must take me straight to your father."

She started away from him, almost falling in shock. "Are you mad? What do you think my father would do, if I walked in with you? What are you thinking to say to him?"

"I am going to tell him that we are in love and I want to marry you. I have met your father, Zeena, and your uncle, we have gone on shooting parties, and played much polo together. He knows that I am not a man who would play with your affections! And I have heard that his love for your mother was the greatest thing in his life – he is a man who understands the nature of love."

Zeena stood listening to him, breathless with alarm. What kind of a man was this that she had given her heart to – a simpleton? She looked into his eyes, and saw that he was not a fool – he was a man of worth, but he did not understand anything about the life of a daughter of Indian princes. She shook her head and said gently, "My lord. There is no way that you can speak with my father on the subject of marriage. Even if I were not betrothed, I think you would find only a blank refusal if you asked for my hand in marriage – though at least, if I were free you would be in no danger – but I am betrothed, I am contracted to a man chosen for me by my family members. It is an unbreakable contract. Do you understand? There is a wall around me, and I cannot climb it."

She paused, and then said very quietly, "Now I see that to be in strict purdah is a good thing. I understand why we are not allowed to meet any man outside our own family. It is not possible for me to wish that I had never met you – but I should say that – because it would be better for us both. I do not know how it is with you, but I do not know how to go on with my life now."

He listened to her without interruption, looking gravely at her veiled face. In the silence that followed her last words, they heard a bugle call made faint by distance. Alan shook his head as he heard it, saying, "That means I must go, though I want you to know that I am as you are, deeply in love. I have no intention of turning away from my desire. You will be my wife – if not with the blessing of your family, then without it. You say next March is the month – we will be here for the September Durbar – and that is when you will come away with me. All I ask of you is this – do not allow your family to make you marry any sooner. I will be here in the first week of September – now I must go – my dearest love. Be very sure that we are going to be together, have no doubts at all. Wait with trusting patience."

He put such determination into his words, such force – he took Zeena into his arms for a moment holding her close, kissed her hands and left her. As long as she could hear the sound of Alan's horse she felt that all he had said would come to pass, but as silence closed over the maidan and all she could hear were the cries of the birds in the trees, she lost this precious certainty.

She rode back to the Chikor Mahal, and went into her room – she had only been away for an hour. She felt that she had entered another country, one in which she must find her way – wait with trust, Alan had said. He knew nothing of her life, all that she had said had meant nothing – or was this feeling of despair what he had tried to prevent her from sensing when he had said, "Be very sure that we will be together"? If he was killed in one of the border skirmishes she had heard her father and uncle speaking of; if she then killed herself – would they then meet? She had no faith strong enough to comfort her. She sent up a wordless prayer to Allah the Compassionate, the Merciful, and prepared to meet the empty year.

There were events that marked the year. The festivities surrounding Gulrukh's marriage to the heir of Panchghar. She missed Gulrukh very much but, in a way, life was easier for her while Gulrukh was not there – their friendship was a very close one, they shared everything but now there was something that she could not share.

Gulrukh sensed the change in her, but thought it was pre-marriage excitement. She was away from the Pakodi Mahal for three months, then came back, glowing with pride – she was pregnant and delighted with herself and with her husband. Zeena, unable to face the thought of her marriage, was quite the wrong companion. Gulrukh began to worry about the change in her beloved cousin, and Zeena, who in desperation had thought of telling her secret, restrained herself under Gulrukh's obvious suspicion, knowing that her cousin would, with the best intentions, go to her mother for advice.

Now on this Durbar night, which was a night of decision for Zeena, she wished Gulrukh was back in Panchghar with her husband. She was conscious of her cousin's questioning stare. She was afraid that all the thoughts that were agitating her brain would show in her face.

"I do not understand why you did not tell me of the Dagshai Lancers riding in. I feel it was very selfish of you – I see so little that is exciting these days. I think I shall ask my lord to let *me* ride with you every morning, and then perhaps I will see what you have seen, the person or the event that has changed you so much. There is something you are hiding, I know it. I am not a fool."

Zeena's heart sank. Then she remembered Gulrukh's pregnancy. She laughed. "Do you think that at two months pregnant you are going to be allowed to ride about with me? Don't be silly! What is there to see, a lot of men in uniform, covered with dust, riding back to the lines. Not very exciting, I think. Now if one of them had jumped off his horse and proposed marriage to me – well, of course I would have told you."

Diverted, Gulrukh giggled. "That would have been exciting. Do you dream of things like that when you sit silent and don't listen to me? That dream could never come true, Zeena! You should decide to be happy that you are to have a husband as rich as Tariq Khan. No Englishman would send you a rope of emeralds. Indeed, I doubt if any one of them would offer us marriage. They are all warned that we are forbidden to them. They are afraid of our men."

Not all of them are afraid, thought Zeena, and at that she found herself back in the maidan, meeting Alan Lyall for the third and most important meeting, on the morning of this day.

She had felt sure that her days of riding out alone were almost over. Chunia had warned her that she had heard a rumour that her rides of the morning would be stopped – it was the wish of her bridegroom. "They will stop you riding alone with me and my companions when your father goes to Amraoti for the tiger shoot," Chunia had explained.

The tiger shoot. The maneater that was ravaging the outlying villages around the Amraoti forest. She had heard Atlar Khan and her father discussing it. It was due to take place in three days after the Durbar. *This* Durbar. It seemed that the rendezvous of the morning would not be a meeting but a farewell. Once the riding alone was forbidden she would never get away to meet Alan. Get away? Get away where – do what?

Without warning the feeling came to her that all she really wanted was to be free of it all, to live somewhere alone

31

without the kind of future that Gulrukh enjoyed. That not even love was enough. The decisions and endeavours that seemed to lie ahead were too much for her. If she could go *now*, riding down the road, leaving everything behind – but go where? There was nowhere she could go. Each day, over these long nine months, she had dreamed of this meeting, longed for this man's return. Now it seemed to her to be another shackle, another prison.

Chunia, riding unusually close behind her said quietly, "Khanum, what are you going to do?"

Zeena answered with sorrow, "I wish I could do whatever I am to do *now*, without a return. Just go and vanish into mist so that no one – *no one* – could ever find me again."

"That is not possible," said Chunia. "Not for you. One of the people you want to leave would find you – your father, out of love, Tariq Khan, out of pique, Zurah Begum, out of jealousy of your mother and hatred for you – or even the Sahib. He would find you. He would search the earth for you."

"You think?"

"Yes. It is plain to see. Do you recall the fortune-teller? The man who came and was called to the Zenana? Think back – remember his words – Khanum, try to recall *all* that he said."

After some time Zeena spoke, as if in a deep sleep, seeing nothing that was around her, not even the passing bullock cart, the clouds of dust, the flat plain of the maidan ahead. "I was a child – I wanted to ride, and you would not come. I remember his words – he said he saw two hearts that cross, he saw lights and heard music. There was a white rose and a long journey, and—" She frowned. "There was more—?"

"Yes. Khanum, you are standing at the edge of this fortune. You can, of your own will, step into this future – or you can render it null by refusing. It is for you to choose – and decide. Chunia paused, then said quietly, "See – the man waits." Zeena looked up and saw that they had reached the maidan. Alan Lyall was standing by his horse. Sakhi Mohammed and Raza had stopped. Chunia turned and joined them, and with nowhere to go, Zeena rode forward to where Alan waited.

In his arms again, in the green shelter of the great tree, it seemed as if everything had been made plain. She had intended to lift her veil, but forgot it in the sweet disturbance of his closeness. He did not ask anything. He stood holding her, and saying her name – then held her away saying, "I must talk to you. There will be time and time again, please God, for me to hold you in my arms. But now time is short. Listen to me carefully."

He had planned during their months apart, he had learned more about the habits and customs that hedged the girls of this country. He had taken advice from a source he trusted, and now laid his plan before her. She listened to him without speaking, with his arms holding her loosely.

"Zeena, my heart. I have three months' leave. It begins in a week. I want take you with me when I leave. It is perfectly possible that we will outwit those who follow, but only if we are assisted. We cannot go by train, we would be caught at any of the stations between Madore and Bombay. So we must go another way, up towards Faridkote and then turn to the bridle paths that climb Tara Devi."

She moved then, saying, "But that is the route that we follow when we return to Chikor—"

"I know, but listen – it would not be expected that we

would go that way." We are running *from* Chikor, therefore who would imagine that we would go *towards* it? I have a friend – he knows your family well, and the families of the hill rulers of Pakodi and Lambagh. He is a strange and interesting man, not a young man but, it seems, not changed by age. He will help us for the sake of an old loyalty to your maternal grandfather, Dil Bahadur of Lambagh. He will guide us to a place where we will be beyond the reach of your family. Will you come with me?"

This question was too sudden – and the plan appeared to be insane. Who was this man who was almost certainly leading Alan to disaster with false promises? She asked, keeping her voice under control, "Who is this friend? What is his name?"

"His name is Rabindra. He said you would ask, and that you would not believe that he is a friend. He said that you must ask Chunia about him. He is known to her family – have you never heard him spoken of? Certainly your uncle, Atlar Khan knows him well – he introduced Rabindra to me. What is wrong, my rose, you look unhappy. I thought you wanted to come with me – am I mistaken?"

Zeena did not know what she wanted to do. Rabindra – the name was familiar, she had heard of him but could not remember what she had heard.

Alan waited and then said, "Do you trust Chunia?"

"With my life. As it is, my freedom is in her hands. If she spoke a few words to Zurah Begum, I would be sent away and locked in somewhere until my marriage. Her life is in my hands and I risk it every time I come and see you – oh Alan, I do not know what to do. I am afraid of this plan – are you sure this is what you want?"

"I am sure. I know with complete certainty that you and I have a life together, you will be my wife – but only if you desire it. Tell me you will come. Trust me, my rose, and tell me I have not spent nine months in a foolish dream of love. Do you love me?"

Suddenly the only answer seemed to be the same as the answer she had given to Gulrukh.

"How can I know if I love you? Who are you? I do not know you, do I? Do you know me? We have met, and talked and touched. Oh, I do not know if I can do this thing." She looked away from him, and said uncertainly, "I am from here, from those hills. I do not know if I can live away from here. Your country is a place one has heard about, a place of travellers' tales, far away from my home. What will I do there?"

"You will live with me, beloved and happy and free to do whatever you wish. Our wives are not locked away from the world. In any case, I am not taking you to another universe! It is the same round world, and our home will be in just another part of it."

"*Our* home? It is your home. I do not understand where it is. The men wear skirts – and it is very cold. Tell me – how will I live there?"

With a patience he did not know that he possessed, he began to tell her of his home in Scotland, half-castle, half-house. A beautiful home standing at the top of Glen Lyall, set in gardens where in summer roses grew. He saw her trying to understand what he was telling her, but he knew that he was not really succeeding. He had so little time, it was pointless to waste it in attempting to paint for her a picture that she was unable to relate to.

He said firmly, "Zeena, there is no time to tell you these things now. I can only ask you to trust me, come with me. I promise you will be happy – I will love you enough for us both until you see for yourself how love can fill your life. Come with me, Zeena, come—"

He spoke with such warmth, and with such absolute certainty that she longed to throw her doubts away and agree at once.

But she could not. It was all too hurried. She was confused and frightened by the decision that faced her, and yet she did not understand her hesistancy. This was what she had wanted, was it not? *Was this not my dream, to go away with Alan at once, to be with him, to have his love and company for the rest of my life?* She did not know how these doubts had come to torment her. She thought of her father! He loved her, she knew, and she returned his love. This would be black treachery and shame to him. Zurah Begum did not matter. She had always known that Zurah Begum felt something for her that was neither love nor kindness. No, it was her father who was important. Everything she had, he had given her – and he had given her a way of life that others in the Zenana envied. In fact, the only freedom she did not have was freedom of choice. The choice of a husband. Suddenly this seemed a small thing.

He was watching her, waiting. She did not know how to tell him.

"I cannot—" she began, searching for words, some part of her clamouring against what she was doing. He stopped her, his eyes desperate.

"Wait. Go back now. I am coming tonight, I have been

36

bidden to attend the Durbar. You will have time to think of what I have said. You need time. When you have considered, can you get a message to me? Just a word? Yes, or no. If, please God, it is yes, then you must be prepared to come here as usual tomorrow morning, but once the hour is up you will not go back and we will leave together. Surely you can get one word to me?"

"How? If I give a letter to be taken to you, it will be taken straight to Zurah Begum." Zeena shuddered at the thought. "I would not see the light of day again until my marriage. I dare not write one word."

Chunia was suddenly beside them. "Khanum, we must go – the time is past."

He turned to look at her. "You – Chunia? You can bring a word to me?" She shook her head. "No. I am as closed behind the Zenana doors as my mistress. But there is something. If you are in the garden below the balcony, on the right hand side, if a flower should fall from above – that will be yes. Then, if it is possible, the lady will be here at dawn tomorrow. If there is no flower she will not come."

It seemed Chunia had taken the arrangements away from them both. Zeena's veiled face was turned from him, and without another word she mounted her mare. In her heart she was saying farewell, and could not look at him. From somewhere she seemed to hear a voice crying out "No! Not again, not again." She felt as if she were being pulled back as she rode away. Chunia, Sakhi and Raza followed, and Alan was left, all his planning in disarray, wondering how he was going to face the rest of his life if no flower fell from the balcony.

That was the morning of the day of the Durbar. The last Durbar of the season. The end of the summer.

Four

Zeena, sitting beside her friend and cousin, had lost herself in thoughts of the morning. She did not listen any more to Gulrukh who was happily chattering on. Zeena looked down into the garden, displayed at its best by the golden light of the lamps, and full of colour and movement as more and more guests arrived. She looked across to the dais, and saw her father sitting with his favoured friends, and her heart went out to him. He had always been gentle with her, protecting her whenever possible from Zurah Begum's stern regime, ensuring that his daughter had a certain amount of liberty. *How foolish I have been*, thought Zeena. *Of course father would not let me go to a monster. I have been disloyal and hysterical – I am sensible now. I* am, she said firmly to the voice that seemed to be sobbing somewhere, weeping for a life that might have been.

There had been new arrivals on the balcony. Two of the ranis from the south, from Bihar and Orissa, were seated on cushions just behind Zeena and Gulrukh. The girls hurriedly stood to greet them under Zurah Begum's minatory eye, then sat down again, grateful that Zurah had not insisted that they gave them the front-line seats. They were not old friends, their husbands did business with the states – they were rich merchants. They were not interested in looking down into the garden, they were busy exchanging news and views, and looking about them on the balcony evaluating the jewels worn by the other ladies.

Zeena was dreading the moment when she would see Alan arriving to stand for a few minutes below the balcony, waiting for a flower which would not fall. She tried to turn her thoughts away from the pain she was going to inflict on him, pain he would have to bear publicly, without showing anything. Now it was possible for her to think, *I wish for his sake that we had never met.* She vowed to herself that she would never again rail against the rules of the harem, never fight against the veil.

Her thoughts were interrupted by Gulrukh saying, "Now who is my father awaiting? See, he has come down from the dais again – look."

Zeena leaned to peer through the lattice of carved flowers and leaves.

Atlar Khan was smiling broadly. She heard him say, "Ah, Alan, you are so late – but I knew you would come. Time to leave your mountain fortresses. You have missed so many good matches this year, and you have some good horses, I hear. We missed you, Alan! Come up to the dais, Sadik Khan is arranging a shooting trip to Amraoti next week – we could bag a couple of tigers. There has been news of two maneaters – if you are interested." Zeena sat rigid, staring down. Another figure had joined Atlar Khan and Alan, just as they were turning to walk towards the dais. This man was not young, his figure was thickening, although he held himself well, and was as tall as the other two. Zeena looked at him with a frisson. Atlar Khan was greeting him without much pleasure, she thought. Who was he, a stranger. He was probably one of the rulers from the far southern states. He was richly dressed, and had a jewelled aigrette in his turban, a fashion that had died out except for very important state occasions. The aigrette was fastened with an enormous emerald. Her hand went to the rope of emeralds that she wore.

She knew who that man was – it was her bridegroom. She looked at the face below the turban, dark skinned, with a loose mouth and pouched eyes. She shuddered and looked away, telling herself not to be foolish and not to imagine horrors. My father would not give me to such a man. He could not approve of a man like that – he would not spend a thought on such a man, so old, so dissipated.

She recalled what she had heard of Tariq Khan, what was supposed to be nothing more than unkind rumour, then she heard what Atlar Khan was saying.

"Tariq Khan – welcome. I hope your journey was not too tiresome. Let me present to you Captain Alan Lyall of the Dagshai Lancers. Alan, this is Khan Sahib Tariq Khan from Sagpurna – he is to be welcomed into our family—"

Atlar Khan said something more that Zeena could not hear through the roaring in her ears. Her uncle looked up at the screened balcony, and Tariq Khan looked up too, and so did her Alan. Zeena, looking down, saw the expression on Alan's face, and could guess what her uncle had said. Alan knew who her future husband was now. He was looking up too openly, he seemed to be looking straight at her, as if he could see through the marble screen. If he was noticed, if Zurah was looking down . . . But nothing happened, Atlar Khan took Alan's arm. "Come Alan – are you trying to see the imprisoned birds of paradise? Do not let my wife catch sight of you, she is up there – she will have you killed! There are tigers up there as well as the beauties you are imagining. Come away, and talk with us about the tigers of Amraoti – they are less likely to harm you!"

Atlar Khan's laughter was warm, but the hand he had placed on Alan's arm was firm, and his eyes held a warning. Alan walked slowly. He was hoping, she knew, to at least see a flower fall, even if he could not pick it up. Why had she been so sure that she would not throw one. Why had she not brought a flower?

Gulrukh was pulling at her arm. "There – quickly, see that man with my father? Now perhaps you will stop worrying. He is no monster, he stands well – and did you see his jewels? That emerald! Such jewels to wear so casually. Imagine the life you will lead in his courts. Nothing in the world will be denied you – Zeena, why are you shutting your eyes?"

"I am imagining what my life would be like in the courts of Sagpurna. I wish I had a flower to throw—"

"Aha," said Gulrukh triumphantly. "So, you are seeing sense about your marriage at last, and you wish to throw a flower at the feet of your future lord? That is wonderful, oh I am so happy for you. Now we can really plan your marriage. To throw a flower to him will be really romantic – and he will be overjoyed of course. He will know it comes from you. But now you will have to wait. He will come back again, I am sure, to stand below the balcony. You can throw the flower then. See, Zeena, let me take the rose from this garland. When he returns you can throw this down. I will shelter you from my mother's eyes, but in any case I think she would be pleased to know that you have accepted your future at last."

41

Zeena saw that the three men had been held up by a laughing group of friends. From this group, Alan Lyall had broken away and was strolling back towards the place beneath the balcony.

The rose that Gulrukh had torn from the garland was drenched with rose water, heavy but still fresh. There was no hesitation in Zeena's mind. She leaned a little forward, put her hand through a curling carving of a marble leaf and dropped the rose as Alan walked under the balcony. She saw him bend and pick up the flower. It was unlikely that anyone else in that crowded garden had seen. All eyes were turned to watch the arrival of the band of dancing girls who were running through the crowd to reach the front of the dais, laughing. And, oh how wonderful, they were throwing flowers in all directions, which meant that her flower could have come from anywhere – except that Alan had already had it in his hand before the other flowers had started to fall. Even Gulrukh, watching to see Tariq Khan had not noticed.

Zeena watched Alan walk slowly away, holding the white rose in his hand. It was done, the first step into a different life was taken. A life where men and women married for love. She was not thinking of her father any more. Tariq Khan was sitting at the table on the dais, and her father was laughing and talking to him as if they were close friends. There was nothing to regret there – her father had agreed to her marriage to Tariq Khan, approved of it. Behind her she heard the voices of the two ranis from the south.

"Eh, Mariama, do you see who is sitting in the seat of honour? The Khan of Sagpurna – what is he doing in exalted company?"

"Why shouldn't he sit there. They are giving their girl to him in marriage – did you not know?"

"That cannot be! No one would give their child to that creature – in any case, I understood marriage was not for him. His court has some of the prettiest boys in the kingdom – well, money talks everywhere, even to the highest in the land."

"Shush – the girl is here, just in front."

"She cannot hear – she is talking with her cousin, the Begum of Panchghar, and *she* is with child. She married well, but of course, Panchghar is not a rich state like Sagpurna. They have sold that girl Zeena – and she will have nothing. Tariq Khan has never produced a child. Not one. What a fate for the girl."

Zeena heard every word. She looked at Gulrukh, and saw that she had heard too, but her cousin said nothing, she would not meet Zeena's eyes. *She knows*, thought Zeena, *it is common knowledge, they all know, and not one of the family has stopped this vile marriage. No need to feel guilt, or sorrow.* She was free of any thought except firm resolve – to escape, to get away.

It was hard to continue to sit beside Gulrukh and talk to her, and smile – but she knew that if she went to her room early, both Zurah Begum and Gulrukh would come to see what was wrong with her. She must stay until Zurah Begum wished to retire.

She saw the guests beginning to take their leave. Saw Alan walk out beside his Colonel and, as he passed beneath the balcony, he glanced up but did not pause. Zeena was grateful for his sense, for Gulrukh immediately said, "That was a handsome man – did you see him? I think he paused – he looked up, I swear he did. I wonder why? If my mother saw, she would be very angry and would send us to our rooms. But he was good to look at, no?"

"I did not see anyone stop and look up – I only saw the Colonel of the Lancers. He *is* a very handsome man. But he did not look up." Zeena produced a jaw-cracking yawn. "I am sleepy," she said, and saw a strange look cross Gulrukh's face, an almost pitying look.

"Do you ride tomorrow morning," Gulrukh asked, and smiled.

Zeena felt her heartbeat quicken. There was something about the tone of that question that worried her. "I usually do," she answered, but perhaps not tomorrow – I am very tired. I will see. Why do you ask?"

"Oh nothing. I thought that after this long night—"

"If I am very weary, I will not go. Or perhaps I will go later."

Supposing Gulrukh came in the morning to see if she had gone or came in just as she was leaving – Zeena felt sure her cousin would do just that. Zurah Begum was beckoning to them, she wanted to send them to bed – at last, thought Zeena. They both said their goodnights, and Zeena, taking Zurah Begum's hand to her forehead and then to her lips in the usual respectful salute, wished that she could sink her teeth into that powerful hand. Something of her thoughts must have shown on her face, for Zurah almost snatched her hand away. "I suppose you are riding out as usual tomorrow morning? Why do you not ride down the river road sometimes – more interesting I would have thought," said Zurah Begum.

"I thank you Begum Sahib – I only go to the maidan because it is nearer, but I might take the river road one day."

Zurah Begum smiled. "Yes," she said, "Take the river road – your mother knew it well. She would frequently visit the Pila Ghar."

Her eyes are like stones, thought Zeena, cold and showing nothing. She was shocked by the feeling of dislike that she was experiencing but Zeena knew that the inscrutable eyes of her aunt also displayed hatred. Zeena was glad to turn away, and say goodnight to Gulrukh, who lingered with her mother. Zeena felt that their eyes watched her until she was out of sight.

Chunia was waiting for her as usual. Her face told Zeena that there was bad news.

"What?"

"Sakhi Mohammed and Raza have been told that their services are no longer needed. They were paid off, just before sunset prayers. There is to be no riding in the morning, we must go tonight."

Zeena, a hand on her heart, stood for a moment with all her hopes crashing round her. She said, "How can we go without horses? And where, at this time of night?"

"Do not be troubled, piyari. This works well for us. *They* know nothing, Zurah Begum and your cousin. But they sense a change in you and want to be sure that you are not planning anything – Zurah Begum wants to have you under her eye until you are safely married. You are to stay in your room for the next few days, the story is that you are unwell. I have to keep the key of your room, and the door is to be kept locked." As she spoke, Chunia went to the door and locked it. "Now," she said, "are you sure of what you wish to do? Have you remembered all that the fortune-teller said?"

"A meeting, two hearts that cross, lights and music, a white

45

rose that is a signal, a long love – and then comes the journey. That is all I heard and it has all come true."

Chunia said, "There is more, and you must hear it before you make your decision. Listen while I tell you what he promised you – he spoke of sorrow and parting, and warned you that if you were not strong of heart you should turn away from the fallen rose, because music would turn to mourning. And there would be sorrow and a broken trust on parting. He spoke of seeing a tomb that is not a tomb. Be very sure of what you do now, Khanum piyari."

Zeena shuddered as she listened. Had Chunia recalled the man's words correctly, or was she using her own words *to frighten me into staying here?* thought Zeena, and then turned away from such ideas. Chunia would never stoop to such deceit. But the prophesy sounded more like a terrible warning than a fortune! She felt her courage begin to fail her and then, just as she was turning to tell Chunia she would stay she remembered Tariq Khan laughing with her father – and a voice within her said, "A long love that never dies." It was the voice of the old man speaking in her heart. There was no turning back, she would remember that promise and forget the rest. She smiled at Chunia.

"Help me to get away Chunia. I am sure of what I need to do."

"Then let me help you change your clothes. You will have to go out with the dancers."

She took Zeena's jewels from her, the pearl and emerald earrings, the jewelled combs from her long hair, and the priceless rope of green fire that circled her neck. She left Zeena's hair hanging loose and lustrous about her shoulders. She dressed the girl in a full swinging skirt of scarlet muslin.

The bodice was of closely fitted muslin, totally transparent, a mist across Zeena's breasts.

Chunia painted her eyes with green shadow and outlined them with antimony, her lips were a crimson flower in a face that was pale with excitement and apprehension. Now the jewels that adorned Zeena were false and glittering, the bracelets on her slender arms were coloured glass: green, scarlet and yellow. Chunia flung a gauze scarf set with diamonds of mirror glass over the girl's head, and stood back to look at her. "Ah – wait – there are bells for your ankles." She knelt to fasten a string of little bells around Zeena's ankles, then stood up and said, "It is well. You will run out with Sunni, the principal dancer. Among the girls no one will recognise you. Listen to the music – it is time. Come, piyari, keep your heart strong. You are following the road that is set for you. Come!"

The music had swelled to a finale, there was the sound of loud applause and men's voices and laughter. The girls were answering and calling back farewells, and the sound of the dancers' running feet could be heard as they moved across the garden.

Chunia opened the door and thrust Zeena out. Scented arms received her, she was surrounded by singing, laughing girls, all dressed as she was dressed. With a girl's arm about her waist she ran down the path, past the guards, down the marble steps to where the *rath*, the domed, scarlet-curtained bullock cart waited. The girl who was embracing her did not let her hesitate to look round for Chunia. She almost threw Zeena into the dark interior of the cart, then climbed in herself, followed by the others, a crowd of giggling, scented girls chattering like birds just about to settle for the night.

47

But as the cart jerked into motion the laughter died and there was silence, and suddenly a deep fear settled over the girls in the dark interior of the *rath*. The curtains were pulled close and tied. Zeena felt fear all round her and shivered. At once warm hands held hers, a voice breathed. "Do not fear. You will be in safety soon—"

"But where do we go," whispered Zeena, trying to see in the darkness where Chunia might be amongst these girls.

"We go to where the master waits for you—"

"The master?" could she mean Alan, Zeena wondered.

"Yes. Rabindra, the Master. He waits with Lalla in her house – the House of Pomegranates where no one will look for you."

Carried through the darkness, among strangers, waves of fear were falling over Zeena, her breath shortened. Where was Chunia? What was this place to which she was being taken, and where was Alan, the reason for this flight? *This is madness*, thought Zeena, *what am I doing?*

The soft whispers all round her spoke of fear. She was not the only one who felt endangered. If she was found among these girls they would be roughly treated, at best. At worst? Oh where was Chunia, if she was left behind in the Chikor Mahal what would happen to her – she lost control and spoke aloud, "Chunia where are you?"

All round her, like a basket of snakes disturbed, she heard "Ssh – sh – sh." The girl Sunni whose arm was around her whispered, "Hush. Chunia comes – she will be with you tomorrow. Do not fear little sister – all is well."

As she spoke the *rath* rumbled over a stretch of paving, then bumped up a rough road. A voice shouted, and the bullocks drawing the *rath* came to a jolting, uneven halt.

Zeena's heartbeat shook her. The curtains of the *rath* were thrown back and a lantern held high shone into the interior, shining on the silks and gauzes, the false jewels and the bright eyes of the girls surrounding Zeena.

She saw that they were moving back from her so that she could get to the opening of the *rath* and step out. She was held by fear, afraid to leave her companions, the last familiar part of this journey. The *rath*, and Sunni's arms had seemed like shelter.

Sunni looked at her "Go – There is nothing here to fear. This is the House of Pomegranates, Lalla and Rabindra wait for you. Go with hope and courage little sister."

There was nothing else to do. With little hope and without courage Zeena scrambled out of the red-curtained *rath* and stood bare-footed on the cold stones of a walled courtyard.

The man with the lantern gestured to her and walked away. The *rath* had creaked into motion, and was leaving. Zeena turned away and followed the lantern light.

Five

The drive was rough to her feet. She had to walk fast to keep the lantern in sight. As she stumbled along she heard the bells on her ankles ringing at every step, and thought of Chunia kneeling to tie them to her feet. *Chunia!* This was the first time she had ever walked alone – and in darkness. She had never been outside the walled garden of Chikor Mahal before – and had never walked anywhere alone. Chunia and Sakhi Mohammed were always with her. She imagined how it would be, if by some extraordinary chance she should be walking up a rough path like this at night with both of them. Sakhi Mohammed would be walking ahead of her with a brightly burning lamp in his hand. Chunia would be beside her – and one of the guards, probably Halkat Khan, with his hand on his sword and his watchful eyes searching the darkness. It helped her to pretend that these, her servants, who were also her dear friends, were with her in this dark strange place. She walked on as quickly as she could and the ringing of the little bells on her ankles were like a friendly encouragement.

The lantern vanished as the drive bent round. In the darkness Zeena called out, but no one answered. She closed her eyes and when she opened them she saw a glow of light,

50

brighter than before, and followed it. Round the bend in the drive she saw a white building ahead of her. The House of Pomegranates? She walked on and saw that the man with the lantern was waiting for her. He walked away as soon as he saw her, taking his lantern with him, but it did not matter. Every window in the house was alight, making the shadows seem so very black by contrast. There were steps leading up to a long veranda, and a door that was half open. Zeena stood at the foot of the steps uncertain of what she should do – where was the man she was supposed to meet, where was the woman, Lara, who owned this house? She wished with all her heart that she was safely in her room in the Chikor Mahal.

A cold wind rose suddenly, and she shivered as it blew about her. It seemed to have a voice – a voice she remembered, speaking broken phrases, words she had tried to forget. "Listen," said the whispering voice, "listen and be wise. Music will turn to mourning, sorrow and parting, a tomb – a tomb that is not a tomb—"

It was the old fortune-teller's voice, now slowly fading as if the cold wind that had brought it was blowing the whispered words away.

The memory of Alan's arms round her, his words of love, his promise of a life together – somehow she had to remember the days of their meetings, of the love she had felt for him. "A long love that never dies" – there were the words she needed to cling to.

She walked up the steps towards the illuminated door, determined to fight off the fears that were trying to break her spirit. As she reached it, the silence of the night was broken by the sound of a horse coming fast up the drive. Alan, at last – or was someone pursuing her? Had her absence been discovered all ready? Surely not – but all the same she shrank back into the shadows of the veranda, away from the well-lit entrance.

It was not Alan. When the horse stopped in a spray of stones and dust, she saw that the rider was an Indian, wearing white robes. As he dismounted a man ran forward from the side of the house to take the horse's reins.

"Is the Begum here?"

"She is here, heaven born – but Lara has not returned yet."

Were these people friends, or had she made a mistake in allowing herself to be left here? It took all her courage to speak, and her voice trembled as she said, "I am here."

The man came up the steps at once. "Zeena Begum – I regret I was not here for your arrival, I had duties. Fool, why did you not take her into the house, send for the servant to see to her comfort?" He had turned on the man who was leading the horse away.

"I did not speak to the Begum Sahiba, she was already afraid." The man sounded as anxious as Zeena did herself, the newcomer's words had cut like a knife. So this was Rabindra, the man they called the Master. When he turned to speak to her his voice was different, gentle and soothing.

"Come in with me, Begum Sahiba. There is nothing here to fear. There is a room prepared for you, and tomorrow your own girl Chunia will be with you." He led the way into a large room, so brightly lit that Zeena was almost blinded after coming in from the dark garden. She was glad to sit on a cushioned divan and look at the man who was with her. He was tall and slender. He wore the usual dress of a hill man of the north, full baggy trousers, a long loose shirt and a velvet waistcoat. But unusually he was bareheaded, his hair, thick and falling to his shoulders was silvery white, and yet he did not look like an old man. His eyes were a clear, pale grey, and he was smiling at her.

"Well, I welcome your safe arrival, Zeena Begum. You did well in a situation that was very strange to you. Now you must put worries and anxieties behind you – you have taken the first difficult step alone. From now on you will be among friends, all desirous of helping you and protecting you. Captain Lyall is most anxious that I reassure you – and he sent to you his warm affections."

"But where is he? How does he know where I am? We are supposed to meet tomorrow morning at the maidan." Zeena felt confused and almost angry.

"Be at peace, Zeena Begum. He knows where you are. But there is no question of you meeting at the maidan! That would be madness. As to where he is, he is in his quarters in the lines, packing what he needs to take on a shooting trip with your father and uncle."

Zeena stared at him, disbelieving. "How can he do that? We are to leave early tomorrow, to follow the road north – it is arranged!"

Rabindra shook his head. "That is not the way to do this. He must not be anywhere near you when your absence from the Chikor Mahal is discovered. The men of your family go off the day after tomorrow – and he, having been invited, goes with them. The *Shikar* trip to Amraoti will last a week or ten days. *Then* Captain Lyall will say farewell, and will make his way to Bombay where he is to take a ship for England. The search will be on for you, but they will not look for you

53

and the man who has just spent time with your family. He will not be under suspicion. Now no more talk tonight – you must rest – and sleep late. I will see you in the morning – go with Chini Ayah now, and tell yourself that all will be well and that you will be with Captain Lyall within ten days – or perhaps sooner. Go, Choti Begum – all is well."

His voice was soft, but so full of confidence that while he was speaking Zeena began to relax and feel quite sure that everything was going to be, as he said, well. He watched her face and satisfied that he had soothed her, he called "Chini Ayah! Come."

The woman who came in was very old, a hill woman but not from Chunia's country. She led Zeena along a passage, and up a staircase to the top floor. The house seemed as big as the Chikor Mahal. Zeena followed the old woman past many closed doors until Chini Ayah stopped and unlocked a door.

The room they entered was very like her own room in Chikor Mahal. There was a large bed veiled in mosquito netting. The curtains at the single window were of heavy silk, and there were carpets covering every inch of the floor.

Zeena was exhausted and all she wanted to do was sleep, but Chini Ayah had prepared a bath for her. The bathroom was floored with marble, there was a large mirror on one wall and Zeena saw her reflection – a drawn, pale-faced figure in tawdry finery. She was glad when the old woman stripped her of the muslins and gauzes of her disguise, and took the false jewellery from her neck and arms.

The hot water was soothing and when Chini Ayah had dried her, she insisted on taking a flask of sandalwood oil and massaging her, until Zeena was almost asleep before she was allowed to climb into the big bed. Even then she was made to stay awake long enough to drink hot, spiced milk – but before she had finished the last mouthful she fell back among the pillows, fast asleep. The old woman looked down at her, satisfied with her work.

The drug Rabindra had given Chini Ayah to put in the milk ensured that the girl would sleep late into the next day and wake refreshed. Chini Ayah wrapped herself in a blanket and lay down to sleep across the door of the bedroom.

When Alan left the Chikor Mahal, a few minutes before the dancers finished the entertainment, he was in a state of some distress and embarrassment. The two rulers, Sadik Khan of Chikor and Atlar Khan of Pakodi had been so friendly, and so determined that he should come with them to the tiger shoot, that knowing what he was about to do made it hard for him to meet their eyes. He had refused the invitation immediately, making the excuse that as he was leaving shortly on a three-month-long furlough he had much to do before he left.

But Sadik Khan declined to accept his refusal. "Nonsense my dear fellow! You must come. It fits in well with your leave – you will be half way to Bombay already when you leave us at Amraoti. Come, do not give me any excuses." Turning to Alan's commanding officer, Sadik Khan said, "Tell me Colonel Gilespie, is it not possible for our young friend to have his affairs in order by the day after tomorrow when our trip starts? You have no objection to him coming with us?"

Colonel Gilespie shook his head. "Your Highness, I have no objection at all. I wish I could come with you but, alas, for me it really is impossible. Alan, you have not so much to do. I give you permission to unload any tasks you have onto the broad shoulders of your adjutant – Chris Walker is a most efficient chap, he will see to anything necessary. Enjoy the *Shikar*. This maneating tiger shoot will be a splendid start to your leave."

Alan was left with nothing to say. He accepted with as much enthusiasm as he could muster and now, riding away, he felt wretchedly guilty. It would have been so much better if he could have gone openly to these two pleasant men and asked outright for Zeena's hand in marriage! Now he felt like the worst hypocrite in the world. Not that his feelings for Zeena had changed. They were as strong as ever.

He arrived at his quarters in the lines, turned his horse over to the waiting syce and told him to have the animal ready at dawn, and walked into his room to find Rabindra waiting for him.

He thought at once that something had gone awry with their plans but, mixed with his apprehension, he felt slight relief. Perhaps after all he would be able to do it his way. When Rabindra told him that Zeena had already left the palace all his anxieties focused on her, and he said at once, "Is she safe, where will she go at this time of night? She could come here. We are due to meet in any case at dawn tomorrow, you remember the plan?"

"Things have changed," said Rabindra calmly. "The old Begum, Zurah of Pakodi, is taking precautions. She is determined that Zeena will marry Tariq Khan. She has sent away the men who rode with the Choti Begum, and there is to be no more riding.

"It is to be hoped that this is not because suspicion points at you! Meanwhile, Sahib, the Choti Begum Zeena is safe. Do not distress yourself about her. Now it is important for you to avoid being suspected of having anything to do with her absence!"

Alan sighed. "Suspicion will certainly point at me when they find the Begum gone, and when I fail to keep my appointment with the rulers tomorrow."

"Yes. Tomorrow you will meet Sadik Khan, as arranged, and who can suspect you – you will be gone with the shooting party."

"And Zeena? They will find her gone and send after her father to tell him."

"They will not find that she is not in her room today. Chunia will keep her door bolted and say that she is sleeping. The two Begums, Zurah and her daughter Gulrukh will think she is sulking because of the forbidden morning ride. They will not go near her. Tomorrow there will be the farewells of departing guests, and Sadik Khan and the shooting party will leave – the place will be like a hive of bees. The earliest that they will notice the absence of the Choti Begum will be at sunset tomorrow after the hour of prayer. That is when the women go into the gardens to enjoy the evening air and talk together."

"But where is she now? I must know that she is safe."

"She is safe, Sahib, and if you do not know where she is you do not have to lie if anyone questions you." He was smiling as he spoke and something in his smile angered Alan.

"Rabindra, do you think I could not lie for my love?"

"No Sahib. But your lies might not deceive our people. But to rest your heart, I will tell you where she is. She is with Lara in the House of Pomegranates."

The House of Pomegranates was a well-known brothel, an expensive place 'for rich men and maharajas only'. Alan had seen it advertised and he was horrified. He was about to protest when he saw Rabindra's smile. "You see Sahib? Now I have told you, and put my trust in you. If you wish you may run now to the ruler and tell him where his daughter is, and that *I* have taken her there. My life would not be worth a grain of rice. Zeena would be found, taken back and married to Tariq Khan. Well? Are you going to trust me when I tell you that the Choti Begum is as safe in the House of Many Pleasures as she would be in her own guarded bedchamber – or safer, in fact. So Sahib. What do you say?"

"It is hard for me to think of her in such a place, but I trust you, Rabindra. I trust you with something that is more precious to me than my own life."

"Well said, Sahib. You will see her again when you board the ship that takes you to England. I will see you myself when all the arrangements are made. Let there be no more names said – neither hers, nor mine. The air itself has ears. Look, we have talked long – the sky grows light."

Alan turned and saw the dawn colouring the sky. Now there was only one day to get through until he went off on the tiger shoot. He turned back to speak to Rabindra, his mind full of anxious questions, and found there was no one in the room with him. Softly, silent-footed Rabindra had gone.

From the lines the bugles began to sing out the *reveille*. Alan was thankful that he still had duties. He could not bear to think of Zeena and how she must be feeling. This was the hour when they should be meeting. He shut his mind to these thoughts as his servant came in with his morning tea. Somehow he had to make sure that no one noticed anything strange about him. He began to give orders for his packing, and told his servant that they were going on to the *Shikar* with the ruler's party.

In the House of Pomegranates Zeena slept half the day away. The old woman, Chini Ayah did not attempt to wake her. The Master had warned her that the Begum must sleep until the drug he had given her had run its course.

When Zeena finally woke it was midday and the sun was streaming through the shutters, so that patterns of light shimmered on the floor of her room. She lay looking at the strange ceiling, and wondered where she was. But she was clear headed, and in moments she had remembered the events of the night and sat up. Had Chunia come as she had promised?

At her first movement the mosquito net was whisked aside and Chuni Ayah smiled down at her. "You slept sweetly, Begum Sahiba. Now I bring your tea, and your bath will be ready."

"Wait – where is my woman, Chunia? She is here?"

"No, no, not yet. But she will come, do not fret. Meanwhile I am your servant, I go to make your tea now—"

Before Zeena could say anything, Chini Ayah was out of the room and Zeena heard the key turn the lock. She was a prisoner. At once all her doubts came back to torment her. Had Alan really agreed to this change of plan? Or did he even know anything about it? There was something strange about the man Rabindra.

I slept too well, thought Zeena. *I was drugged last night.* She got out of bed and hurried to see if there was any other way out of the room. There was. The bathroom door was unlocked. Still in her muslin nightrobe, she rushed out and found herself on a balcony high above a garden. A twisting iron staircase was the only way down and at the foot of the stairs two men were standing guards. Zeena realised this and drew back.

The fresh air cleared her head. She was being foolish, there was no way that she could escape dressed in a muslin robe with bare feet. She must wait, find out more. She went back to the bedroom and found Chini Ayah entering, a tray in her hands.

"Why is the door locked, Chini Ayah? I am a prisoner of the Master?"

"Nay child! Never! It is locked for your safety. Many come and go in this house – next time I leave you, I will give you the key and you will lock the door after me. Do not open it until you hear my voice. Now. Here is your tea, jasmine tea, as you like it. Drink it, Begum Sahiba while I see to your bath!"

How did they know, these strangers, that she preferred jasmine-scented tea?

Zeena heard Chini Ayah shrilling from the balcony. "Ho, you two! Bring up the water now – and be sure it is hot. Quickly."

Not guards then, just the *bhisti* and another servant – a sweeper probably. Zeena drank her tea and forgot to be afraid that it might be drugged. *I must* trust, she thought, and when Chini Ayah came to tell her that her bath was ready, she went with the old woman, hoping that Chunia might come at any moment.

But no one came. With jasmine–scented oil and wrapped in warmed towels after her bath, Zeena tried once again to find out when Chunia would arrive, and again Chini Ayah said she did not know.

"All I know is that she will come. Be patient, child! When

she leaves the Chikor Mahal she is leaving for good. No doubt she has much to do before she comes away. Also she must choose her moment. She does not wish to be followed. Does *my* work not please you that you ask every minute for Chunia Bhai? Be still, flower of the heart, and I will bring you garments for you to choose from."

"Chini Ayah, wait. Listen to me. This is not a matter of liking your work or not liking it. Chunia has been with me since I was five and she was ten. She is more than my servant, she is my friend of years. I wish to be told the truth. Someone must know when Chunia will be here, and also how she plans to make her escape. When it is discovered that I am not in the palace, Chunia will be in danger, and you – and others here – must know that. Now. Tell me what you know, for I am sure you know plenty."

Chini Ayah turned from the wooden chest she had unlocked and faced Zeena. "I cannot answer you, *nabibi*. I do not know any more. When you are dressed I will take you to the Master and he will give you answers. I am only his serving maid and I must tell you nothing."

She went back to the chest again and Zeena realised that Chuni Ayah had been ordered to be silent. There was no question of bribing her – Zeena knew that the old woman was like Chunia and the bribe might be accepted, but she would not talk. The other reason was that Zeena had neither money nor jewels – she had left them all behind. She remembered the necklace of emeralds lying like a coiled snake on her bed where Chunia had thrown it. The emeralds given by the Sagpurna Nawab to his future bride. Whatever her future was now, at least she was free of that horror . . .

The silks and brocades that Chini Ayah was pulling from

61

the chest were making rainbows of colour all over the bed. This was not cheap finery, these were robes and *saris* that a queen would be content to wear.

"Chini Ayah – these are very beautiful. Who do they belong to? If I am to borrow clothes, I should at least know the name of the owner so that I may thank her. Is this her room? Where does she sleep while I take her bed?"

"The lady who slept in this room has been gone from these parts for many many years. She sleeps now beneath the soil of the country over the black waters, or at least her body lies there. Her spirit roves free. Her name was Muna, the Rose of Madore. The greatest dancer of all time. She would be happy to think that one of her blood is making use of her house and her possessions."

Everyone had heard of Muna the dancer. Down the years her name had come to represent beauty and grace. She had been a legend in her lifetime and the legend had lived on. Zeena, touching a fold of gleaming satin, could not believe that she was in Muna's house, and would wear some of her clothes. Chini Ayah had shaken out the folds of a green *sari*, and a brocaded *choti*, found an underskirt and slippers. She dressed Zeena as if she were robing a queen, combed and coiled up Zeena's hair, and all the time Zeena was puzzling over something the old woman had said: "one of her blood".

Finally Chini Ayah was satisfied and led Zeena to stand before a long glass, so old that it was fogged and bloomed with age. The reflection was not clear, it was doubled in the glass so that it seemed that two women looked back at Zeena. Then Chini Ayah turned the glass away and Zeena heard her mutter, "They will say the dancer has returned."

Zeena said, "I am no kin to the beautiful Muna, alas. My mother was Yasmin Begum, the daughter of Amora of Jungdah and my father was the Nawab of Chikor, as you know. But I am proud to wear her clothes and use her room."

Chini Ayah, busy folding away the silks that littered the bed said, "There are many stories of Muna – you should speak to the Master. He knows. He served the great Dil Bahadur, the son of Muna."

"When may I see the Master? I have many questions to ask him. "You said I might go when I was dressed."

"Yes. But wait, you have no jewels. Here are earrings." She opened a small wooden box and brought out a pair of earrings, circles of jade surrounded by pearl drops. As she was fitting them onto Zeena's ears, a knock sounded on the door. Zeena was full of hope as Chini Ayah unlocked the door, but it was not Chunia. It was a girl with a tray placed on which was a spray of jasmine flowers.

Chunia Ayah said "Ah. The Master waits for you – wait, let me put these in your hair." Five long minutes later, enveloped in a *burkah*, Zeena was at last on her way to meet the man who she hoped would answer her questions.

Six

Alan was to meet Sadik Khan at the fourth milestone down the old river road that ran between Madore and the walled city of Safed. There, Alan imagined, they would join the road to Ranaghar in the jungle country, below the foothills of the Himalayan mountains Nanda Devi and Nanda Kot. Tiger country was thick with deodar and shisham, and broken with dry gullies and deep rocky ravines. It would be a week's riding at least, which meant that it would be over a fortnight before he would take the train. Alan understood that, together with the week's journey and the ten-day *Shikar*, he would not see his beloved for what would seem an eternity. If only he could be sure that Zeena was safe! He had Rabindra's word – he must trust him, there was no alternative.

Alan was riding Sultana, his Arab mare, but his baggage was stored on a pack mule led by his syce. Alan had made arrangements for Sultana to be left in the care of his friend Christopher Walker while he was on leave. "Should anything happen to me, then she is yours to keep, Chris."

"Well, that is a remarkably decent offer – but what do you imagine is going to happen to you? Nothing, you fortunate chap, getting away early to go shooting tiger, and leaving me all your work! I would change places with you any day. I suppose the loan of Sultana is to sweeten me. Don't worry I'll look after her well and hand her back with regret when you return in three months. Goodbye old fellow. Have a good leave."

Alan said goodbye trying to hide the sadness welling up inside him. He was sure that he would not be returning. The scandal that would follow after the discovery of Zeena's departure would ensure that he would have to send in his papers. There was no way that Zeena's escape would not be connected to him eventually. Someone – one of the servants – however faithful, would break down and talk. This would be his last ride on Sultana, and the tiger shoot his last excitement in beautiful India, the fascinating and dangerous country that he loved.

He had left the lines early, thinking it would be more civil to be there at the tenth milestone than to keep the two rulers and their entourage waiting for him. But when he arrived at the meeting place, they had already arrived. They had not brought many followers with them, only a small company of uniformed men, troopers of the state force, and two cooks and two body servants.

Both the Nawabs greeted Alan warmly, and both admired his mare. "She is magnificent, but if you will take my advice," said Atlar Khan, "you will send her back to the lines. She is too good for the rough roads we will travel. Take my second horse – imagine what could happen to those legs, and she will be a temptation to every dacoit who sees her. It would be wiser to return her as you only have your syce to guard her."

Alan had been looking forward to his last ride with Sultana, but he saw the sense of Atlar Khan's suggestion and agreed. He watched his syce ride away on her, leading his beloved mount, and Sadik said consolingly, "Do not look after her as if you are never going to see her again my friend! Three months will pass quickly and she will be here, waiting for you. You will find Atlar Khan's second horse, Sikunder, an interesting ride, I think. He is very fresh, having been under exercised."

In fact the animal was almost unmanageable and Alan, for the first day, had no time to think of anything except staying on Sikunder's back. The exercise, the concentration and the feeling that Atlar Khan was watching his struggles with admiration helped to keep his mind away from his anxieties and, by evening, when he had control of the wily Sikunder, he felt cheerful and relaxed. He was going on an exciting expedition with men he already thought of as friends. And more and more he began to enjoy himself. Of course he had not forgotten Zeena – she was part of everything and indeed the colours of the evening were brighter because of her. Alan was certain of his love for her and now the fact that she had braved the night and gone with strangers to an unfamiliar place gave him a reason to feel sure that she loved him as much as he loved her. She had proved it.

There was no urgency in his thoughts of her. She was always there, in the back of his mind, a pleasure and a pride. He had one regret: he wished he could have asked this man, Sadik Khan, for his daughter's hand in marriage. He hated having to play this devious game. If only he could be honest. This was the only shadow on his enjoyment, and it was a shadow he could not throw off.

The more he talked with Sadik, the more he liked him. He saw, during the second day that both the Nawabs were popular, the people who drew off the narrow road to let them pass did so with good grace and called out greetings.

He remembered another shooting party he had attended, down in the southern state of Simunder, when the ruler had not been popular, and never went out so lightly attended. When this ruler travelled around his state he had an armed escort of twenty or thirty men, and his jails were said to be full of malcontents who objected to his punishing taxation. Alan remembered the feeling of fear that brooded over the state.

When Sadik Khan called a halt to breathe the horses and quench their own thirsts, too, Alan mentioned his visit to Simunder four years earlier. Sadik Khan said, "Ah it is always so. That ruler had a bad reputation. He was the choice of the men in Delhi after the last ruler died leaving no heir of his blood. The ruler they chose was a bad choice – a Moslem ruler with a Hindu minority, and no conscience. There is always trouble in those southern states – Simunder, Kakikar and Sagpurna. They have all been merged now, into one state called Sagpurna. The man you visited died last year and there were strange rumours about the manner of his death. Those are the states of devil worshippers."

And you, thought Alan, *are sending your daughter down there!* He said, "I met the ruler of Sagpurna at your table at the last Durbar I think?"

"Yes," said Atlar Khan. "Yes, you did meet him. Tariq Khan. He is going to join our family by marrying into it. Zeena Begum, aged seventeen, is to be married to him in two months. He is a bad choice for a husband."

Sadik Khan's face set in displeasure. He said nothing for a minute. Then he stood up and called to the syces to bring the horses. He looked towards Atlar Khan and said quietly, "As you say, my brother. But your wife chose—"

"My wife indeed – and she is your sister. Do you have no say in such matters? Do you not rule your own house? She listens more to you than she does to me."

"I have as much say in my women's quarters as you have in yours. I, alas, have no wife to advise me, and I am grateful for the help Zurah Begum gives me. Well, in this case I see no way to change what has been done. If Zeena had immediately told me that she was against the marriage I could have stopped the negotiations before the bond was signed. But Zurah Begum said that she was agreeable and the thing was done." Sadik Khan spoke slowly and shook his head, looking away from Atlar Khan.

"The girl has changed – in this last year she has turned against the marriage. And now it is too late." He spoke with firm finality.

"Why is it too late? Can such a contract not be broken if the girl is unwilling?" Alan questioned, trying to appear interested rather than concerned.

But the two men looked at him with surprise, detecting the anger in his voice. It was Atlar Khan who answered him.

"Once a marriage contract is signed it is binding, and a girl whose family breaks a contract would have difficulty in finding another suitable husband for her. It brings shame to her and to her family for all time. It is not so in Belait, I know."

Alan said, "No. it is not so. A couple may break an engagement if one of the two wishes to do so. One may be unhappy, but there is no shame. A broken marriage, that is different, that could be a matter of shame."

Sadik said coldly, "In this country the customs are different. Enough. It is time to continue our journey if we are to reach the camp site before dark."

He mounted and rode off, not waiting for his companions. Several of the troopers scrambled onto their saddles and hurried to canter after him. Atlar Khan spoke. "He is angered because he knows he is wrong. He has every reason to break this contract and he knows it. He has allowed Zurah Begum to over-rule him, and he cannot face the scenes she would make for him if he goes against her now. She is a very strong woman and always gets her desires. I can tell you that, for I am married to her. But I think perhaps Sadik will for once surprise her – and may Allah protect us from the fury of my wife. I will be brave and stand with him – I will enjoy it."

Alan rode beside him in silence. He was horrified by what he felt was Sadik Khan's weakness – that this man he had begun to like and respect should be swayed by an old woman's words made Sadik a lesser person in Alan's eyes. He now began to lose all feelings of guilt about deceiving Zeena's father. He had always liked and respected Atlar Khan, and that feeling remained.

Later that evening, sitting beside a campfire, comfortable on thick carpets and many cushions, Sadik Khan asked him where he had learned to speak Urdu. "You speak as one of us. I have never heard an Englishman speak thus. How is this? Who taught you? Did you have a girl from Lucknow to share your bed?"

"No. My father and my grandfather served here in my regiment. I was born in Mhow. Urdu was my first language."

"Eh well, you could be one of us when you speak. Why do you return to Belait for your leave? Stay here, come up

69

to Chikor and Pakodi and fish our rivers and see our way of life. Why not?"

Before he had heard Sadik betraying his weak behaviour over Zeena's marriage Alan might have said, "Thank you – I will stay, as I wish to marry your daughter." But not now. No. Now he searched Sadik's face, wondering if this was a trap. Had he heard a whisper about the meetings between Alan and Zeena? *Perhaps*, thought Alan, *perhaps I have been brought away so that Zeena can be taken out of my reach.*

He felt uneasy. "The offer is a wonderful one and I would accept if I could. But my father and mother are both dead and I must go back to see to the estate. My leave may not be long enough for me to complete all I have to do."

"Well, I understand that," said Sadik, "but the offer is open." Who knows, you may find life in Chikor so pleasant you do not wish to leave. There are several British men in our hill states, acting as advisers to the rulers. It is a good life for a man of your ability. Give it a thought, Captain Sahib."

"I am honoured, your Highness."

If Sadik Khan was disappointed that Alan did not immediately accept, he did not show it, but he went early to his tent. After he had left them, Atlar Khan lit a fresh cigar and seemed prepared to stay talking. Alan felt an overwhelming desire to confide in this big friendly man. Warmed by the brandy he had enjoyed after dinner, Alan seemed to lose caution. "Atlar Khan. I would ask you something – I need your advice—"

Before he could say another word Atlar Khan held up his hand and said in English. "I am your friend Alan, but ask me nothing. My advice to you is that you keep your thoughts to yourself. Do not speak of what is in your heart. I must not allow you to speak. There are certain things that are forbidden. One thing I will tell you. Madore cantonment is a very small place, there is much coming and going between the cantonment and the various homes of the visiting rulers. I can say no more, but, I repeat, I *am* your friend, remember that."

He smiled and rose to his feet, throwing away his cigar. "I am for bed now – we have an early start in the morning. Goodnight, Alan."

Alan sat alone beside the fire until the wood burned down to embers and a servant came to renew it. Then he went to bed, but found himself lying awake thinking. It was plain that Atlar Khan knew of the meetings on the old polo field – but Alan know that he would not talk. However, when he returned to Madore and Zeena's absence was discovered would he still keep what he knew to himself? If Atlar Khan spoke, would they send people after him and find him in Bombay. The night was full of hideous anxieties. *When* was Rabindra going to contact him, as he had promised? Or was this all a trap to get him away? Eventually, not being able to find any rest, Alan got up, heavy eyed and unhappy. The sky now bright with dawn, the servant called him and harded Alan a cup of tea.

When the three men met over an early breakfast, Alan was only partially relieved by the friendly greetings of the two Nawabs. It was hard for him to meet Atlar Khan's eyes and he longed for the trip – which had only just started – to be over. As the day wore on, however, he began to feel better. The friendly atmosphere seemed genuine and the country through which they rode was beautiful. Everything became easier, and he tried to enjoy the moment.

Five days later they walked up to the Rest House which would be their base for the time of the *Shikar*. It was about five miles, as the crow flies, from Ranaghar, buried deep in the jungles of Sakapura. The house was built on a ridge so that it was possible to see for miles over the thick green jungle that surrounded it.

They arrived at midday, having climbed from the village of Ranaghar where they had left the horses with the syces and five soldiers as guards. The rest of the company of state troopers came with them, and the cooks and body servants too.

Tired and sweating after the long steep climb up the bridle path that led to the rest house, all three of them were thinking of cold baths and cold beer. They were not best pleased to see a small group waiting for them, and Sadik Khan was about to order them away but his brother-in-law, Atlar Khan, stopped him.

"Wait, brother. Two of these men are our *shikarees* and, see, there is Buldo, the headman of the village. I think something is wrong."

Buldo, an old man, approached and saluted Sadik Khan, bending to touch his feet and then bowing over his folded hands.

"Protector of the poor, the beast we told you of has killed again. We left a man nearby and he has come to say the tiger is back at the kill now. If it pleases you we can take you there. He hasn't yet fed fully, he will not leave that spot. We have the elephant ready." Buldo paused to look appealingly at Sadik Khan and added, "There is a suitable tree and a *machan* has been prepared, or your honour may shoot from Kushi's back."

Sadik sighed. "This does not please me, but we must go.

Alan, this could be your first tiger. Or are you fatigued? Would you rather rest here? There will be other tigers."

Alan refused the offer of a rest. "This is my first tiger," he said.

Sadik smiled, "Well said. The tiger you will never forget. Let us go."

Alan had expected to enter the forest on foot. Instead they went in and perched high on a shooting pad on the back of the largest elephant he had ever seen. The pad, he found, was stuffed with lumps of cotton and strapped round the elephant with thick ropes. It seemed to Alan a precarious perch.

The mahout was an elderly man, obviously well known to the two Nawabs, who called him "Nasir". He spoke to the elephant as he might have spoken to an adored woman, his voice low and wooing, calling her "piyari" and "habbibi", the beautiful one.

They were soon in a thick part of the jungle, tall trees and tangled canes and creepers were interspersed by patches of high grass, which was good cover for tigers. The elephant moved slowly on, pushing his way through everything with ease, gliding silently while all around them the noises of the jungle made a steady undertone to their progress, rising and falling as they passed through. A jungle fowl rocketed into flight screaming. A skein of monkeys leapt from one tree to another above their heads, chittering in fear and fury. Suddenly Nasir pointed. Ahead, the high grass moved and parted, and Alan saw a big striped body briefly before the grass closed over it like water covering a rock. A few steps further on they came to the kill. Shocked and silent Alan stared down.

It had been a woman. A wisp of scarlet cloth still covered

part of the body and her long black hair mercifully hid her face. She was a young woman who had still got coloured glass bangles on one rounded arm.

Sadik Khan leaned to whisper to the mahout. "Nasir, where is the *machan*, can you get your beast closer, the Sahib will shoot from the *machan*."

Nasir nodded and urged Kushi on, whispering endearments. Atlar Khan put his mouth to Alan's ear. "As this is your tiger it is better you shoot from the *machan*. You will be ready to climb up into that tree *there*. Kushi is trained, she will kneel, and we will keep you covered."

Tiger shooting was even more exciting than Alan had expected – he wondered exactly how far away the tiger would be as he stood on the ground after Kushi had kneeled. But all went well, he jumped from the elephant's enormous leg and ran the few yards to the tree indicated. There were knotted creepers growing up the trunk of the tree and Alan knew that it would be as easy to climb as a ladder. But did tigers climb too? Like big cats?

He put his foot on a limb of the creeper, his hand reached up to grasp another branch. There was a crash and a thud behind him. He turned to see what had happened, assuming the tiger had been driven away.

Sadik Khan had leaned over too far, had slipped and had fallen from Kushi's back. He had fallen heavily and was lying unconscious a little way from the kill. The elephant had been moving back – now the mahout was trying to turn her.

Alan, the tiger now forgotten, was walking towards Sadik when a ripple, like a breeze, moved over the long grass and the great amber-eyed head appeared. The head was so beautiful, the eyes so hypnotic that Alan stood still in admiration more

than fear, looking at something he had never seen before . . .
This great creature free and in his own environment. The
thought of danger did not come to him at first. He expected the
tiger to back away. But when this did not happen, a warning
rushed through Alan's mind.

The whole scene was would be etched on Alan's memory
for ever more, a nightmare in full colour. The elephant was
standing still, a grey shadow against the green of the jungle.
Sadik was lying, a tumble of khaki with his yellow turban
fallen beside him. Then the tiger emerged and stood arrested,
a silent snarl of white teeth in his black and gold mask.
He was about five yards from where Sadik, who was now
stirring, lay.

As if he were watching a scene on stage, Alan thought this
was going to be a devil of a shot. *If Sadik Khan sits up he
will mask the tiger. I must shoot before he sits up.*

Everything seemed to happen in slow motion. His hands
were loading his gun. A total silence had fallen on the jungle,
everything was still. The click of the bolt as he snapped it
forward sounded like a shot, loud in the unnatural stillness.
The tiger's eyes moved, his furred chin lifted and he roared.
The noise, an ugly sawing sound, tore through the silence
birds and monkeys gave voice and suddenly Alan fired. He
put one bullet into the beast's barely seen shoulder, the other
into his eye. The tiger fell across Sadik's lower body, his legs
and his hips were imprisoned while the animals great paws
clawed at the ground. Was it a dying spasm, the tiger now
still appeared to be dead. But Alan could not be sure.

Looking up, Alan saw that Atlar Khan was aiming at the
tiger, but could not shoot because the body of the beast
was lying across Sadik. Alan walked towards Sadik and the

animal. The tiger had not moved, though it was hard to be sure of this as Sadik himself was trying to sit up.

"Sadik, keep still—" Alan called and hurried his steps. He bent down and saw that the animal was certainly dead. There was no need to shoot.

It was then, at that moment of release from tension that Alan began to shake. He could do nothing to help Sadik who was still struggling to kick himself free of the tiger's body. Alan stood helpless, trembling and sweating, and in the end it was up to Atlar Khan, who had descended from the elephant's back, to drag the tiger's body to one side and help Sadik to stand up, dusty and stained with the tiger's blood.

Both men then turned to Alan and Sadik, who felt shattered and helpless, embraced him. "My brother, you have given me back a life I had lost. I will say – I *can* say no word of thanks, words are too small, but you have my life for yours. I will never forget you." It was Atlar Khan, in his strong silence, who helped Alan to gain command of himself. Atlar Khan pulled a flask from his pocket and put it to Alan's mouth and the gulps of brandy that burned their way down his throat pulled him together quickly. The three men stood quietly, their arms about each other, and looked down at the dead tiger at their feet.

"Well," said Atlar Khan. "There lies your first tiger, Alan. I do not think you can do much with that skin. We told you that you would never forget your first tiger – how correct that has become!"

"Indeed he will remember the tiger and we will remember him. Alan, your name will be written in our history books for our grandchildren to read – and their children after them. Your name will never be forgotten. You are a member of my family now." Again, he embraced Alan and over his shoulder Alan saw Atlar Khan's eyes. He was not smiling but nodded his head gravely, "Yes Alan. Your name will long be honoured – your bravery, walking towards a tiger to save the ruler. Well, that will be known throughout the hill states."

It was all too much: the relief of course, but also the realisation of what he would really be remembered for. Alan felt himself lose control. He burst into hysterical laughter and could not stop.

Sadik Khan held his shoulders. "He is overthrown by his own bravery. The English are all like this. This is a show of modesty, they always laugh about such things. Give me more of your brandy and I will laugh too – come Alan, my brother, let us praise you, it is no small thing that you have done."

The mahout brought Kushi to her knees and the two *shikarees* who had come running, with Buldo at their heels, bent over the kill with shouts of praise and gratitude. Sadik Khan was assisted up onto the elephant's back – Atlar Khan and Alan followed. With the brandy flask being passed from hand to hand, not forgetting Nasir, Kushi swayed off through the jungle to the rest house. The *shikarees* were left measuring the tiger from nose to tail, while Buldo took the beast's whiskers.

Later, villagers came with a *charpoy* to carry away what was left of the girl who had been collecting firewood and had met the tiger in the cool early morning of her last day.

Seven

Zeena, in the House of Pomegranates, followed her guide down a long passage and two flights of stairs to reach the same room that she had entered on her arrival the evening before, but this time the Master was not there.

A girl was sitting among the piled cushions beside the window. The light was behind her so that her face was not clear, but she appeared to be very beautiful. She was richly dressed in a long red and gold brocade robe which she wore over full red silk trousers. Her veil had fallen back and there was a gleam of gold at her ears and at her throat. Her voice was deep and husky as she said the words of greeting to Zeena.

"Welcome, Choti Begum, come and sit here with me, be at home, and we will drink tea together and talk while we wait for Rabindra Sahib. He has been delayed. I am Lara, and this is my house. Rabindra Sahib told me that you would have many questions for me. Ask, Choti Begum, ask me what you will, and I will try to answer as many questions as I can. There are some answers that perhaps I may not be able answer."

She had risen as she spoke, waving Zeena forward with a graceful gesture of small henna-tipped hands. Her fingers were laden with jewelled rings and the gold bracelets on her arm rang and tinkled with every movement. Zeena obeyed her gestures, and sank down among the cushions. She tried to smile as she thanked the other girl, and began to ask for Chunia. But before she could say anything more than Chunia's name, her companion said, "Did you sleep well? I hope so. Sleep is sent by the gods to soothe away anxieties and fears."

Zeena, convinced that the woman was avoiding her question said flatly, "I was drugged."

Lara showed no surprise. "Yes, that is very likely. Only a drug to make you sleep. You were very afraid and overtired."

"I was worried, and I still am. I have been given no answers to any questions. I ask about Chunia, my maid."

"Do not be worried. You have shown great courage, you have the heart of a lion – let no fears disturb you. As for Chunia – did not Chini Ayah please you? She has worked in the palace of Chikor, the old palace up in your hills. She was pleased to be given the duty of seeing to your comforts here. She is old, but very faithful."

Lara had turned to face the window as she spoke, and the light was full on her face. Zeena, surprised, saw that this was no girl, this was a woman of some years, many years – still beautiful but not at all young. It was impossible, looking at that perfect face to judge how old, but the thick shining hair that fell to her shoulders was streaked with silver, and her painted eyes were not the eyes of a young woman. *Lara*! She had heard of Lara, of course. She was famous, a courtesan of the time of her father's youth. Now Zeena remembered hearing her name spoken in the long evenings when the women gossiped together, speaking of the past.

Lara of the House of Many Pleasures, the dancer from some foreign place – Serbia, or perhaps Turkey.

For a moment Zeena forgot her fears and stared at her, fascinated. There was Lara, glittering with beautiful jewellery, dressed like a queen, and speaking with the assurance and courtesy of a great lady – Lara the harlot, the heart-breaker.

Lara had stopped speaking and faced Zeena's wide-eyed stare with smiling equanamity. As if Zeena had asked a question she answered, "Yes. I am that Lara – but grown old and now I no longer live that life. I sit in peace and watch others and remember the past. Are you distressed to be under my roof? You do not need to fear anything here, Choti Begum. Be at peace. My past is my own, and when you leave here no one will know that you have sat with Lara."

Zeena felt her face burning with embarrassment. She had stared like a peasant at this elegant woman, who had rightly said that her past was nothing to do with Zeena. Quickly, Zeena said, "Sahiba, I am grateful for your hospitality. You have given me shelter from danger. But I fear for Chunia – she should have come with me, and it is almost midday and she is not here—"

"She will come. Chunia knows that you are here. There are reasons for this delay, we know. She has to be very careful to chose the right time to leave the Chikor Mahal. She must leave before it is discovered that you are not there, otherwise they may prevent her going, or worse, follow her to find you. So she will wait, perhaps hide herself away for two or three days before she comes, and she will choose a way that will confuse any pursuit."

Zeena found no comfort in these words. She imagined what might have happened to delay Chunia. Her fears for the girl grew. "Oh she should have run out with me! I am afraid for her. Afraid of what my father and Zurah Begum may do when they find me gone. They will think of her at once."

"Your father," said Lara, considering. "Your father will do nothing. He is already well on the road to Ranaghar with Atlar Khan and your Captain. But indeed, the old Begum – yes, we have reason to fear her anger. She has a score to settle with your mother which goes back to their youth, to the time of Zurah Begum's marriage with your uncle, Atlar Khan, your mother's half-brother."

"A score to settle with my mother? How can that be. My mother died at my birth."

"Ay, the beautiful Yasmin died, and broke your father's heart – and it was not only your father who was desolate after her death. Her presence had given happiness to so many people – including the members of her own family."

If Lara had intended to divert Zeena from thinking about Chunia, she had succeeded. The girl was listening to her, astonished. Lara leaned forward and took Zeena's hands.

"This is a tale as long as the serpent of jealousy that coiled secretly in Zurah Begum's heart. She had cast her eyes on Atlar Khan when she was a girl of seventeen – before your mother, beautiful Yasmin, married the ruler, Sadik Khan. The two girls met when Yasmin was brought before the parents of Sadik Khan to see if she would be a suitable bride for their son. Everyone loved your mother, including her own brother – and then the whispering started. It was said that her brother loved her as a man loves a woman, not as he should love his sister. This was the usual, jealous whispering which creeps in when women are idle and envious. The slander went round and round and grew into dangerous gossip, and

Zurah Begum, who has always had a jealous nature, became convinced that Atlar Khan had delayed asking any woman to marry him because he nourished an unhealthy passion for Yasmin, his own sister."

Zeena drew in her breath, outraged, but Lara held up her hand. "Wait, Choti Begum. Of course this was not true. The gossip of women should never be believed, but sadly it stayed in Zurah's heart, and poisoned her thoughts. Yasmin knew that Zurah Begum, who she thought was her friend, had given her heart to Atlar Khan, and urged her brother to ask Zurah to be his wife. But your mother never suspected that Zurah was believing the evil words that were being said about her – indeed, how could Yasmin know? She heard no gossip. If Zurah Begum had had any sense, she would have either banished the bad thoughts from her heart, or refused to marry Atlar Khan. Her parents would not have forced her. But she was determined to have Atlar Khan and accepted his suit.

"Atlar Khan was a mature man, who had, for his own reasons avoided marriage – his seventeen-year-old bride pleased him greatly, but her jealousy grew, and finally if he turned his head to look at Yasmin when she came to visit Zurah, his wife made a jealous scene. As time went on Atlar Khan, an even-tempered man, grew tired of constant scenes. After his son and daughter were born, his shoes were seldom outside the door of Zurah's chamber, and she began to have reason for being jealous, for Atlar Khan was a man of warm passion, and he quenched the fires of his body with other women.

"On the surface, there was a friendship between the two women, Yasmin and Zurah, and it seems that Sadik Khan knew nothing of his sister's jealous feelings towards his beloved wife. When you were born and Yasmin died, Sadik

82

Khan took comfort in you, his daughter – and Atlar Khan also gave his love to you – and Zurah's jealousy had a new focus, a small, harmless little girl. She took her revenge by choosing to marry you off to an evil-living man – and now you have thwarted her plans. Yes, indeed, there is cause to worry about Chunia – but she is a girl of courage and good sense. And it is my guess that she has hidden out of sight, and will come once it is safe for her to move.

"Rabindra Sahib is making quiet enquiries as we speak. We will soon know some answers, and perhaps he will bring Chunia with him when he returns." Lara smiled at Zeena, shook her head and sighed.

"Beauty is so much desired by men and by women, but it is sometimes dangerous to be beautiful. Yasmin was *so* lovely that she took the heart of every man who saw her – and you, Choti Begum are the image of her. She in turn, was the match of her beautiful grandmother, the great dancer, the Rose of Gold, Muna."

Zeena stared at Lara, astonished. "*I* am the great grand-daughter of Muna the dancer? No one has ever told me this. Are you sure? I think I must ask my father to tell me."

It was then that she remembered where she was, and what she had done. The possibility that she would never speak with her father again beat like a bell of mourning in her heart. She was silent, looking down at her ringless hands clasped in the slender ringed fingers of Lara, who said quietly. "I do not think that your father will ever tell you about Muna. Your uncle might have done, but it has never been spoken about in your family. Ask Rabindra Sahib. He will perhaps tell you the story – or perhaps not."

Now Zeena was beginning to understand how her life had

changed. She had entered another phase of her life and, every day, from now on it would bring new experiences, and new mysteries. She suddenly longed for everything to be as it once was, with no shadows on the bright days of life. No knowledge of Tariq Khan – it seemed to her that his presence in her life, and all the other troubles and discomforts, went back to the death of her mother, and the position of power that Zurah Begum now had. She began to say to Lara, "If only Zurah Begum would go back to her own state and stay there, and leave my father and me alone all would be well. She has caused all this unhapiness. I would never—"

She saw Lara's expression change, and stopped speaking. What *had* she said? Lara released her hands and leaned back, almost as if she were withdrawing from Zeena.

"What were you about to say, Choti Begum? That you would never have run away if she had not been in charge of you? I thought you ran away out of love for the handsome Captain – am I wrong?"

Zeena looked away from the grey eyes that were almost frighteningly penetrating. She said quickly, "Of course I ran away because I fell in love with Alan Lyall, but also because I was being forced into a marriage with Tariq Khan, who is a cruel man – you yourself have said so."

"Yes, it is true, your marriage to Tariq Khan would have been unsuitable. But my child, are you sure that you truly love your Captain? Because if you do not, you are running away from something very bad, to something that could be worse. You must search deeply for the answer to my question, and you must remember that your Captain is not of your race. Look into your heart and be very sure of your answer."

Zeena felt that she had already studied her feelings enough.

"What could be worse than Tariq Khan and a life in the far south many miles away from my father, and from my own country? What is wrong with marrying a man of a different race?"

Too late she saw that she had fallen into a trap. Lara repeated Zeena's words. "Many miles away from your father and from your own country. Yes, and how far away will you go to be with your Captain, who belongs to a race of people who are in fact more strange to you than even Tariq Khan – who is at least a man of Islam. Alan is a Christian – and to live with a man you do not truly love can be as difficult as living with one you hate. Zeena, think well. You are leaving one life and going to one about which you know nothing. Love would smooth your path, without love your new life could be very hard for you. Are you sure of what you should do?"

Of course I am sure, thought Zeena. *I wish that this woman would not put doubts in my mind. I am perfectly sure. I have been told my future* – "a long love that will never die" – and I am sure of it. If only others doubts were not put into my mind. All the uncertainties I feel exist because everything has changed and I have nothing familiar to hold on to. *I know*, thought Zeena. *If Alan were with me I would have no doubts at all.*

Zeena looked across at Lara and said, "I am sure. I love Alan and I do know what I am doing. If he is with me, everything will be right, and he will teach me how to live this new life in his country."

Lara looked at her in silence, and Zeena tried to avoid meeting her eyes, which seemed to see straight into her mind. There *were* doubts and fears, and of course she was conscious of them. But underneath these surface fears there was a core of certainty. Lara continued to study her in silence, until Zeena grew restive under her gaze. "Why do you look at me thus? As if you do not believe me?"

"Choti Begum, of course I believe you. It is a good sign for the future that you are sure of yourself. Good, too, for your Captain. He is, of course, a very beautiful young man. And you are indeed like Muna. You have set a seal on this man's heart, he will never change now. He is giving up his life for you – a hard and unusual thing for a man to do. To give is expected of us women, but it is very unusual for men."

To Zeena, Lara seemed to be censoring her. "But I too have given up my life for him. I have nothing – it has all been left behind."

"True," said Lara, smiling, "You have given much. A way of life you know; riches, jewels and the love of your father. Silks and brocades, and you will find that you have given up the warmth of the sun – the long, lazy warm days and the sweet garden evenings under the star-covered skies of our summer nights. The running feet and willing hands of many servants. All these things you have given up.

"But Alan Sahib – ah, he has given away a life's training and a way of life and work that he was born for, and the greatest loss of all, his regiment, his friends and the men he has fought beside and trusts – as they have trusted him. It will be hard for him to throw that trust away and trample on all his dreams of the future, and lose his good name for the sake of being with you. Your love must fill a great many empty spaces in his life and must heal many wounds. Is your love deep enough to help him build a new and satisfying life? Think, Choti Begum. Is love enough for you both?"

Lara's voice seemed to echo strangely in the room, recalling words spoken in voice many years ago. Zeena became a child again. She felt the burning heat of a summer morning, heard the voice of an old man speaking to her from the past. Another warning: "She who accepts this fortune must be strong of heart or I see sorrow that is unending—"

Zeena felt a cold wind blowing from the sunny garden, although the roses at the window did not move or bow their heads.

Who was this woman, Lara? A witch to call up the past? How did she know so much about Alan: what he liked and valued, and what he felt? A little snake-like thought wriggled through her mind. This woman was a harlot. Her house was a brothel. How much time had Alan spent here, opening his heart to some honey-tongued long-eyed beauty – even perhaps to Lara herself, an older woman but skilled and still radiant. *I was not told his thoughts and his desires,* thought Zeena. *I know nothing of his way of life. There was so little time – I only had his kisses, and perhaps some other girl, more knowledgeable and clever in the arts of love had more than kisses, perhaps she shared his love and his deep thoughts. Cheap kisses, cheap love, to be shared with any woman. What do I know about this man?*

She sat silent, downcast, all her ideas about love twisted and confused. She had spoken so lightly about finding some wonderful man to share her dreams and her love. Had she found him? Was Alan to be her long love – would he love her forever? Why this strange talk about sacrifice and Alan losing the life for which he had trained – what did this mean? She knew nothing of life outside the Zenana. How could she? She felt that she could answer no questions, either her own or

Lara's. Lara – this strange woman who spoke so gently and said such hard and dismaying things! What warning was she giving, and why?

Zeena turned to face Lara's questioning eyes. "Oh how can I say I love him. How do I know? We had so little time to talk, a few weeks every year – then the long days of separation when I did not see him at all. And always the danger of being seen with him – danger for us both. I can say that to look at him makes my heart beat faster, and his kisses take my breath away. I thought of him all the time, longed for the night, praying that I would find him in dreams. Is this love?"

Zeena's voice was trembling as she spoke, partly with anger that she should be made to feel so uncertain, partly with fears about the future. Unending sorrow? How was she to face that? She repeated, "*Is* this love? I do not know."

"Poor little one. How can you know? Yes, it is perhaps the beginning of love, the first bud of the rose. Perhaps with time, with Alan beside you, the bud will grow and bloom in beauty. I have no doubts about his love for you. As for you – you will learn about love. You have a good teacher who will find his reward in you, if he is patient, and you are willing. But—"

She paused, and raised her head to listen, and Zeena, too, heard the noise that had disturbed Lara. A carriage and several horses were coming up the drive, and over the sounds made by the coach party a single horse could be heard – ridden hard, coming fast into the courtyard. Lara came to her feet as lithely as a girl, and took Zena's arm.

"Quickly, child, into this room, and do not come out until I call you – I must find out who it is that comes. Draw the bolts across the door, and be silent until we know that all is well."

Lara's obvious anxiety startled Zeena. She ran to the door that Lara had indicated and, opening it, she slipped through and shot the two bolts across. She leaned back against the door, and listened. Lara had been frightened, Zeena had seen her fear, and realised that Lara was concerned for *her* safety. Lara had thought that people from the Chikor Mahal had come looking for Zeena. *If Lara feared for me*, thought Zeena, *how much more should I be anxious about Chunia. I am safe here, but what dangers is Chunia facing for me?* She turned her head and put her ear against the door, trying to make sense of the murmur of voices. One of the voices was a man's voice. Rabindra? There were other voices, too – she strained her ears but could not make out any words. Then, clearly, she heard Lara's voice.

"Very well. I will tell her. Poor girl, she is very afraid for her maid – you must talk to her soon, Rabindraji."

Something bad had happened – Zeena was sure of it. She put her hand up to draw back the bolts, and heard Lara's voice calling to her.

"Come out, Zeena piyari – Rabindra Sahib is here."

Standing behind Lara, Zeena saw Rabindra's tall figure and, beyond, standing in the drive was a carriage, and two men she knew. Sakhi Mohammed and Raza. But how different they looked! She almost did not recognise them. Sakhi Mohammed was bareheaded and his magnificent moustache was gone. He was not wearing his usual immaculate uniform, but was dressed in a dirty shirt and loose white trousers, also torn and soiled. Raza was in rags, and both man appeared tired and distressed. They both salaamed to her, but before she could speak to them Lara took her arm.

"Come, piyari, come into the other room, Rabindra wishes to speak with you."

But Zeena was staring at the carriage with dilated eyes, and resisted Lara's gentle pull on her arm.

"What are Sakhi Mohammed and Raza doing here, they were sent back to their country. What has happened to make them look as they do? And who is in that carriage – that is one of the Pakodi carriages – who is there? I *know* who it is, it is Chunia. Why does she stay in there? Chunia, come out, I am here – Chunia!" She was almost screaming. Horror had seized her. Lara moved swiftly to put her hand across Zeena's mouth.

"Hush, piyari, come inside quickly, we will tell you what has happened, come."

Only the hope that they would answer her questions made her obey Lara and go inside. Rabindra was there, and he led her to the piled cushions in the window and made her sit and sip from a glass before he would let her speak. She was cautious about drinking from the goblet he put into her hand, remembering that she had been drugged the night before. But as she looked up at Rabindra with suspicion in her eyes he said quietly. "Drink, Begum Sahiba. It is only brandy and water – you have had a shock, and will hear more unpleasant news. Drink, and then listen to what I have to say."

She drank obediently, and looking at them both she asked, "It is to do with Chunia, is it not – is she dead?" Lara came to crouch beside her, and took both her hands and held them closely as Rabindra began to speak to her.

Eight

Zeena's absence was discovered the day Atlar Khan and Sadik Khan left with Alan on their journey to Ranaghar. It would not have been found so early but for Zurah Begum's determination to return to the Chikor Mahal sooner than she was expected.

Zurah Begum and Gulrukh had gone back to the Pakodi Mahal, the small palace that was only used when the family came down from Pakodi for a wedding party or the yearly Durbar festivities. Atlar Khan was very fond of the old palace, and in his bachelor days he had used it a great deal. After his marriage, however, he had not come down so often. Zurah Begum did not like the little palace, feeling that it was too small and unpretentious for a ruler of Atlar Khan's status. And after Yasmin's death, when she had been given the role of hostess to her brother Sadik Khan, and the status of senior Begum in the two families, Zurah much preferred to stay in the larger and more imposing palace, the Chikor Mahal.

Now, on this morning, she watched her husband Atlar Khan go off to meet Sadik Khan for the *Shikar* trip, and decided that she would not stay in the Pakodi Mahal until his return. There were a great many important matters that she wanted to deal with in the Chikor Mahal. She would go back there as soon as her daughter was dressed, and had finished her Choti *hazri*. She called to Gulrukh to hurry, and then issued enough orders to her servants to ensure that they would be kept busy for the next two weeks. She greatly valued her position as senior Begum of the two families of Pakodi and Chikor. She was treated with respect by all – including her own daughter and her easygoing husband. There was only one constant irritant in her life, and that would soon be removed.

The marriage arranged for Zeena had a great many advantages. Quite apart from the man's wealth, the position of his kingdom – far down on the southern coast – meant that Zeena would be well out of the way and would not be able to visit very often. Zurah said as much to Gulrukh when she joined her daughter on a shaded balcony, to drink a glass of lime-scented tea with her.

"Sagpurna is the best place for Zeena. She will have to learn to be a good wife and will not be able to run to her father every five minutes. Indeed there will be no one to run to if everything is not to her liking! Tariq Khan will no doubt know how to deal with a spoilt girl who has always had everything her own way. It is time Zeena grew up and learned what her place in life actually is. Zurah sipped her tea with a wry twist to her mouth as if the thought of Zeena took all the sweetness from the tea. She put her glass away and continued, "I have been able to alter some arrangements. I have brought the marriage forward a month. Tariq Khan was agreeable to this, and will be coming up to Chikor – I think he starts his journey only two or three weeks after we get there."

"But Ma-ji, will the passes be open by then? Imagine if the bridegroom gets snowed up in one of the small villages – with the kind of entourage he travels with they would not have enough room in the houses. Oh my, what a *tamasha* that would cause!" Gulrukh giggled at the thought.

Zurah Begum waved away the matter of the passes – she felt that no weather could hold back an eager bridegroom. "The snow fall has been light this year."

"So far, Ma-ji," said Gulrukh low voiced, and again Zurah Begum ignored her.

"All that remains to be done is the blessing in the mosque in the presence of her father and myself. After that there will be a party for the family and those of the hill rulers who can get through the passes, before Zeena leaves for her bridegroom's home. We will have the great parties for the birth of your child – inshallah you have a son. My good and obedient daughter, Allah the Beneficent will reward you." Zurah Begum sighed with deep satisfaction, leaning back among her cushions. But something about Gulrukh's silence caught her attention. Was it a critical silence? Zurah turned, frowning to look at her daughter. "What are you thinking, Gulrukh, with such a long face? Do you not approve of what I have arranged?"

Gulrukh made haste to disavow any criticism. "No, Ma-ji, I am sure it is all arranged well, of course. Only – my uncle. Will he approve of the marriage being put forward?"

Zurah laughed. "Your uncle will come back from his shooting, and find everything is arranged, and will be glad that he does not have to do anything."

"And Zeena?" asked Gulrukh. "Will she be pleased?"

"Well," said Zurah, "I have not told her yet, but I will tell her today. She will be upset, no doubt, but it does not matter. Tell me, daughter, do you know what has turned her against the marriage? She was content enough when she was first

93

told about it. Now she is behaving as if she is being sold into slavery. What has got into her mind?"

"I think" answered Gulrukh, "her horror of this marriage started when there were stories about Tariq Khan and his part is the death of that concubine. Also, he is very old – not even his riches will make him any younger. And, of course, she does not care to go so far from home."

"Bapri Bap!" exclaimed Zurah, looking ruffled. "What a basket of excuses – and none of them true. All this distaste for marriage and the complaints about going far from home are so sudden. What? No, do not start to tell me any more stories. *I* think she has seen, or even met someone else. It is perfectly possible, with all this riding by herself. These morning rides! Foolishness. I should have forbidden them immediately."

"But my uncle gave her leave to ride alone, you remember Ma-ji?" Gulrukh was being increasingly daring, her mother's eyes were as hard as stones as she looked at her daughter. Gulrukh gritted her teeth and continued. "My uncle said that she could ride as often as she wished, provided that she took Sakhi Mohammed and Raza with her, and a guard – and of course Chunia. She always had Chunia with her. I do not think she met anyone on those rides. She would have told me if she had seen some exciting man! She always told me about her rides. She would go to the old maidan, to the polo field, and spend perhaps an hour there, and then return. I once asked her if she had seen anyone who took her eye, and she laughed at me. Truly, Ma-ji, you do not have to take all these pleasures from us, because I too enjoyed her rides."

"What are you saying, daughter? *You* enjoy the rides? If I find that you have been riding out alone with that girl behind my back—"

The Palace Garden

The anger in Zurah's voice made Gulrukh shudder inwardly, but she managed to laugh as she said, "Ma-ji. of course I did not go out riding with Zeena. I am not mad! No, I did not go with her but I enjoyed it very much when she came back and told me about all that she had seen. Why, only two days ago she saw the Lancers riding in after their time in Afghanistan—"

"There!" said Zurah, "I knew it! And you saying that she did not meet anyone on those rides! You are a fool, Gulrukh. Of course she met someone. I saw the way those men looked up at the balcony. I saw it. I was watching, and I saw the way she leaned out and stared down – bright eyed and ready to catch the eye of any man. Oho, I saw her, quite plainly."

Gulrukh said triumphantly, "Yes, she leaned over and threw a flower – did you see *that* Ma-ji. She threw a flower to her own bridegroom. It was he that she was looking at – Tariq Khan. When she saw him, dressed so splendidly, with that great emerald in his turban, she was quite taken with him. It was very romantic, the way he paused below the balcony and looked up, and she snatched up a rose and threw it to him. She was smiling to herself afterwards, like she does when something gives her pleasure. She will give you no more trouble about the marriage, I am sure. So do not take her riding from her – you know how quickly her temper turns."

Zurah Begum snorted. "She can turn any way she wishes, it will not alter anything. There is no chance now of her meeting her lover if she has one. I have stopped her riding. I have paid off her guard, and that man Sakhi Mohammed and the syce Raza. All three of those men were chosen by Chunia, all of them, people from Jungdah, people who had been part of the Begum of Jungdah's court. Amora Begum's men – and everyone knows what *she* was."

Gulrukh was shocked. "Ma-ji, what are you saying? The beautiful Amora Begum? My father's mother, my grand-mother – you speak ill of *her*? Why? My father loved her dearly, and I have always wished that I could have met her. What do you mean, Ma-ji!"

"Never mind what I mean. She was Zeena's grandmother too – and I see her in that girl. But never mind. I am slowly cleaning our own court. It only remains to be rid of Chunia. Chunia has been by Zeena's side for too long. She must go. I shall send her off to her own country. As for you Gulrukh, I shall be glad when your cousin has left us. She is a bad influence on you."

Gulrukh thought of her charming, warm-hearted cousin. *I shall have no one to laugh with when Zeena is gone, I shall be so sad. I love her very much.* But she did not say this aloud. She had never seen her mother in such a bad temper.

Mother and daughter sat in silence, neither of them happy to be together. Zurah Begum's eyes rested on her daughter with a hard, considering stare, and Gulrukh sat very still aware of the meaning behind that look.

Zurah stood up. "There is no time to waste now. Be ready, Gulrukh, I am about to tell them to bring the carriage round."

Gulrukh had been trying to summon the courage to make one last protest on Zeena's behalf. *I must say something immediately*, she thought, *now, before we get back – because when we arrive in the Chikor Mahal there will be a terrible meeting with Zeena, who will be enraged about the loss of her freedom to ride. And the unkind way in which my mother will certainly speak to her. She has already spoken to me as if I was a dog*, Gulrukh reflected indignantly, *so the way she will speak to Zeena will be worse.*

Speaking quickly as her mother turned to leave the room, Gulrukh uttered the words "Ma-ji – you are not going to send Chunia away are you? Zeena loves her. In fact, so do I. We think of her as a member of the family, an elder sister. Please do not send her away."

Zurah Begum looked at her daughter with such a cold glare – and for so long – that Gulrukh could feel herself beginning to tremble. Then Zurah said in a tone so harsh that Gulrukh winced, as if she had been struck. "You, Gulrukh, my own child – what you have just said makes it even more imperative that Chunia must go. An elder sister indeed! That little low-caste Ladakhi, an idol worshipper, a cleaner of stables – she is more like a syce than a maid. Like her mother, she is a witch, and she has put her finger on you. She must go.

"As for you, I do not wish to hear you plead for any more worthless creatures. You have become a rebellious daughter, and I know why. Be silent now, or I will send you back to your husband before we leave for the hills. Mind what I say! All this talk of 'Love' for the people around you – it is not healthy. One does not love one's servants! One loves one's husband, the lord of one's life, and after him comes the love one feels for one's children. When you speak as you did this morning I find it hard to feel any affection for you. This is all Zeena's doing, taught to her by that Chunia. I will not have that nest of serpents in my house any longer."

Gulrukh bowed her head. She would have been pleased to return to her husband, whom she adored. But her husband was not in Panchghar, and would not be there for another ten days or perhaps more. He had gone to a distant village further down the valley to settle a lawsuit. If Gulrukh was sent back now, there would be no one there but her old mother-in-law and a collection of the old ruler's concubines, now of advanced age and full of gossip and bitterness. It was not an inviting prospect. Besides, she wanted to stay in order to try and turn her mother's extraordinary rage away from Zeena and Chunia.

Heavily veiled, Gulrukh followed her mother's cloaked figure out to the carriage. She was anxious to see her cousin – together they needed to plan how to save Chunia from being sent away. However angry Zeena would be about her loss of freedom, she would be even more distraught by the thought of losing Chunia. Zeena would think of something to prevent it. She was better at evading Zurah Begum than Gulrukh was. She was not afraid of Zurah. Perhaps she would speak with one of the guards and send him off with a letter to her father, that was the kind of thing she was quite capable of doing. The Chikor servants all adored Zeena. They would do anything for her.

When she and her mother arrived at the gates of the Chikor Mahal, Gulrukh was surprised to see that the sentries on duty were wearing the uniform of the Pakodi state forces. She had become used to the elderly retired men of the Chikor forces. Now, though, there were young men, and she did not remember seeing them before. She remarked on this to her mother who replied tartly that surely she did not imagine she knew the faces of every man in her father's army.

"Of course not, Ma-ji," said Gulrukh, "I wondered why our men were on guard duty at this gate."

"Because," said Zurah, "Sadik Khan took his best men with him on the *Shikar*. Not only that, the usual gate sentries were too careless in their duties. They had served the family too long, and were too old for their work. Why, anyone who wished could come and go. My men are better trained. No one can get in or out now without first obtaining permission from me." Zurah Begum wore an expression that Gulrukh and, indeed, all Zurah's household had learned to dread. But Gulrukh forgot her fear in astonishment. Zurah Begum had dismissed the guards that Sher Ali employed – and she spoke of the new guards as being 'her' men. Gulrukh was concerned. She had no idea what her mother would do next.

"Ma-ji, you speak as if the Chikor Mahal is a prison! What makes you so angry? Do you think Zeena will run away? When you look as you do now, and speak so harshly, I too become afraid and want to flee!"

They had drawn up at the steps leading to the Zenana, and Zurah said nothing until they were inside the doors. Then she turned on her daughter, her eyes blazing.

"Then run away if you feel so, and take Zeena and that little snake with you. Do not try to return! Go back to your husband and see if he will be joyful to see you once he knows that your parents have cast you off. I do not wish to keep you here if you are going to argue over everything I do. Go!"

Gulrukh stood still in total dismay. There was certainly something wrong with her mother. And she was not going to tolerate it.

"My father is also part of my family – and he has not cast me off! I will go and find my father and tell him that you are very unwell. He must return at once, he will be distressed when he hears what I have to say, and so will Sadik Khan – and they will return with me at once."

Zurah continued to glare at her daughter, her face distorted with anger. She said, "Indeed, you have been well taught by your cousin. She runs to her father all the time to make trouble. Do not speak so lightly of going to find your father! How will you find him, a young girl in your condition going up and down the roads of Hind, crying for your father! Very good for our name! Leave being foolish, I spoke in rage – I only wish to keep that girl from blackening our faces. She will bring shame on us if I do not watch her. But I will safeguard our honour, that is all I wish to do."

"But mother. What has Zeena done to enrage you so bitterly?"

"Who knows what she has done, alone here all last night. I should not have left her, I should have taken her with us. Now I will go and question her. And *you* are not coming. Go and rest and think of your child, your son, inshallah."

"I think of my child both night and day. But I must say to you, mother, that you seem to me to have run mad! You threaten to turn me away from my father's house and now I am afraid that something terrible will happen." Eventually, Gulrukh in tears, ran from the room.

Zurah Begum stood looking after her for a few moments, then she shrugged and turned away. Zeena was her first problem – she would deal with her daughter later. She hurried out to the kitchen quarters, throwing off her veil and calling for her maid as she went.

Nine

Safely in her own rooms, Gulrukh grew calmer. She was relieved to find them empty, as the maid her mother had provided for her was – she was certain – apt to go and tell her mother everything she did. And certainly everything she talked about with Zeena. *A spy*, thought Gulrukh, who now began to think of occasions when she and Zeena had not been very careful about what they said.

Gulrukh decided that before anything more happened she would have to go and talk with Zeena, warn her that Zurah was in one of her very worst tempers. Gulrukh knew that Zeena would have to prove that she had accepted the thought of her marriage and was willing to go through with it. Perhaps Zurah would then grow calmer, and Chunia would not be sent away.

She waited until her mother's voice could be heard in the kitchen quarters: one of the servants was being questioned, or scolded – or both. Gulrukh went out of her living quarters and hurried down the passage to Zeena's room. She tapped gently on the door and lifted the latch. But the door was locked and no one came to open it. Gulrukh put her ear to the door. No sound of voices. No movement came. The silence frightened her. Chunia should have been there, as she always was, to open the door.

Gulrukh stood in the passage and suddenly shivered. Something was wrong. Gulrukh could sense the stillness coming from Zeena's room, but she still felt that perhaps someone was there, paralysed by fear and unable to answer her calls. Again, she held her breath, listened and then whispered, "Zeena – it's me. Let me in."

No one stirred behind the door, no one came. Gulrukh crept away and went back to her own room and sat beside the window, feeling shaken – by a fear she did not understand. She thought of her mother's hard voice – her bitter words, the way she spat out Zeena's name as if it left a sour taste in her mouth – and shivered once again. She had not realised before that her mother really despised Zeena, and she could see that all Zurah's actions were directed towards hurting her cousin. Certainly, Chunia's dismissal was nothing to do with the way the maid did her work. It was to make Zeena's life miserable.

Where *was* Chunia? There was no sign of her. It was all too strange: that locked door, bolted on the inside, and no one in the room. Or was there someone . . .

Suddenly, though, Gulrukh's fears turned to her cousin. Suppose Zeena had tried to go riding, but had discovered that her syce, her manservant and her guard had all been sent away. What if she had felt imprisoned and had, in desperation, carried out her threats: having swallowed her earrings – or taken poison – was she now lying dead behind that locked door? *Oh, Allah the Compassionate, make none of this true. Save my beloved cousin!* Gulrukh was trembling with horror at her own imagination.

Staring out – full of anxiety – into the green and gold of the garden, Gulrukh focused on a movement beyond the long beds of flowers, on the far side of the lawn. She couldn't make the figure out at first. But soon she realised it was a woman moving cautiously from one patch of shadow to another, bending low and finally disappearing behind the thickly planted bushes of jasmine and plumbago that grew along the wall. Gulrukh was sure that the woman was Chunia, but dressed as she had never seen her. Wearing dark robes, the bareheaded figure was scuttling like a frightened animal between the deep shade and the trees. Gulrukh stood up and was about to call to the woman, but stopped herself sharply. *If that* was *Chunia, she was running away*, fearing for her life. Something very bad must have happened to make Chunia so frightened.

Gulrukh waited a few minutes to see if the woman reappeared, but there was no sign of her. Gulrukh was still looking out of the window when her mother burst in.

"What are you doing, standing unveiled in front of an open window? Be ashamed!"

"There is no one there, mother – who would see me?"

"No one?" questioned Zurah. "There will be soon, though." I have ordered that the garden be searched – I am not going to allow our family to be disgraced. They cannot have gone far—"

"Who? What is it mother, who are you looking for? Not Zeena? Mother be careful, you are behaving very strangely. What is it with you? Zeena has done nothing wrong and you know that – and this is her home. You must not behave as if she has no rights here. She is her father's heir, and it is *only* her marriage that is preventing her from becoming the Begum of Chikor."

Her mother was infuriated, her glare quite mad, and Gulrukh faltered into silence. This lasted for a few minutes

103

while Zurah Begum attempted to gain control of herself. When she finally spoke, her voice was as harsh as the cawing crows that were protesting against the disturbance in *their* garden. There were men walking about in the garden, carrying long staves with which they were beating the bushes and areas behind the trees.

"I do not know why you believe these men are searching for Zeena. Zeena is asleep in her bed. But Chunia is missing, and so is a quantity of Zeena's jewellery – not least the emerald chain that she wore last night."

Gulrukh just couldn't imagine Zeena asleep in her room while Zurah Begum searched for missing jewellery in the dressing room next door. This was very unlikely – as unlikely, in fact, as Chunia having stolen anything. But Gulrukh kept these thoughts to herself.

"Mother – you said 'they' cannot have gone far. Who has gone with Chunia?" As Gulrukh spoke, she looked carefully at her mother's face, and thought she saw a flicker of uncertainty in her eyes.

"How you question me. My own daughter! As it happens, we think the kitchen boy has gone with her, he cannot be found either. Are you sure you saw nothing while you were standing by the window? No one at all?"

"I saw no one," said Gulrukh steadily, knowing that the only way to help Chunia was by convincing her enraged mother to leave the garden be. "Only the peaceful garden." *Which is destroyed now*, she thought, *I shall never be able to look out of this window again without seeing Chunia running in fear*. And Zeena? Gulrukh could not believe that her cousin was lying asleep, with such a huge commotion going on. She became dreadfully suspicious. Her mother's story that the kitchen boy had run away with Chunia was ridiculous. The more she considered the situation the more afraid she became, on Zeena's behalf.

Looking away from her mother's angry eyes, Gulrukh asked, "Mother – is Zeena really asleep?"

"Oh may Allah protect me from the ingratitude of my daughter. Are you implying that I lie to you?" For one moment, Zurah appeared so outraged that Gulrukh felt sure that her mother would strike her. To protect herself, the young girl stepped back holding her arms in front of her body. Zurah saw the movement, and the fear in her daughter's face, and made another effort to control herself. "Yes, she is asleep. What else?"

"I wonder at her sleeping so soundly, when there is so much noise. I am afraid for her – very afraid."

"Do not be foolish. No one is going to harm your precious cousin! Are you now accusing me of doing her wrong? You are becoming fanciful – but of course, this can happen when you are carrying a child. Be calm, my daughter, do not imagine such ludicrous things." Zurah now had control of her voice. She spoke tenderly as she usually did, and put her hand gently on Gulrukh's arm. "What is it, my daughter? Do you not trust me, your mother? When have you ever seen me harm one of my family? Even when I have been greatly provoked?"

This was true – Zurah had often raged, but the rage had never led to violence. But Gulrukh, while longing to believe her mother, was still doubtful. She had never seen Zurah Begum in such a fury, so full of bitter anger – and her actions had been so strange." She had dismissed the Chikor guards, ordered a search of the garden, while accusing Chunia of theft – none of this was right. She looked up to meet her mother's eyes.

Zurah repeated her question, "What is it, Gulrukh piyari? Do you feel ill?" The question was tenderly spoken, and Gulrukh's eyes filled with tears. This was the voice she was used to, this was the Zurah Begum that she knew – and loved. Gulrukh longed to cast herself into her mother's arms, pour out her fears, and have them all soothed away – and yet something stopped her.

Addressing her mother with the loving diminutive once again, Gulrukh said,

"Oh Ma-ji, I am so afraid – if Zeena is so soundly asleep, I am afraid that she has done what she said she would do, that she has taken poison and died. She *said* she would do that if she was forced into marriage."

"What foolish thoughts you have! She is sleeping peacefully, with the curtains drawn and the shutters closed. She can hear nothing. In any case, I will call off the men if it is distressing you so much. But you must see that I cannot allow a servant to run from the house if there is jewellery missing."

It all sounded so sensible, and her mother spoke as she normally did. But Gulrukh's fear remained. Her mother noticed her daughter's unease and said at once, "Gulrukh, what is it? You are over-tired, come and lie on your bed and rest. I will go and give some orders, bring back tea, and we will speak together, mother and daughter, and you will tell me what Zeena has said to you: where she rode and what she saw. Poor foolish Zeena. I am sure that when she is married she will be happy, as you are, my good obedient daughter."

Zurah left the room smiling – *perhaps my worries are ill-founded*, Gulrukh thought. But then she remembered Zeena once saying, "When your mother smiles be careful – it means she is plotting something that will not be pleasant for us. It is a smile of power."

Gulrukh lay obediently on her bed and watched the door close behind her mother, her own mind full of half-formed plans. But when she heard the key turn in the lock she started up, appalled. Her mother had locked her in! This was enough to cement the decision she had been making

She lay still until the sound of her mother's footsteps had faded into silence, then she got up and went into the bathroom. Here there was one door that was never locked. The privy door was always unbolted so that the sweeper, with his conical basket, could get in to carry out the pan from the commode. She opened the door a crack, listened, and then slipped out into the hot dazzling sun. She kept close to the wall of the house as she walked quickly to Zeena's bathroom door.

The searchers were still about – she could see them in the distance moving like shadows along the wall that surrounded the property. They were intent on their business, and did not see her. She tried the door beside her and, as she had expected, it was unbolted. She went in quickly, closing the door behind her. Now she would see if her mother was telling the truth. If Zeena was in her bed asleep, she would never doubt her mother again . . .

The bedroom was dark, the mosquito net drawn close about the big bed. She could see a figure lying on the bed, covers pulled up around the shoulders.

"Zeena!" she whispered, but Zeena did not move. Gulrukhh went closer and lifted the folds of the net. There was no movement. *Merciful Allah let her wake, let her not be dead*! With trembling hands Gulrukh drew down the covers and stood back with a gasp.

There was no one there. Just a roll of bedding, carefully arranged to look like someone sleeping. So carefully done that there was even a dark wisp of veiling where the head might have been resting!

Gulrukh dropped the netting and stood back. Who had arranged the bed so carefully? Chunia, to hide Zeena's escape – if she had escaped? Or Zurah, to make her story seem true? It did not really matter. Zurah had lied. Zeena was not there. Was she safely on her way, or was she being hunted by those men who were investigating, beating every inch of the garden? There was no time to look for answers. Only time to get to her room before her mother came back.

She was at the bathroom door when she heard her mother's voice, somewhere outside. Her tone was low, but the words were perfectly clear. "You have only found one? Then widen the search – outside the gate, and into the walled city. There is a great reward waiting for the man that finds her and brings her back – widen the search, and be quick."

Gulrukh heard every word, with shocked amazement. Her mother *had* gone mad. She was speaking of her niece, the ruler's daughter, and Chunia, a faithful servant of the family. Gulrukh knew that she had to get news to her father.

Atlar Khan had always seemed distant from her mother. He always seemed to be amused by his wife's commands and her determination to rule both her own household and the Chikor family. But surely this was more serious and he would not allow Zurah Begum to behave in this way. Gulrukh had to get word to him.

She was safely back in her own bed, lying as her mother had left her, trying to quieten her hurrying heart and catch her breath when her mother came back. Zurah put a soothing hand on her head, and looked startled.

"You are sweating Gulrukh. You have allowed yourself to develop a fever with all this worrying about your cousin – I am sending for the hakim in any case. Zeena is not well. She complained of a headache in the night, it seems, and now, this morning, she is burning with fever. The hakim can see you both when he comes – but once you have become calm and have perhaps slept a little I am sure you will be well again. Drink this – it is fresh orange juice, it will cool you better than tea. Drink it, and then I must go and see Zeena – foolish girl, she must have been very unwell in the night. Chunia should have sent one of the men for me."

The orange juice was cool and sweet, and Gulrukh drank it all with her mother's kindly eye resting on her. Had she been dreaming, or had she imagined everything? Her mother was so plainly her usual self, bending to take the glass, then smoothing back Gulrukh's hair, saying softly, "Now sleep, my daughter – remember your child, and for his sake, rest."

It was while she was watching her mother move about the room, drawing the curtain to darken the room, picking up the veil and the cloak that Gulrukh had discarded, that Gulrukh heard what she thought was the wail of a baby – distant, somewhere across the garden and down towards the stable.

"Mother, did you hear that cry?" Her mother, standing by the open window said, "I heard no cry – try to sleep, Gulrukh, you are distraught."

"No – listen, there it is again. It sounds like a baby? But Mohammed has gone already, with Zainab—"

"Then there is no baby here. You are imagining that cry. Unless, perhaps, one of the servants has his wife here, and their child. Yes that is what it is." Her mother pulled the window shut, and drew the curtain across it. But the sound, though muffled, could still be heard.

Gulrukh moved restlessly, raising her head from the pillow. The cry was so desolate, as if the child was lying alone. She put her hand on her stomach, feeling the curve, wondering when she would first feel her own child stir in her womb. Her mother was about to leave, but before she did so she came to the bed and adjusted the quilt over Gulrukh's shoulders. Her eyes seemed to be staring. She was angry once more.

"Why don't you sleep, Gulrukh? Why are you lying there imagining the cries of a child in the servant's quarters. If you cannot sleep perhaps you have something on your mind – have you been honest about all you and Zeena have talked about? Do you know anything you have not told me?"

Gulrukh was cold with fear, a feeling she associated with a time, long ago, when she had found a cobra in her bathroom. This was not her mother bending over her, with staring eyes, this was a terrifying stranger. Something evil had fallen on her mother, a bad spirit had entered her and taken away her soul. The room seemed full of coiling shadows, drifting smoke, and in the distance Gulrukh could hear the desolate cry. Gulrukh tried to sit up, but the shadows in the room towered and grew and, before she could move, the darkness overwhelmed her and she fell into a pit of drugged sleep.

"At last," said Zurah Begum, drawing the quilt up over the

girl's shoulders. "Sleep, my daughter, and let me do what I must." She went out, locking the door behind her.

The drug in the orange juice was strong. It had taken a long time to work. But now Gulrukh would sleep for the rest of the day.

Ten

Outside, in the paved courtyard of the House of Pomegranates, a fountain tossed a plume of sparkling spray into the air, and a carriage waited.

The horses stamped and rattled their harnesses. These were pleasant sounds, familiar to Zeena – a reminder that life had once been ordinary and normal. Sakhi Mohammed and Raza, having changed their clothes after carrying the sheeted body of Chunia upstairs, had returned to sit by the fountain, talking in low voices – a picture, to Zeena, of a past that seemed to have gone forever as she listened to what Rabindra was telling her.

"Chunia took too long to make her preparations. She was trying to ensure that you would not be missed too soon – but Zurah Begum, who was not expected for another day, returned earlier. Chunia had to leave by daylight, instead of waiting for darkness. Also Zurah Begum had changed the guard on the gate – she brought her own men and dismissed your father's troopers. If she had not done that, Chunia could have walked out without trouble. As it was, she was caught." He paused and looked into Zeena's face. She sat so still, her face without expression, a beautiful mask. He wondered if she had heard what he was saying. He repeated, "She was caught

112

– and taken down to the stables at the end of the compound." He saw Zeena pull her shoulders in as if she dodged a blow. He knew then that she had heard him.

"She was beaten, Zeena. Badly beaten and brutally treated. She has the heart of a lion. She bore it all and did not tell them what they wanted to know. When she could keep silent no longer, she screamed without words, until the merciful gods sent darkness over her mind and she was out of pain."

Zeena said nothing for a few minutes, then she freed her hands from Lara's grasp and said, "She is dead. I want to see her please."

Lara moved closer to her. "No, no, she is not dead. She lives, though her injuries are terrible – a hakim has been sent for."

"Yes," said Rabindra. "The man who is coming is from the mission hospital. Doctor Robert. If anyone can save her, he can. With the help of the gods he will do it."

"Let me see her." Zeena could not hold back her tears, as she pleaded with the Master.

At first Rabindra refused, but Lara said, "Take her up, let her see the girl – the pain is greater when someone you love is hurt and you are kept from seeing them. It builds nightmares."

"Nothing could be worse than what you will see, Zeena, but I believe there is wisdom in Lara's words. Come then, Zeena, for only a minute, before the hakim comes. He must not see you."

Upstairs, in a big, silent room, Chunia was lying on a high bed. She was covered by a sheet, which was now stained by the deep red blood that had seeped from her injuries. Zeena stood at the foot of the bed, while Rabindra lifted the cover.

Zeena's eyes fell on a stranger. This was not Chunia – this battered, soiled person, whose draggled hair had been pulled back from her face. *A face?* There was nothing to see but a profusion of blood and dark, hideous markings. "But this is not Chunia, you are wrong!" said Zeena, shuddering away from what she saw.

Rabindra with a steady hand raised the sheet more, and Zeena saw the woman's hands: one hand was sheltering another. The hand on top was untouched – long fingered, work worn, with a ring on one finger, a band of thin silver, set with a blue stone.

Zeena looked back to the head on the pillow, then back to the hand with the ring, and cried out, "Oh Chunia! Chunia."

At the sound of Zeena's cry, the battered head on the pillow moved and the whole body convulsed, as if the injured Chunia was trying to respond to this heartfelt wail.

Rabindra pulled Zeena back from the bed. "Hush, be silent. She must not be disturbed!"

"Disturbed? *I* disturb her?" Zeena burst into tears as Rabindra took her out of the room, directing her back to Lara.

"Well?" said Lara.

Rabindra nodded, "The Begum saw Chunia. Now we must take her away from here, find somewhere safe for her, in case Chunia was followed."

"No! I will not go. Do you think to take me away from Chunia now when she needs me most? *Me*, not you. She was lying like one dead until she heard my voice. I must stay with her, I am her life. She has been with me from the day I was born. She needs someone close to her. How can she find her way back from the threshold of death without a known hand to hold hers, a loved voice to call her name? Surely you can find somewhere in this great house to hide me until the hakim has been? I can hide every time he comes – I must stay. I *will* stay. If that carriage is waiting for me, send it away."

Rabindra said slowly, "This is a risk I did not wish to take. If you are discovered, all that Chunia has endured will have gone for nothing. There is another matter. Should you be found, and the connection between you and the Captain is made, his life will not be worth a handful of dust. He will be hunted and killed, either by men sent by your bridegroom, whose face your actions have blackened, or by Zurah's men. Think well, Zeena Begum."

"I will stay. If Chunia dies, I will return to the Chikor Mahal and throw myself on my father's mercy. As for Alan Lyall, they can do nothing to him – there is nothing that links our two names. Our meetings were not seen – and you yourself have arranged that no suspicion could fall on him. It is settled, I stay."

"So, you stay." At that moment both Lara and Rabindra knew that this girl had her own power; she was no weakling certainly, she seemed to be growing up in front of their eyes. But only Lara wondered, a little sadly, how important Alan Lyall was to the young, headstrong Zeena. She had not heard Zeena mention him once all this long morning.

The hakim arrived. He was a man Zeena knew by sight, Dr Robert Maclaren – he had attended her father two or three times, and was often invited to the Chikor Mahal as a guest. A man from Scotland, from Alan's country – and for a moment Alan flashed into her mind. There was only room in her thoughts for Chunia. It did not seem possible that Chunia would ever recover. Zeena stood behind the closed door of the room where she had hidden before, and strained her ears for sounds from upstairs, but she could hear nothing. What would he do with that broken body – surely any touch would be agony for Chunia? *I should be beside her, I should share her pain and her fear. I who have caused all this horror.*

Zeena's thoughts drifted to Zurah Begum – but she could not connect the dignified figure of her aunt, the woman who had ruled her childhood, and had looked after household affairs in the Chikor Mahal, with the monster who had ordered such a brutal beating. It was not possible – unless Zurah Begum had lost her mind.

Zeena had never thought of herself as being her father's heir, as the future ruler of Chikor state. She had taken it for granted that, should anything happen to her father, Atlar Khan would inherit Chikor state – and after him would come Gulrukh's brother, who had already been given the title of Nawabzada Sahib. She had often discussed Zurah Begum with Gulrukh, when some stern stricture had been laid on them. They had often laughed about her jealous love of Zeena's father, and her possessive hold on Atlar Khan. Now Zeena began to see that perhaps they had not understood the strength of Zurah's passions. Her thoughts roved over the past, but always returned to Chunia – what had happened to her and what was happening upstairs.

The sound of the doctor's deep voice was suddenly clear, he must have been making his way downstairs. "She would be better in our hospital, Rabindra. Surely you do not belong to the uncivilised, who imagine that we murder our patients. So, tell, what is your objection? I can send a nurse, of course, but really her wounds need careful dressing, and constant care – she is in a shocking state. I doubt if we can save her eye but I should insist on her coming to the hospital."

"Yes, and you could refuse to attend her if we do not agree to let her go. You have had patients from here before. We know well how skilled your nurses are. But for the sake of Chunia's safety, we cannot let her go. She is being hunted now – here she is safe. No one will look for her here – she comes from a respectable family."

"A respectable family; she has been beaten almost to death – and you will not send for the police? I do not understand, Rabindra, this is not usual for you. I would have expected you to go at once to the police *Thana*, and to have reported this affair to the Residency. This is still British India, you know."

"Not so, Robert. This house is across the border, and you stand on land ruled by the native states."

"You are splitting hairs, my brother. Any one of the rulers who has property here would be against such violence."

"In *this* case, the girl would be in danger from those who you assume would help her. I ask you to trust me – that could not be dealt with by the British without confusion, and possibly more trouble that could become widespread. Will you continue to attend her here – she is in safety, unless of course you speak."

"I do not think that you need to mention that. Of course I will do what I can for her – I am a doctor, and I hold my vows sacred. But after all these years of friendship I am confounded by your refusal to contact either the police or the British authorities. The people who performed this brutality are criminals and should be brought to justice. Not only was she almost beaten to death, but she was also raped by those monsters as well. By not taking up her case, you are protecting people of no value."

"Not so. Be very sure that vengeance will be taken. But in my way. If I take this to the police or to the authorities, you already know, from experience, what is likely to happen: endless paper-work, a long case before a magistrate – either British or one of our own venal *Thanadars* – and possibly imprisonment – unless a suitably large bribe buys their freedom. This is part of the reason why I do not want to contact the authorities. And if I were to bring this injured girl before the eyes of the administration, such a catastrophe would ensue. Two good families would be destroyed, so many lives ruined." Rabindra sighed and shook his head. "I cannot think of all that would follow. But I know this kind of action would be the cause of terrible confrontations."

There was silence for a few minutes, then the doctor said quietly, "I will return as soon as I can and will bring with me all that the girl's 'nurse' will need. I hope for her sake that you have someone intelligent and compassionate."

As soon as the doctor had gone, Zeena rushed upstairs to Chunia, followed by Lara. Two ayahs, and Chini Ayah were in the room where Chunia lay. The torn, bloodied clothes and been removed, and Chunia's head and face had been cleaned. Her hair was combed back from her face – now bruises and contusions were clearly seen. Her right eye was covered by a pad of white linen, the other, surrounded by bruising, was closed, with the lids terribly swollen. Did Chunia sleep, or was she still unconscious?

Zeena sat on the floor by the bed and whispered, "I am here, Chunia. We are both safe – I will never leave

118

you." This time there was no sign that Chunia had heard her.

Lara was speaking quietly to Chini Ayah, but returned to Zeena in no time at all. "She has had a powder mixed with warm milk, it has been dripped into her mouth, and Chini Ayah thinks that Chunia has swallowed some of it."

"The doctor said that she was to be given nothing at all – you heard him," said Zeena crossly.

Lara shrugged. "I heard him – but Chini Ayah did not. She is a very wise woman. The herbs and powders that she makes are good. See, already Chunia sleeps quietly."

Zeena had no way of telling whether Chunia was sleeping, or whether she was comatose. She took Chunia's uninjured hand and held it. There was a tap at the door and Lara went to answer it. She had been called by Rabindra: "I will come and warn you when the doctor returns. There is a dressing room through the door, where you must hide before he comes in."

After Lara left the room, Zeena was conscious of a feeling in the air of expectation, of patient waiting for some event. *What event?* she wondered. *Chunia's death? No*, she thought, *no, I will not let her go! I will keep her alive by every memory I have of her – she cannot die, love alone will protect her from death.*

At intervals, Zeena whispered Chunia's name, but there was never any response, and Chunia's hand was very cold. Zeena rubbed it gently. "Come back, Chunia, you cannot go – I need you." Where ever Chunia was, she might hear and answer – she had never ignored any call from Zeena.

Time wore away, and the hand that Zeena held remained

119

cold. But Zeena would not give up. She was whispering Chunia's name once more when she heard a sound and noticed someone in the room behind her.

"That is good. You must also talk to her, just as if you believe that she can hear you. We do not know how much the soul hears when a person lies in the stillness of a coma. Now, let me take your place for a time. Bring me some drinking water."

The doctor had returned, and no one had warned her. Her veil lay round her shoulders – bareheaded she stood up and met his interested gaze. She saw a tall Englishman, with very bright, observing eyes. She looked into his blue eyes, which reminded her – but they were not as blue as the eyes that she was remembering . . .

This man was not young. He was perhaps her father's age. He had an air of command – like, her father, Sadik Khan, he was used to being obeyed instantly. No one had ever ordered Zeena to bring anything.

The doctor took the glass from her, bent over Chunia, and poured the water, drop by drop onto the cotton pad that covered Chunia's right eye. He then tried to lift the pad from the eye but it resisted him. He asked for more water and when one of the other women brought it, he said to Zeena, "Could you try to lift off the pad as I pour the water. Do not force it, if it does not come easily." Zeena's hand shook as she took a corner of the pad in her fingers and pulled gently. She watched to see if Chunia was in pain, but there was no sign. The pad lifted off easily and she gasped as she saw what it covered. There did not seem to be any eye, only a mass of blood. The doctor did not touch it. He took a fresh pad from the box he had brought with him and covered the eye once more, and Zeena was glad not to see the wound any longer.

She said softly, "Oh Chunia piyari, what have they done." And then, looking up at the man she said,

"You can save her eye?"

"I can try, but – it is a very bad wound." He shook his head and Zeena thought she saw hopelessness in his look. He stood back from the bed and beckoned to her. "When did this happen?" he asked.

"Perhaps last night – I think." She wanted to go on her knees to him, to beg him to work a miracle, to save Chunia's eye.

As if her thoughts were plain to him he said, "I am only a man. I cannot work miracles. It will be God's work if she survives. You had better pray to all your gods."

Zeena's head went back in instinctive pride, even at such a moment she was angered that he should think she was an idol worshipper. She said, "I will pray to Allah the Compassionate, the Merciful, the only God. I am of the only true faith."

"Ah. You are a Moslem. This wounded girl is not, she is a Hindu, surely – perhaps a Buddhist?' He spoke as if he were surprised that she would pray for someone of another religion.

"We both bleed," Zeena said forcefully, "we both feel pain – and she is my friend, my elder sister, even though she is not of my faith, or of our blood."

He was looking at her with interest, her fair skin and the light eyes that met his so proudly. She was different from the other women in the room; different build, different colouring, different bearing. She was like Rabindra in a way, he thought, but she could not be a member of his family if she was a Moslem. Rabindra was a Hindu – if he was anything.

"Of what race are you?" The doctor looked at Zeena, curious. He seldom saw the women of the princely houses. This girl could not be the legitimate child of a good family, not living here in the house of Lara, the madame of a high-class brothel. He waited with interest for Zeena's reply.

"I am from the hill country," said Zeena, unable to claim her family name. She looked away from the intent blue gaze that reminded her of Alan, and fumbled for her veil, feeling naked without it before this strange man. She pulled the veil up over her head and face.

The doctor had watched Zeena cover herself and reflected. *This is no whore, the veiling was not done provocatively. What on earth is this girl doing here?*

The oldest woman in the room, a fierce-eyed old crone, came forward to stand beside the girl, and pulled Zeena's veil straight. The elderly woman's glare reminded him that he was in a purdah quarter, one which he could never penetrate except in his capacity as a doctor. He turned to his patient quickly and yet he knew that there was nothing more he could do for her at that time. Without looking directly at any of the women he said, "I will come back tonight." Robert left the room, determined to ask Lara, or Rabindra, about this very different girl. He wanted to know why she was caring for a badly wounded woman of a different caste and religion.

But he did not get his answer. Instead he was frustrated to find that neither Rabindra nor Lara were there, and so he walked out to the veranda, where he saw a man he recognised at once.

"Sakhi Mohammed, how are you – no more fever?"

"Nay, Sahib – I am well, your medicine cured me."

"You are shaven – was that because of the fever? Or are

122

you chasing a younger woman, a second wife? You appear younger without your beard."

Sakhi Mohammed laughed awkwardly, looking away from the doctor, "What would I do with a younger wife?"

"Well, this is an expensive house to visit – it might be cheaper to marry." He saw that the old man was embarrassed and wondered why. This was of course a strange place to find one of Sadik Khan's senior servants – perhaps his joking was rather heavy handed.

Sakhi Mohammed had come forward to hold his stirrup as the doctor mounted. He looked up at Robert and said quietly, "I brought your patient here. Will she live?"

This was surprising. Robert saw real anxiety on the old man's face. "I will do all that I can, Sakhi Mohammed, but she is grievously wounded. If God wills, she will recover."

"Inshallah," said the old man and stepped back.

Robert Maclaren rode down the drive, more puzzled still. He began to think deeply. First, the call from Rabindra, begging him to come to deal with a badly hurt woman. Then the strange girl of a good family – he could have sworn she was – who was apparently staying at the House of Pomegranates to look after the wounded woman. And now Sakhi Mohammed, a trusted senior servant of the Chikor ruler, was here. And equally mysterious, neither Lara nor Rabindra waiting to see him go – this was unheard of discourtesy.

Something very interesting was happening under that roof. But he felt sure that any questions he might ask would go unanswered if what he was beginning to suspect was true.

Eleven

It was sunset in the jungle country of Ranaghar. The last evening of the shooting party was unfolding. In the morning they would all ride to Safed where Alan would catch the mail train to Bombay.

The two princes had declared that this last evening was to be a celebration of the successful *Shikar* and of a new and valued friendship. "We will do this every year," said Sadik Khan, his arm across Alan's shoulders. "Every year on this day we will meet – even if there is no shooting, we will meet and rejoice in our friendship. You must be always sure to arrange your leave so that it falls at this time."

Laughing, Alan said, "I will do my best but who knows where we will all be—"

"We know where we will be. We will be in Madore for the Durbar. And you – you are not thinking of leaving your regiment, surely? Of course you will be in Madore for the yearly Durbar and you will get leave and be with us on this evening a year from now. It is decided."

Alan wondered bleakly where he *would* be. Probably not in India – or even if, by some miracle, he was allowed to stay in the Indian Army, he would likely be in Grass Farms, or Remounts. Not in his own regiment, not after the scandal.

The news of Zeena's absence must have broken already – it must have been discovered.

I know nothing about what is happening to her. Alan drifted off into his own world. Rabindra has not kept his promise – and yet I had such a strong feeling that I could trust him. I should have followed my own instincts, I should have told Sadik Khan what was happening. Should I tell him now? He is my friend, I would trust him with my life – and yet . . .

He sighed, and saw Atlar Khan look at him sharply. Sadik Khan spoke, "You sigh, Alan? What is this, you are unhappy?"

Alan, his glance held by Atlar Khan's warning look, knew he couldn't mention anything of his true feelings. "It is only that these days it is difficult to think of the future – there is talk of war in Europe, and if that happens none of us can know where we will be—"

Atlar Khan's chest rose in a silent breath, and he looked away, but Sadik interrupted.

"There is *talk* of war, but talk sharpens no swords, and indeed none of us know where we will be at any time – the future is known only to God the Compassionate, the Merciful. We are in his hands. Let us remember that, and enjoy our days, without looking for shadows. I have reason to speak in this priestly fashion – I have not forgotten the real reason for our celebration. I have had a wonderful ten days – and if you had not jeopardised your own life to save mine, with no thought of your future, I would not be here today. Is this not a good reason for a yearly meeting?"

With that, Atlar Khan spoke, "It is the greatest reason of all. Alan is too modest to admit that he had no thought for his life at that moment. Alan, it does not matter where we are a year from now. We, my brother and I, will always remember you for *that* action if for nothing else."

Returning in his mind to the night when he almost confided in Atlar Khan, Alan now felt sure that his friend knew . . . *He knows about my love for Zeena and probably suspects our plans*, thought Alan, *but he is surely telling me that he will not talk, and warning me that I must not either. It would be so easy to tell this man, Sadik, whom I know and like so much. So easy to tell him the truth, to ask him for his daughter's hand in marriage. It seems so right to do this, and yet, I cannot forget Rabindra's warning that I must be silent. And now it is so clear that Atlar Khan is warning me. I must leave tomorrow, and say goodbye to these men with whom I have found friendship, and whom I doubt I will ever see again.*

Alan understood that soon his new friends could very well be hunting for him, with murder in their hearts. But he soon dismissed the notion, and instead determined to enjoy the celebration of this new-found friendship.

It was the night of the full moon, and the small gathering watched it rise above the trees and flood the clearing where they sat around a table glittering with crystal and silver – there was even a delicate bunch of jasmine in the centre of the table, the scent and the texture of which reminded all three men of women.

Only Alan remained silent as the other two spoke of famous beauties they had seen and known, and remembered aloud evenings of dalliance – "Long ago, long, long ago," said Atlar Khan, who smiled at his brother, Sadik Khan. "You, my brother were known to every dancing girl in the north, and your absence from their courts has always been spoken of with regret – your sudden change to chastity broke many hearts."

"Ah well – there is a poem written by one of your poets, Alan. A man who wrote his poem for a woman called the Winter Queen. Do you know the one I mean? I cannot remember it well, but the poet speaks of the moon and the stars."

"Ye meaner beauties of the night, where are you when the moon shall rise—" said Alan quietly.

"Hah! Yes, that is it. Well, the moon rose for me when I saw Yasmin, and I have never looked with love at another woman since," said Sadik Khan, who lifted his glass to the moon.

After a moment, Alan did the same, and Atlar Khan shrugged, "I will drink, as always to the many – the stars that look kindly on all men, asking nothing of love in return."

The glasses were drained and filled again. The night wore on, and still they sat, reluctant to part, talking – the two older men sharing memories, and Alan listening, enjoying their stories. It was the setting moon that lit up the paths to their beds, the long ride to Safed ahead of them but now forgotten.

At Safed station, Alan walked on to the platform escorted by the two princes. He was assured of a clean first-class compartment to himself. While they stood saying their farewells, Alan's bearer checked that his baggage was in the guard's van, opened the bedding roll and made the bunk ready for the night.

Doors were slamming all the way down the train, and Alan began to say his thanks and farewells.

"No," said Sadik Khan, "do not say farewell. We shall meet again many times, please God. You are our dear brother."

Both men embraced him, and as the train departed they stood waving until it was out of sight. Alan was glad to stretch his tired muscles on his bunk, and fell asleep within minutes of putting his head on the pillow.

He woke to daylight coming through the window, and to the noise that his bearer was making by trying to pull his boots off. The train had arrived at a station: there were shouting crowds pushing past outside, and a man selling tea passing by the window.

"Which station is this, Iqbal?" Alan asked as the bearer put the boots side by side, and began to undo his tie.

"This is Kuddasa, Sahib." He saw Alan looking at the tea-seller outside and explained, "Sahib, that tea is no good. I have tea ready for you from the refreshment room."

Alan, now in his dressing gown, sat at ease, drinking fresh tea and looking out of the window. "When do we reach Bombay, Iqbal? Tomorrow morning?"

"Yes, Sahib, but not morning. It will be in the evening."

A slender girl, in full swirling skirts, with a basket of fruit balanced on her veiled head, passed them by. She walked like a dancer, and Alan immediately thought of Zeena. His graceful, seductive Zeena. Bombay tomorrow – would she be there? In the station? Impossible. But if not, then where? How would he find her? Rabindra should have told him. He felt desperate. What if Rabindra had lied to him – if Zeena had never left the Chikor Mahal. What then? He would have to go straight back to Madore and tell Sadik Khan.

He bathed under the tap in the inadequate *ghusalkhana*, and sat in the compartment while Iqbal shaved him with a cut-throat razor, timing each sweeping stroke to the rocking rhythm of the train. Had Iqbal's hand slipped, Alan would not have noticed. He was too busy making plans for finding Zeena – if she was in Bombay, or getting her out of the Chikor Mahal if she was still there. None of his plans seemed very likely to succeed. He asked Iqbal how he would set about finding someone who was supposed to meet him in Bombay.

"Friend of Sahib's?" enquired Iqbal.

"Yes."

"I would go straight to Tajmahal Hotel. All Sahib go there. Very easy to meet there. All officer and rich men and Maharaja, all go to the Taj." Iqbal looked keenly at Alan. "You are expecting Rabindra Nath-ji, I think, Sahib?"

Alan was surprised "Yes."

Iqbal nodded. "Tajmahal, Sahib. You will need a room there for two nights – the boat does not go for two days, I think. So you go to reception desk and take one room, then you go to the veranda and sit – and Rabindra, if he is in Bombay, will come to look for you there."

Alan was always amazed at how much his bearer knew about his movements. He wondered how much of his conversation with Rabindra had been overheard.

"Do you know a man called Sakhi Mohammed?"

"Oh yes, Sahib. Very good old man, my father's cousin brother. Long time in service of Begum of Jungdah – now he is servant of young Begum, daughter of Chikor."

Alan felt he was going to learn where Zeena was with no trouble. He thought for a minute, then said, "Iqbal, if you see Sakhi Mohammed in Bombay, tell him I want to see him."

He looked enquiringly at Iqbal, who showed no surprise at his request. "Very good, Sahib," he said, and continued to put away Alan's shaving gear and to tidy the compartment, just as he would have done in Alan's quarters in Madore.

They arrived in Bombay in the late evening. The sun had set, and the sky was fading from the lurid reds, yellows and purples that marked the end of the day. His luggage piled round him, Alan stood waiting, while Iqbal bargained with a vociferous old man driving a well-cared-for Victoria.

Alan, standing in the shadows of the entry hall looked about him without hope. There was no one standing near him, no one waiting to meet him. He longed to call to Iqbal, "Leave it, Iqbal, I do not care what it costs. Let us get away from here." But for some reason he felt vulnerable. Who was going to attack him? There had not been time for anyone to get here from Madore – and he was not afraid of anybody else. He could not understand why he felt that he was being watched. But he had had felt troubled from the moment he he had left the train and walked to wait in the entrance of the station. This strange feeling reminded him of his days on the frontier to the north, riding through narrow defiles with the high rocky ridges on each side of him and his company. In those places, he had every reason to be on edge, for he knew that they were always being watched by the fierce men of the tribes who know their passage. There he was used to this sense of apprehension – before the first burst of firing. But here? Surely he had no reason for his taut nervousness.

At last Iqbal finished his bargaining and, with a smug expression on his face, he returned with the Victoria, and a tonga for the baggage. As they set off, Alan found himself looking over his shoulder, as if an enemy were following him. They were moving through crowded streets so, even if he was being watched, it was senseless to look back. Among the thronging crowds, it would not have been possible to pick out any one face.

He gradually relaxed and, by the time he reached the Tajmahal Hotel, he had nothing on his mind but the hope of a meeting with his beloved Zeena – and if not a meeting with her, then at least some news of her.

At the reception, he was told. "Your room is already reserved for you, Captain Lyall. We had a telegram from Safed – and there is also a telegram for you." Alan accepted the envelope hoping that it was from Rabindra – but suspected that this was unlikely. Rabindra was too secretive to risk contacting him by telegram. He was right – the message was from Sadik Khan and Atlar Khan, wishing him a good voyage and a happy return.

Alan walked out to the veranda and ordered himself a whisky, which he badly needed. If by evil chance Zeena's absence had been discovered and his name was already connected with hers, the family now knew where to find him.

At this time in the evening the veranda was crowded. Every table appeared to have a large party round it. He was fortunate to have a table for two. He was by this time quite prepared to believe that the two rulers had booked it for him. He sat drinking his whisky, hoping that among the crowds there was no other brother officer on leave – he could see several uniforms but no one he knew. Alone in the crowd, Alan waited with optimism.

Twelve

Late that night, after a busy day, Robert rode to the House of Pomegranates. As he walked up the drive, he heard music and the sound of voices and laughter. He had been to the house many times before, in his capacity as a medical officer, or sometimes at Rabindra's invitation to sit and talk over a meal or a drink, in the long hot weather evenings.

With night-time came an excitable, vibrant atmosphere to the House of Many Pleasures. During the day it was silent, sleeping under the sun, but on this night – as on many nights before – it was busy: lamp light spilled golden from most of the windows, and the hum of many voices above the music could be heard from afar.

The beautiful girl he had seen tending his patient that morning had returned to his thoughts many times during the day. What could have brought her to this place? He was almost sure he had guessed who she might be, but if his guess was right it made her presence in the House of Pomegranates even more unbelievable.

He dismounted at the veranda steps, and was surprised to see the same old man, Sakhi Mohammed, coming forward to take the reins and lead his horse way.

"Sakhi Mohammed! Still here? Do you work here now?"

"Only for a friend, Sahib. I will put your horse in stables until you wish to leave." As he walked away he said over his shoulder, "I no longer find employment in the Chikor Mahal."

"After so many years, Sakhi Mohammed? You have grown old in their employment. Did you leave of your own accord?"

"Zurah Begum desires younger men – I am too old to take orders from her. So, I have left."

Beneath the quiet tones of Sakhi Mohammed's voice Robert thought he detected anger, as well as sorrow. It was plain that Sakhi Mohammed didn't want to answer questions on the subject. But Robert had some questions he was determined to ask.

"Sakhi Mohammed. The injured girl you brought here this morning, was she known to you, or was she a stranger that you helped?"

"She was known to me, Sahib. She was also a servant in the Chikor Mahal, as I was."

"Then you can tell me – was it by someone's order that she was beaten so cruelly? Who in the house of Chikor would order such a punishment?"

But it was not Sakhi Mohammed who answered this, it was Rabindra's voice that spoke quietly from the shadowed veranda.

"I can tell you all that you need to know, Robert. Sakhi Mohammed, take the Sahib's horse to the stables."

"Good evening, Rabindra – I did not see you there. I will be glad to have some answers to my questions. But first I must go up and see my patient – and her beautiful and mysterious nurse."

Rabindra said calmly, "Of course. I can guess what makes

133

you ask. I will wait for you here." He had come down the steps and stood beside Sakhi Mohammed, looking tall and elegant in his usual white robes.

Robert heard Rabindra tell Sakhi Mohammed to go to the stables and, as the old man led the horse away, Robert became convinced that Rabindra was determined to prevent Sakhi Mohammed answering any questions about the wounded girl. There was nothing he could do to speak to Sakhi Mohammed, so Robert went quickly up the stairs, now sure that he had corectly guessed the identity of the beautiful stranger.

In the room where the girl Chunia lay, the noise from the house was muffled by the thick walls. Robert saw the exquisitely pretty girl seated on a stool beside the maidservant's bed. On the other side sat the old woman. Chunia lay very still, her breathing barely stirring the sheet that covered her. The pad was still over her eyes, but he saw that her face and throat were covered with a thick coating of greenish-grey ointment. A strong scent of herbs and spices stung his nostrils. God alone knew what they had put on her face and body. Robert was quite used to his patients being treated by their relatives, who treated the sick with various noxious pastes and potions, but this one smelled better than most. This was probably the work of the old woman. Robert, even-tempered and open-minded, was interested to know what the paste was, and so he asked the old woman, who was avoiding his eyes, but answered quite fearlessly when he spoke to her.

"It is an ointment made from herbs and spices. I have cured worse wounds than this, Sahib."

"I see. You are a healer, no doubt. Tell me, old one, have you moved her at all?"

"I bathed her, Sahib, therefore I moved her. You think of

134

broken bones? Her body is whole, bruised and torn, but the bones are not splintered or fractured, except the fingers on the right hand. There is not a whole bone in that hand, and her fingernails are gone. It will be many moons before she is able to eat, as is suitable, using her right hand."

Privately Robert doubted if the girl would ever eat again, but he changed his mind as he felt her pulse – faint but steady, stronger than it had been that morning. This was wonderful, more than he had hoped for.

All this time, Zeena had sat without speaking. She had only moved to veil herself to his regret. Now he turned to her and said, "Has she been conscious at all?"

"No. She has not moved all day."

"All the same, she is better. Her pulse is stronger and the simple fact that she still lives is miraculous. Has she been given anything by the mouth – I had better ask the old lady, what is her name?"

"She is Chini Ayah. She is greatly respected as a healer Lara-ji told me."

It was when Robert spoke to Chini Ayah in Urdu that Zeena realised that he had been talking to her in English, and she had replied in the same language.

Fool! she thought to herself, *I have given him a reason to be curious about me. It is unlikely that a girl in this house would be fluent in English. Was he suspicious, has he been trying to trap me? How he stares, even though he is talking to Chini Ayah. He is looking at me, as if he was trying to penetrate the veil.*

She lowered her head before his interested blue stare, and at once he looked away and returned his gaze to Chini Ayah who was still describing to him the herbs she had used.

"Have you given her anything to drink?"

"Only the powder you left for her. I dripped it into her mouth as you would feed a wounded bird. Did I do wrong, Sahib?"

Chini Ayah was hungry for praise.

"No, Chini Ayah, you are indeed a healer – you had the courage that I lacked – to try and restore the life that was almost gone – and you have succeeded. See, she is sleeping quietly, and that alone is a sign of her healing. I leave her in your hands – as for *her* hand, I can do nothing until the swelling goes down."

As he turned away, the old woman stopped him.

"There is something I would ask, Sahib – it concerns this other one, who is as close to my heart as any child has been."

Robert looked quickly at Zeena. "Yes, old one – what is it?"

"She will not leave the bedside. She should sleep, she should eat – or at least drink some warmed milk. She will do nothing. She just sits here like a hen on her eggs, growing old before her time. If you, Sahib should give an order—"

Robert looked at Zeena and met her furious eyes as she dropped her veil to say, "Old woman! I do not need you to speak to the hakim about me! You forget yourself!"

"Nay, Begum Sahiba, I only ask that he sends you to your bed before you become sick yourself."

"Begum Sahiba?" said Robert. "So I was right. You are Zeena Begum, the Choti Begum of Chikor. Don't be angry with Chini Ayah, she is quite right, you are exhausted. I don't want you as my next patient. I suggest that you go to your room and sleep. You can be sure that your maid will be

well cared for, and you will be able to sit with her tomorrow
– perhaps hear her speak. So do as Chini Ayah says – have
a hot drink, and sleep."

Zeena did not move. She looked up at him and asked,
"How do you know my name?"

"Partly, it was a guess. Then, this morning I met an old man
Sakhi Mohammed outside. He told me that he had brought the
wounded girl here – and I remembered that I had treated him
for a bad bout of malaria in the Chikor Mahal. Then in my
dispensary I heard two of the nurses talking about jewellery
that had been stolen by a maidservant at the Chikor Mahal
and that men were searching the roads for two missing girls
– it was not hard to guess. But I would like to know what
the only child of my friend Sadik Khan of Chikor is doing
in this place."

Zeena was not listening to him. She had heard nothing he
had said after the words, "Men sent to search the roads for
two missing girls."

Chunia lying helpless, and men searching – danger was
moving closer. And this man, this doctor – if he talked! She
looked up at him and he saw terror in her eyes.

"My dear girl – what is it?"

"They are searching for us – Zurah Begum's guards. You
said it was not hard for you to guess who I am – how easy
then, for them to find out *where* I am if you speak of seeing
us. And if *you* do not speak there may be others who will."

"I will not say a word, I promise you. I will not mention
your name outside this house. But, surely, even if you are
found you will come to no harm – you are the daughter of
Sadik Khan himself! Who will dare to touch you?"

"I should be lying where Chunia is – she was almost beaten

137

to death because she wouldn't say where I was hiding. And if Zurah Begum finds me—"

"I don't understand? Why would you be beaten? What have you done?"

"I have run away."

"For what reason?"

"I ran from a marriage that I do not want, and a family I can no longer trust."

"But your father loves you, Zeena Begum, and I am sure he will not force you to marry a man you do not want?"

"How can you say that he is a loving father? You know nothing. Look at Chunia – do you think I can ever trust any member of my family again?

"I told my father that I did not want to marry, but he signed the marriage contract before he went away – and this marriage contract cannot be broken. Well, now I have broken it – and I will never go back. I never want to see my father again."

Robert found it hard to believe that the man whose friendship he had enjoyed for years could have a servant – a woman – punished with such brutality. Somehow Zeena's story seemed to be confused and incomplete. But he saw that she was exhausted and overwrought, and decided that he should ask no more questions of her. He would talk to Rabindra.

"I think you are too tired to make such decisions tonight. Sleep now – you and Chunia are safe enough here. We will talk again."

She looked back at him with fear in her eyes. How could such beautiful, speaking eyes hold such fear?

"Please do not be afraid that I will give you away. I give you my word, Zeena Begum. Trust me." As if he was sealing a vow by the gesture, he took her hand and kissed it before he walked out of the room. He heard the bolts being drawn across the door before he had taken three steps. He found it unbearable to think of this girl lying awake behind that bolted door, starting up at every sound.

In the big room downstairs, he found Rabindra waiting for him, and said at once, "I know who you have upstairs: Zeena Begum, the only daughter of Sadik Khan, and her maid Chunia. She has run away from the Chikor Mahal, and she is terrified. Can you please explain why she is so tormented, because her terror will certainly make her ill."

"Did she tell you why she ran away?"

"Yes. The reason that girls so often run away. The dread of the husband that her family has found for her."

"In this case, the arranged marriage was organised three years ago."

"Good heavens – and she is so young!"

Rabindra smiled. "Your people look at age differently to us. She is seventeen, that is not too young to be married in this country."

"So she was fourteen when the man was chosen. How could a girl of that age choose a husband?"

"Quite so. But our girls do not choose. The husband is chosen for them. Most accept this. In fact Zeena Begum made no fuss about her marriage being arranged. None at all. The girls of princely families are well used to arranged marriages. They know that they will have little say, if any, about the choice of a husband. Like all of them, Zeena disliked the idea, but accepted it as a fact of life. Then two things happened: she heard some talk about her future husband – gossip among the women – which frightened and angered

139

her; and at the same time, she met, while out riding, Captain Alan Lyall, a most personable and charming man." Rabindra was looking keenly at Robert as he spoke.

"Alan Lyall?" said Robert. "I know him. He is a very pleasant fellow – you say he *met* Zeena Begum? I have been to the Chikor Mahal many times, and have never even seen her – and you say they met?"

"Oh, not an official meeting, you understand. As you know, the young Begums do not attend the regimental balls or dinner parties. But they met, and continued to meet secretly, for very short periods over the last two years. It seems it does not take a long time to fall under love's dangerous spell?"

"No." said Robert thoughtfully, "it does not take very long. I know young Alan Lyall quite well. Sandeman House, where he was born is just across Loch Lymon where my parents live. Both his parents are dead, and his elder brother, the heir, was killed in Africa, so Alan inherited the title. He is the fifth baronet. The people of the village and the glen will be all agog to see the new lady of Sandeman House. I wonder, does the Choti Begum have any idea of how her life will be up in the wilds of Scotland? I think my parents' house is the nearest for miles – the new Lady Lyall will feel very isolated there." Robert spoke slowly, frowning over his thoughts.

"So it is more than just running from a future husband she does not want – she is running to a lover. That makes it more serious to the family, I suppose. But surely – I know Sadik Khan well. He is a most civilised man, and I am certain he would not force his beloved daughter into a situation she does not want?"

"Robert, you are not thinking as we think. Your ways are different. How many years have you spent here, yet parts of

140

our lives and customs are still hidden from you. None are more hidden than the customs of the harem – the closed place, the Zenana. Sadik Khan would not even consider this marriage to be a question of force. He has arranged a suitable union with a ruler of another state, a state that is as wealthy as his own. The girl will live, wrapped in a kind of luxury. These girls – they know from childhood what their lives are to be. Girls dream of handsome princely lovers, of course, but they marry as they are told. As Zeena would have done, had she not met Alan Lyall. A marriage contract, once entered into and signed, cannot be broken."

"Never?" asked Robert.

"Never. Well, not without a great deal of trouble, and disgrace for the girl – and the family – who breaks it. The Chikor family would find it difficult to arrange another good marriage for Zeena. Oh, they would be able to find a husband for her, but he would be a man who, already married, wants a second, younger wife. Sadik would consider that kind of marriage beneath his family. Zurah Begum of Pakodi, Sadik's sister arranged this marriage and was well pleased with it, and Zeena, at first, made no great objection – until she met Alan Lyall."

"So Zeena Begum ran away for love," said Robert. "And that unfortunate maid of hers was so badly beaten on the orders of – Zurah Begum? In the absence of Sadik Khan? The girl is fortunate to have survived but she will be scarred for life. I am sure that had Sadik Khan been in the palace this outrage would not have happened."

Rabindra sighed, "Who knows? I am sure the girl would not have been raped – a reward for the man who caught her – if Sadik had been there. But if Zurah Begum told him that his daughter had run away and only Chunia knew where she was – oh yes, I think he would have approved of such a beating to make Chunia talk. Sadik Khan is a man of strong passions. He is possessive and jealous of temperament, and his daughter is his most valued possession."

"Strange. He loves his daughter, yet he will not give her freedom of choice over the man with whom she must spend her entire life. Who was chosen for her?"

"No doubt you have met him. He goes out and about a great deal when he attends the Durbars. A man of great wealth. He is Tariq Khan of Sagpurna."

"You lie! *That* man? He is well over sixty and even I have heard rumours about him. I cannot believe what you tell me." Robert's tone was full of anger.

"Well, it is true. Among the women, it is said that Zurah Begum has fixed her sights on the Guddee of Chikor for her son Mohammed Khan. So she wants Zeena Begum to marry a ruler whose kingdom lies a good distance from Chikor. Zeena cannot make a claim to her father's inheritance if she marries a Mohammadan and Sagpurna lies far away on the western coast. She has persuaded Sadik Khan that Tariq Khan is ageing, and that he will not live long. She claims that then Zeena, a childless widow, can return to Chikor – what a fool Sadik Khan is. Tariq Khan may well live on for years – and Zeena Begum could die young and broken-hearted. Hearts wither and die, and the body soon follows.

"There are many other things that could hasten Zeena Begum's death – not least, a Zenana full of jealous concubines, all hoping to have a son and become Tariq Khan's Begum. How the name of Tariq Khan stinks in the nostrils of all good men, though there are many villains full of flattery, who frequent his court. I wonder – did Zurah Begum's new guards come from Tariq Khan's stable of *goondas*. I must find out about that."

Outside in the courtyard the moonlight gave the fountain a magical quality and each spray of water glistened like silver, Soft music floated in the air, and everything seemed so peaceful that Robert could hardly believe what Rabindra was saying. To think that he had urged Zeena to return to her father. Such a father!

"I used to admire Sadik Khan." Robert could not hide his distress. "I did not see very deeply into his heart and mind, it seems. How could I imagine that he loved his daughter."

"But he does! With all his heart. Zeena has helped to heal the wound that her mother's death caused. Zeena has become his *reason* for living. You cannot possibly think as we do. Our attitude to certain things is so far from yours! It is because Sadik loves his child that he accepts that she should marry an ageing rich man, whom he trusts will die soon. He is only going ahead with Zurah Begum's plans so that his daughter will return to her rightful home. Perhaps Zurah Begum, has promised him that a poisoned cup awaits Tariq Khan and that he will soon be removed from this world that his presence pollutes. Zurah Begum is capable of anything, and will certainly lie to get her way."

"This kind of love," said Robert, "I certainly do not understand. But I know that I should not meddle in lives that—" Robert, his face contored by sadness, sighed, "lives that, alas, do not concern me."

"But I am about to ask you to concern yourself more deeply in this affair, Robert – out of friendship for me, if for no other reason. But first I must warn you that you will be at risk, if not of danger of death."

"Danger of *death*? Rabindra, you are spinning such a story that I feel you are making dramas out of this whole affair. How can I concern myself in this tangle – what do you want me to do?" As Robert spoke, Rabindra stood up and went to a table upon which there was a decanter and several glasses. He poured two glasses and brought one glass over to Robert.

"Drink with me while we talk, listen to me and try to believe that what I am telling you is not moonshine but the truth. Remember, we have differences between us which have never spoiled our friendship. I am going to ask you to risk perhaps not your life, but certainly your *way* of life. You might lose your position as Chief Medical Officer of this province, and all that it means to you. That is one thing. I ask you to look again at Chunia, and understand that this could happen to you – a beating so severe that you might well die as a result. These are the things you risk if it is ever discovered that you have helped me."

Outside, there was a sudden outcry, a man's angry shout, and running feet. Then the door was flung open and two men dragging a body between them, burst into the room.

144

Thirteen

Five days had passed since the two rulers had ridden away to Rhanaghar, light-hearted and free of responsibility.

Life in the Chikor Mahal had become strange to those left behind. Suddenly, from one day to the next, things had altered. Part of the Zenana had been screened off at Zurah Begum's order.

"No one is to come past these screens, for an evil disease has fallen upon us," Zurah Begum had said. A guard had then been placed outside the screens to enforce obedience. Nobody could believe it: a man, a soldier in uniform, a male guard, and armed, standing there in the Zenana, a guard who was changed every two hours – day and night, one stood there. The women of the Zenana whispered together, peeping with caution round the edges of doors to try to see the man standing on guard half-way down the long hall.

"Zurah is mad," said Merabhen, the oldest concubine, who was much respected as the favourite of Sadik Khan's father. She was allowed to speak her mind and frequently did. "Zurah has been mad at certain times all her life. See the moon, my sisters? It is coming up to the full. That is always a bad time for Zurah. Her mother used to lock her up for the week of the full moon."

145

The listening women made big eyes and looked over their shoulders and begged her to guard her unruly tongue.

They were all speaking of the disease that had struck the Choti Begum, Zeena. With lowered voices they said how strange it was that the sickness should have fallen on Zeena Begum as soon as her father, Sadik Khan, had left for his tiger shoot. "Let us hope that he returns as soon as he hears the news that she is ill."

It was said that a messenger had been racing after the ruler's party. But as the days went by and Sadik Khan had not returned, the women began to ask each other who had been sent? No one knew. Soon they were not even allowed to walk in the garden, and gradually the women grew afraid. When they saw that the soldier on guard had been joined by two brawny women from the city, everyone grew more unsettled. Merabhen dared to ask Zurah Begum what these two low-caste women were doing in the Zenana, walking wherever they wished – in the kitchen, in and out of the bedrooms, listening at doors and looking through windows.

"They are from the City Medical Department, checking that this pestilence, this terrible contagion does not spread," explained Zurah Begum, and her tone and glare were so awful that even Merabhen asked no more questions and retreated into her own quarters, longing for the ruler to return.

Gulrukh stayed in her room during these strange five days. She had slept heavily most of the time, through the days and nights, and woke only for short spells, She accepted that she had a fever, her mother had told her so. When she woke, her mother seemed to come to her almost at once, telling her to rest. "Bismillah, thanks be that you have a light fever, not like your cousin." she would say. But each time she refused to allow Gulrukh to go to Zeena.

"You cannot see her, she has a contagious disease. You could became infected too, and then what of my grandson? For his sake, I change my clothing every time I come to you, as nothing from Zeena's room must touch you. Now, be still, rest yourself and be thankful that your fever does not pose as much threat as Zeena's sickness does. I will come every day and bring you news of your cousin, even if it means all this dressing and undressing. For the unborn boy it must be done."

Gulrukh, still unable to believe her mother, said, "Mother – is my cousin really sick?"

"She lies at the door of death, my daughter. The hakim comes every day. Do not doubt the danger you are in – you are not to leave your room, think of your child and behave with sense. I have told that girl of yours, Sushi, to stay with you and she will come for me if you need me."

Gulrukh watched her mother whisk out of the room and listened for the sound of the key. Yes, the door was locked, she heard it – but only faintly. Her head felt as if it was full of water. She lay still and looked up at the ceiling which moved and billowed like silk in a high wind. Then sleep fell on her and she saw nothing more, remembered nothing.

She usually slept deeply for the rest of the day. When she woke it was always a sudden awakening. She would try to collect her wits, and keep still. If she moved, or turned her head, everything would swing round her and she would fall into a strange state of unknowingness. Then she would open her eyes again to find Sushi bending over her, making soothing sounds.

Zurah Begum came twice a day, early in the morning and at night. She spoke sadly of the advance of Zeena's illness. It no longer seemed to concern Gulrukh. She listened to her mother, drank whatever she was given and saw her mother leave. Her inner confusion increased to such an extent that sometimes the room seemed to be a different place, a place of deep shadows and moving walls, melting one into the other. The bed floated on a dark sea, and Gulrukh lay still, and tried to remember . . . But what? It was important, but sleep overtook her before she could catch the tail of the thought.

Three days passed, and Sushi, the maid, sat by the bed, watching and waiting for the key to turn, the door to open and to see Zurah Begum's appear with a glass. Sushi was beginning to wonder what was in the glass. Whatever it was, it held her mistress in a deep sleep. But on this, the fifth day, Zurah Begum did not come with the glass. Gulrukh slept on, and at midday Sushi went out through the sweeper's door to go to the kitchens for drinking water, but she also took from the harried cook some chicken broth. She returned to Gulrukh and found her still sleeping.

Sushi bent over her mistress and touched her, speaking softly, "Gulrukh piyari – wake, you should eat a little." She had no success, and Gulrukh slept on. By nightfall, Zurah Begum had not come and, as the hours passed, Sushi watching, saw her mistress grow restless. Finally, late in the night, Sushi tried again to wake the sleeping girl. "Khanum – it is time to wake." This time Gulrukh groaned, and opened her eyes. She lay for a few minutes, while the sleep cleared from her head. She felt unwell, with a throbbing head and burning eyes, but the walls of the room were solid and she knew where she was. She tried to sit up and, at once,

148

Sushi put her arm about her and pulled cushions up behind her back.

"Sushi, I am thirst—"

Sushi heaved a great, relieved sigh.

"Of course you are thirsty! I have water for you – and also soup, but it has grown cold."

Gulrukh put her heavy throbbing head in her hands and asked for water, which she drank with desperation. Handing the glass back to Sushi, she asked for more. When she had finished the second glass, she lay back on her cushions and tried to sort out her thoughts. She had been very afraid – but of what? She put her hand gently on her stomach, as a horrible thought came to her. Sushi leaned to cover her hands gently. "Nay, piyari, do not think such a thought. All is well with you – only you have slept long hours . . . days."

"*Days*, Sushi, how long? I feel as if I have slept for weeks, my head aches, and my mouth – ugh, what a taste! Give me more water, let me wash this taste away."

The foul taste in Gulrukh's mouth was one thing, but her suspicions were more important. Sushi wondered if she should tell Gulrukh that Zurah Begum had probably been drugging her daughter for all these days. "You have slept for five days, Khanum, and have eaten nothing but milk, or soup that your mother brought you." She hesitated, but before she could speak Gulrukh said, "Sushi, you said you had brought soup. Where did you get it from?"

At once Sushi knew that she did not have to say anything about Zurah Begum – not in words. She gave Gulrukh a glass of water and said, "When you have drunk this water, you may drink the soup. I myself brought it from the kitchens, and no one saw me go and come from the sweeper's door. I, too, have had some of this soup, and I have sat beside you since without closing my eyes. The soup is cold, but you will only sleep if you want to."

"And I have slept for five days. Five days of my life, just to keep me quiet."

Gulrukh lay back, and sipped the cold soup, and slowly began to remember. First the orange juice – her mother said she was fevered then – and the bundle of rugs in Zeena's bed. It all began to come back. But Gulrukh couldn't stop herself from thinking about what had been happening while she slept. She would ask Sushi. Sushi was a girl from the Panchghar. She had come back with Gulrukh to Madore after the marriage. She could be trusted.

Gulrukh put her hands to her head once more and said, "Sushi, come here, close to my bed, come and tell me what has been happening here while I lost so many days."

Sushi remembered: the tense atmosphere in the kitchen, the wild-eyed cook and, before that, Merabhen asking about the stange women, the screens across the hall. Her mistress knew nothing. Would it harm Gulrukh to tell her all these things? And would she not be in danger if she said anything? There were orders, nothing was to be discussed – silence had been imposed on the frightened women of the Zenana. But not to speak might be just as dangerous.

Faithful Sushi inched herself nearer to the bed, leaned even closer and, low-voiced, told Gulrukh that her cousin was said to be dying.

Gulrukh asked at once, "Where is she?"

"She was carried from her room, down the hall to a room near Zurah Begum. That part of the hall has been screened off, and guarded. No one can go there."

The Palace Garden

Strangely, this seemed to relieve Gulrukh, who asked if Sushi had seen Zeena carried from her room.

"No. It was deep in the night and I was here in your room. No one saw this. We were told that she was ill, and that the illness was contagious, a disease like cholera." She paused and looked at her mistress." I have also been given an order: you are not to be disturbed, as you too have been very ill. But thanks be to the Gods, it is not an illness like the Choti Begum's.

"I am not ill, Sushi. You know what is wrong with me – my heart fails me when I think of my own mother putting my child at risk. Who can say how these drugs will have affected my child? Helpless within my body, drawing sustenance from my blood – may Allah the Compassionate, the Merciful, protect my child, and let no harm have come to the precious unborn. Oh Sushi, I am so afraid."

Sushi said sadly, "At first, I did not see what was happening. I could not believe that you would be given any noxious substance by the hand of your own mother. If I had guessed, I would have run for help – but where could I have gone? There is no one to turn to here, Khanum, life has become very strange. But do not think solely of evil. Remember your mother is anxious for a grandson, and I truly do not believe she would make you take anything that might harm your child."

Gulrukh was not so sure, but tried to rid herself of her fears. As the clouds lifted from her mind, and her thoughts grew clearer, she said, "You are right when you say we can get no help here. Tell me more – I must know as much as I can, and then we will make a plan to get away from this place before anything more happens."

Sushi thought of the guards and the two women who roamed the corridors of the palace. What plans could her mistress possibly make to get her away from her mother? All Sushi knew was that she would try to help Gulrukh Begum. What else could she do? She leaned close to the bed again, and resumed her low-voiced words about what had been happening during Gulrukh's long sleep.

"Khanum, it is said that the disease was brought to the Choti Begum by her servant, Chunia."

"Chunia! Where is Chunia now?"

Chunia, the last time she had seen Zeena's maid servant she was running and wearing strange clothes: Chunia hunted by the new men from the gate, afraid and accused of being a thief. Gulrukh could not bear to think of it.

"Where is Chunia?" she repeated.

Sushi stared at her.

"Gulrukh Begum, do you not remember? It was said that she ran away."

"It is *said*, it is *said*! What is the truth? What do you think, what do the other women think?" Her voiced was raised and forceful.

Sushi looked over her shoulder into the shadowed room and listened as if she could hear footsteps. Her fear was obvious. "I do not know what the other women think. I have not spoken with them – we are all too afraid to speak."

She told Gulrukh about the two great women who now haunted the Zenana. "Truly, Khanum, they are as big as men, with arms like tree trunks. Their eyes betray their desire to hear and see everything – trap someone or something. All of us are afraid of them, even Merabhen. No lover has ever longed for the return of a beloved as the women of the Zenana long for the return of the two Nawabs." Just talking about the two imposing women made Sushi tremble, but her mistress was waiting for an answer . . .

"But about Chunia. Khanum piyari, I am reluctant and afraid to tell you this, but it is necessary for you to know how bad things are. The other night, after all was quiet, Zurah Begum took a lantern and went down to the stables. I do not know anything of what happened there, but I heard the sound of screaming. Terrible screams without words. Then Zurah Begum came back in a great hurry, and within a few minutes she entered your room with a drink. Her face was smooth, but I was afraid to look at her eyes. Khanum, if the person who screamed was Chunia, then I think she no longer lives."

"May Allah protect her! Did you see Zurah Begum, Sushi?"

"Yes, I saw her clearly. I was sitting on the steps outside the bathroom."

Sushi has reason to be afraid, thought Gulrukh. Her mother has eyes and ears all around her head. *Oh Zeena, where are you? What trouble we are all in.* Gulrukh was certain that wherever Zeena was, she was not lying ill in the room down the hall, behind the screens that Sushi had described. What were these schemes of her mother's that were worth taking so much trouble for? Poisoning her daughter with drugs, then acting out this strange charade – changing her clothes, speaking all the time of a terrible infection, putting guards in the Zenana – what could it be?

Like an echo dying away in the past, words she had once heard came into her head – "What a trouble the Choti Begum has brought to Zurah. He will have made her his heir." *Had* she heard these words or was she dreaming them? Or was she making them up to have a reason for her mother's behaviour?

153

Zeena had always been Sadik Khan's heir. She must have dreamed those words. But there had to be a reason for Zurah's behaviour – unless, of course, she was mad.

"The sound of screaming." The words were there, but they were nothing to do with Zeena. Gulrukh would not connect them to Zeena. Instead she thought that perhaps Zeena had escaped and was hidden somewhere in the grounds of the palace. Not all the servants were the paid hirelings of Zurah. Then she remembered that the three most trusted servants, faithful to Zeena, were gone: Sakhi Mohammed, Raza, and the beloved Chunia. Who was left? She looked at Sushi, who had come from her husband's state, and was proving to be a friend, as well as a servant. She could trust her, but it meant that she was risking Sushi's life. But what else could she do. They had to get away from the palace, even only as far as her father's palace in Pakodi. There Zurah Begum, the Begum of Pakodi, had less authority than she had in the palace of Chikor.

Gulrukh continued to press Sushi for information. "Sushi, tell me, have all the men at the gate been replaced? Are any of the men who came down from Chikor still there, the older men?"

Gulrukh saw with a sinking heart that Sushi had guessed what this question might lead to. "Oh, Khanum. I do not know, I have hardly left your room since your mother called me and said I was to stay with you – and then locked us in. If I do go out, I go by the sweeper's door, and I cannot reach any of the women now. There are guards about the garden all the time, but I have not seen any that I know. None of our men from Panchghar are here. But if you wish me to go and see—"

"No, I cannot let you risk your life. Tell me, do you believe that the Choti Begum lies ill behind those screens?"

154

"Gulrukh piyari, you are my father and my mother. I am afraid of this question, but I must answer it. A *dhai* from the city is the only one allowed in there, through the screens. Zurah Begum takes in food and water. There is a smell of heavy unguents and burning herbs, and Zurah Begum washes her hands and feet and changes her clothes whenever she comes here from that room. Indeed there is someone very ill behind those screens. That I do believe – but who it is, I cannot say."

"You think it may not be my cousin? Why do you think that?"

"Because you do not think it is her. You think that she has run away – I heard you speaking with your mother just after we came here to the Mahal. There is so much that cannot be believed: the tale that Chunia has run away with stolen jewels is not true – Chunia was my friend and I know that she wouldn't have taken anything from the Choti Begum." Sushi stopped, and went quietly to the door and listened, her ear against the wooden panels. She thought of the extra guards who had come; strange dark-faced men, who were constantly moving around the gardens and even prowling silently in the corridors of the palace. Had she heard a footfall – muffled, creeping? She went back to sit close to Gulrukh, now even more concerned. Who could say if those women in the house would dare to come in here?

"Khanum, I am afraid to speak any more of these matters. We are forbidden."

"At this time in the night," said Gulrukh impatiently, "surely no one is listening. Please Sushi, tell me more, it is important. Speak, we are safe here."

Sushi heard the desperation in Gulrukh's voice. Poor

Sushi! Torn between saving herself, and protecting her mistress.

"Gulrukh piyari, I risk both our lives by speaking. You did not hear those screams in the night! No one is safe here these days. But I will tell you. How can I refuse you? These are my reasons for thinking that the Choti Begum is not here: the searchers were looking for two girls. I think one was taken. I think it was Chunia. No one would dare to lay a hand on Zeena Begum." She paused for a while, to concentrate.

"You did not hear the screams. But if Zeena Begum is lying sick in that screened room, why are the men still searching? You see, a reward has been made and has since been doubled for the person who finds her. That is why I am sure that Zeena Begum is not here. She has escaped."

Gulrukh sighed deeply. "Inshalla." She reached for Sushi's hand and held it tightly. "Sushi, I have never been so frightened."

"I am also afraid. Let us leave this place, Khanum. Evil has made its home here. Let us go back to Panchghar, before it is too late."

Both girls were whispering, but suddenly Sushi shuddered, her eyes focusing on the door. The shudder that shook Sushi conveyed itself to Gulrukh, who felt the child within her stir, as if her fears and activities were touching the unborn. She loosened her hold on Sushi's hand and folded both hands over the small mound that held her most precious possession.

"Sushi, we must not fear for ourselves." Gulrukh took a deep breath and said confidentially "Zurah Begum will not harm me because of my child. She will not dare to harm you because you were given to me by the Begum Sahiba of Panchghar. She would have kept you away from me otherwise. We are safe. But oh, Allah, what has happened to Chunia – and where is Zeena?"

It was almost dawn. The cool silver light that appeared around the edge of the shuttered window spoke of the coming day. The night was over at last. Sushi rose and went to the window and flung back the shutters, letting the cool air flood in. As she turned to go back to raise Gulrukh's mosquito net, they heard a cry from somewhere close by, a wail that rose and hung quavering in the quiet air. It was taken up soon, echoing, by every woman in the Zenana. These were mourning cries. Hired mourners were women who came from the city, tore their bodices and raked their nails through their hair and down their cheeks. They were paid for their noisy grief. The women of the Zenana were not slow to join in, but their grief was *real*, it was their Choti Begum who they mourned for, their bright laughing princess, dead of a horrible sickness, gone into the shadows untimely – a sad loss to the family.

Gulrukh and Sushi, alone in the bedroom, sat staring with horror into each other's eyes.

Dry eyed, Gulrukh said, "It is a lie, Sushi – I do not know who has died, but it is not my cousin. But for our own sakes, we must give the cry – for our lives." She flung her head back and gave the high, shrieking cry of sorrow, and Sushi was able to do the same, letting her fear and anxiety lend realism to her cries. Within minutes the door was opened, and Zurah Begum ran in. She had put on the white clothes of mourning, but did not weep. She put her arms around Gulrukh, sitting rigid in her bed, and admonished her.

"Stop – think of your child. You may harm him – be silent. Weep, weep with grief, but do not waste your breath in screaming. Be quiet my daughter."

157

Gulrukh took a deep breath, screamed again, and then said, her voice rasping, her throat already raw, "I must go now, and see my cousin. I must take my last farewell of her."

"Are you mad? You cannot see your cousin. No one can go near her – everything in her room will be burned and it will be closed away for a year." She looked at her daughter's distraught face, and Gulrukh, conscious of dry eyes buried her face in her arms and wailed aloud.

"Calm yourself my daughter. Come, Sushi, cease your wailing. Help my daughter to bathe. You must both dress in the white cloth of mourning and then you must go and join the others, to watch the body carried to the burial ground at midday. We cannot wait until sunset. The hakim says that, by order, the body should be burned, but I said no. She will have to be buried speedily, deeply. There is no danger of infection then, if the bed and everything else is burned. So that is how it will be."

Gulrukh knew that bodies could not be dug up, and that Zurah Begum would think herself safe. Aloud, gasping between sobs Gulrukh said, "I must at least see her carried out – I must do her that little honour."

"But of course you can do that. You will join the other women in the Zenana and pray with them. Now I must go – and you must be good and save your strength." Glaring at Sushi, Zurah made her final order. "She is not to wail – you may wail for her."

At last she left them. Sushi had wept genuinely, from sheer fear, but now she dried her eyes and began to prepare the bath for Gulrukh, who was in deep thought. All she wanted now was to escape from the Chikor Mahal – but how? She had not thought of a way when they left the bedroom and went off, suitably dressed, in white kudda and no jewellery, to join the other women.

One of the women guards was on the door that led to the rest of the Zenana. She unlocked the door, and let them through onto the veranda, which was hidden by pierced marble screens. It was possible to see through the decorative panels, but no one could see in. The woman guard locked the door after them. "Thank God she stayed on the other side," said Merabhen coming to greet them.

All the women were in white clothes, and their hair was disarranged. There was true grief on all their faces, and in their hearts. For the first time, Gulrukh felt hatred for her mother and then she thought with horror of her uncle, Sadik Khan: he would believe this taradiddle, as he trusted Zurah Begum. *Sadik Khan might very well die of sorrow.* As this awful thought came to her she saw Merabhen looking in her direction. *She doesn't believe any of this either.* Gulrukh realised, and drew the other woman aside. With every caution, Gulrukh whispered, "My uncle – has word been sent to him?"

"I do not know – but it will very likely kill him. And we are here like caged birds – with no way of getting word to him. He will believe every word she says."

"And you don't?" asked Gulrukh, barely moving her lips.

"Do you, Begum Sahiba?"

There was a cry from outside and the mourners appeared, flinging their arms above their heads and screaming, their long hair covering their faces, their clothes in rags hanging from their scrawny bodies. They were the only women in the funeral cortège. Women never attended Moslem funerals.

The body, wrapped in a sheet, lay on a string bed, carried by

159

four men. There were marigold wreathes and green garlands lying over the stiff form. The women fell silent as the corpse was carried by. They watched it being taken through the gate and then the procession disappeared out of sight. Merabhen, Gulrukh, and Sushi stood a little apart from the others.

"Who – who could have been lying on that bier," Gulrukh was impatient to find some answers.

Sushi shrugged, but Merabhen quietly spoke, "Some poor creature from the city hospital, brought here to breathe her last conveniently – what else?"

The women did not start to chatter when the funeral cortège vanished, leaving only dust clouds behind. They waited for the door to be unlocked, and slowly dispersed to their rooms. Merabhen went with Gulrukh and Sushi. Gulrukh wanted to talk to the much-admired concubine, at a time when it should have been safe. Zurah Begum would be occupied with visitors who had come to commiserate, sit talking sadly, drinking tea and eating funeral cakes.

Sushi asked if she could bring tea and cakes for them, and Gulrukh was pleased that she had made the offer. It would be expected of them. Normally she would have been with her mother, accepting the condolences of the callers. Her excuse for not being there was of course her pregnancy, and the fact that she had also been ill. Sushi hurried off and Gulrukh turned at once to Merabhen: "Do you think that Zeena has escaped?"

"Surely. Zurah Begum's rage tells me that. She will have gone off with her officer, no doubt."

"What? What are you talking about?"

"You do not know? She has been meeting an Angreze in the old polo field – whenever the Dagshai Lancers are in the cantonments, she meets him. We all know about it."

"I did not know! I had no idea." Even as she said the words, Gulrukh remembered being puzzled by what had made Zeena suddenly so against her marriage.

Merabhen said. "I am not surprised that you did not know. Who was going to gossip about such a thing before you? You are Zurah Begum's daughter, after all. None of us wished to make trouble for our loved Zeena. Nearly three years ago it started. Poor girl – she will now be dead to the family, whatever happens – and there will be no consolation for Sadik Khan."

"But – but you know she is not dead. Of course he will be consoled when we tell him – we can prove it."

"Gulrukh Begum, open your eyes and consider clearly this situation. Do you think that he will be consoled to know that his daughter is not dead, but has run away with an Angreze, and brought the head of the family into the dust with shame? Is that going to make proud Sadik Khan happy? Console him?"

Gulrukh was silent as she mulled over these facts, and confronted the reality. Sadik Khan was a very proud man, that was true. But better dead than disgraced? She looked into Merabhen's eyes and knew that the old lady was right. She could not speak. For the first time, since the mourning for Zeena had started, she wept. She wept for her cousin, who was dead to her family and who would never be able to return.

Fourteen

Sakhi Mohammed and Raza released their prisoner and he fell face down on the floor and remained there. Robert admired how calm Rabindra's voice was when he said enquiringly, "Sakhi Mohammed?"

"Rabindra-ji, he was listening at the door. He did not see us, we were in the shadows by the fountain."

"Who is he?"

"He is a man of the far south – his name is Rallia Ram. He serves the ruler of Sagpurna."

Rabindra turned away, saying over his shoulder; "How long did he stand by the door?"

"With his accursed ear pressed to the panel? Long enough, lord."

Rabindra seated himself, "Raise him. I would see his face."

Sakhi Mohammed and Raza bent down to lift the man up, but he avoided their hands, and stood up by himself. He stood, defiant, looking at Rabindra with no fear on his face – only, Robert thought, something of resignation. Rabindra looked back at him, and after a moment said, "Did they pay you well?"

"Not enough – Rabindra-ji."

162

"No. Not enough. But you will be paid – for the task you accepted, taking the risk?"

"Taking the risk, as you say – Rabindra-ji. I may ask a question?"

"Certainly. Ask."

"Do you go south sometimes, Rabindra, my brother?"

"I go sometimes, yes."

"Then, when you next go, please take my ashes and throw them into the great river. I only did what I was ordered to do."

Rabindra nodded. "Very well. Now, Sakhi Mohammed, take him."

Rabindra turned immediately to Robert and picked up the conversation that had been interrupted by the men bursting in. Robert had been listening to Rabindra with growing alarm, but now he told himself not to be imaginative. He was absorbing too much of Rabindra's love of drama and excitement. All Indians loved drama; play-acting, colourful speech.

Rabindra spoke. "It is necessary for you to understand the risks you will take if you agree to help the Choti Begum, Zeena." What was that sound outside – a choked, gurgling? Robert, for a moment, lost the sense of what Rabindra was saying. He listened, straining his ears for sounds from the garden. All he heard was the fountain, and faintly, music and a drum beating somewhere – nothing else. He must have imagined that he heard a cry – but it was only the fountain or a singer in the other part of the house. But all the same, the air now seemed charged with menace! Perhaps it was time for Robert to admit that he could not continue to be connected with Rabindra, the Begum and her servant – perhaps he should refuse to help.

Rabindra's earlier words – "Lose your way of life" – had worried him. His life was a pleasant one: he enjoyed his work and could do it well; he was important in this place. He was respected and liked because he could give help where it was needed. He thought of his busy clinic, of his many grateful patients, of his skills, which were given freely in the native hospital, and the mission hospital. He would miss his way of life – no doubt about that. But could he turn his back on Rabindra? Could he walk out on that frightened girl upstairs – and go on living contentedly without being constantly plagued by visions of what had happened to her after he walked away? He knew what the answer was. Crossly he said, "Less chatter about the risks and dangers and life-threatening villains. Tell me what you want me to do and let us get on with it."

Rabindra's smile was wide and charming. He looked incredibly young when he smiled, which was seldom. He rose and, having poured out two more drinks, sat forward in his chair. "We have to get Zeena Begum away from here and out of Madore as soon as possible. That man was one of Tariq Khan's creatures – if the ruler of Sagpurna is on the hunt with Zurah Begum, that is very serious. Of course, Rallia Ram may have been left in the household of Chikor some time ago to spy on the actions of Tariq Khan's future wife – and I do not think Zurah Begum would want him to know that Zeena has run away. One of her greatest desires is to preserve the family name, and one of the quickest ways to disgrace a great family is to break a marriage contract. So I think we can hope that Rallia Ram is paid by Zurah Begum, and that Tariq Ali knows nothing of Zeena's disappearance.

"It is being rumoured that Zeena Begum is not appearing in public at present because she has fallen sick with some dreadful disease – I wonder if they will send for you? Highly unlikely in this case. Zurah Begum will no doubt call in some character of her own, one of those wonder barbers who do doctoring on the side."

Robert shuddered. "Don't even think of one of them touching Zeena Begum. In any case, won't that man Rallia Ram give the game away when he returns to the Chikor Mahal?"

Rabindra said thoughtfully, "Yes, no doubt he would have done, no doubt at all. He would also implicate you, and tell Zurah Begum exactly where you had taken Zeena. But as he will not be returning, we do not have to think about it."

Robert did not hear the last part of what Rabindra had said. He only heard that he was taking Zeena away. "But will she come with me? And where do I take her?"

Rabindra nodded. "She will come. Chunia has almost lost her life trying to keep Zeena safe. When I tell her that it will all be wasted – all Chunia's efforts – if Zurah Begum's searchers come here, Zeena will agree to go with you. As to where you take her – well, it is necessary to get her safely to Bombay, where Captain Alan awaits her. By now he must be there, wondering where I am and what has happened to Zeena."

Robert leaned forward, as if he could not understand what Rabindra was saying. "Do you mean that Alan Lyall is in Bombay, waiting for her to join him? Not a very passionate lover! How does he imagine she is going to get to him – with the whole of Madore being searched and eyes around every corner watching for her? Not at all the way I would have imagined he would behave – a daring brave man, or so I thought."

And not at all the way you would behave, my friend Robert,

165

thought Rabindra. *My friend Robert has tumbled into late love, alas, seduced by a pair of pleading eyes.*

"You should remember, Robert, that Alan has no idea what is happening here – and as to passionate love, well, I have no doubt of his love for Zeena."

"And the Begum? Her love must be warmer, more intense, than his, to drive her into running away, coming here and trusting strangers. To elope as she has done, she must be passionately in love," said Robert.

"I think there is a burning passion between Alan and Zeena, but it has not yet been tapped. Her love at present is directed at Chunia, her maid who is both mother and sister to her, the one solitary person she trusts. I think Zeena was at first in love with an idea – but was also determined to escape from Tariq Khan."

Robert shivered inwardly as he imagined Zeena in the hands of the man he had sat beside at dinner only a few days ago, in the Chikor Mahal. "I can understand very well why she ran from that man. But it seems to me that these two young people need time more than anything else. Time to think – and at least get to know each other. Surely to set off into marriage, neither of them knowing anything about the ways and customs of the other, would be a recipe for disaster."

"It will be easier for Zeena Begum than for him," said Rabindra. This shocked Robert.

"You think it will be easier for *her*? Going off with a stranger, to a strange country? How much do you suppose she knows about life in northern Scotland?"

Rabindra shrugged his shoulders. "She knows nothing, of course. But a woman expects to conform to the ways of her

166

husband and his family. It is, after all, part of her life – to mould herself to her husband's wishes."

"Good God!" said Robert. "Have you ever been married, Rabindra?"

"No. But one does not need to wear the fetters of matrimony to understand women, my brother. You are not married, I think?"

"No, and I do not pretend to understand anything about women. But I do know what is expected of the women of my country. I have watched my mother and my sisters. Zeena Begum belongs to a different culture. Nothing is going to be easy in Scotland for a Mogul princess, which after all is what she is. If she was passionately in love with this young man, that might help her over the changes she will have to face, but you say she is not in love?"

"I do not know. It does not matter in any case. Women are taught to please their husbands in every way. She will learn about passion from him, I have no doubt. I think the eyes of her spirit were caught by him. Now the only thing that remains is the awakening of the body."

Listening to these words Robert felt his heart sink. If only he could be the one who awakened that girl's desire – he could not bear to think of her in another man's arms.

Rabindra sensed what Robert was thinking and felt pity for his unfortunate friend. *She has taken you heart. How sad that it was not you who caught her eye! How much more simple that would have been – this love affair is following a tortuous route.*

"Robert, I hope this coupling does not lead to the disaster I fear. Her life will be in grave danger if we do not get her away from Madore. Every moment that she stays here

167

puts her at more risk. Events have moved swiftly. They say Zeena Begum is ill and close to death – I now await news of her death."

Robert stared at him aghast. Rabindra put his hand on his arm to stop him rising to his feet. "Wait, Robert, listen to me. You think I am being over-dramatic. I am not. I tell you that death is the only way Zurah Begum can allow the marriage contract to be broken without destroying the good name of the Chikor family. The reputation of the family lies in the hands of the women of the family."

Robert made a dissenting movement, "My impression, after many years of work among the families of this country does not bear that out. Women here appear to be of very little importance. Chattels, to be used as financial pawns in some cases, they have, as you yourself have told me, no say in their lives at all."

"You think that because you have never passed beyond the walls of the Zenana. In fact, the women of Islam are precious. They are loved and protected, valued and respected – as long as they conform. To you it must seem strange. A man may do anything he likes, break any rules. His own reputation may be tarnished, but it will not affect his family name. But if a woman breaks with tradition . . . I tell you, that old woman in the Chikor Mahal will kill to keep the Chikor name unsullied. That is one thing. There is also the fact that she would like her son to be Sadik Khan's heir – and Zeena stands in the way of that. Of course, Zurah Begum is quite mad. She has always been jealous, and unstable. Her jealousy has grown with her age and evolved into insanity. Listen to what I say. We have to get Zeena out of danger – away from Madore!"

Robert listened, engrossed as if he was being told a strange, fictional tale. He could not believe anything that Rabindra was saying. Rabindra recognised his friend's expression and sighed.

"Robert, my friend. Would you say that I am a man of a murderous nature?"

Robert shook his head smiling. "What are you talking about? No. I do not always understand you – I think you have a love of drama, but you are certainly not a killer by nature."

"And yet I had a man killed this evening, not a hundred yards from this room – you must have heard his dying cry?"

Robert jumped up. "What? Rallia Ram, that man? You had him killed?" Robert remembered the choked off sound he had heard, and said, in horror "Is this *true*?"

"You can believe me. If I had not had him killed he would have gone straight from here to Zurah Begum, and her guards would have arrived before Zeena had escaped. She would have been dragged back to the Chikor Mahal and, I think, dramatic or not, Zurah Begum would have poisoned her. Believe me now, Robert?"

Robert had to believe him. Because he wanted to see Zeena safe, Rabindra had ordered – so coolly, so calmly – the death of a man. Robert was beginning to feel that a nightmare was beginning to unfold, that it was becoming a reality.

"Very well. I believe you. But how do we get her away? For one thing, I do not think she will leave Chunia, and the maidservant cannot be moved, and do you think the man, Rallia Ram, was sent here because someone saw her come in? Are they watching this house?"

"Certainly. They are watching all the roads in and out of

Madore, and there is, I know a spy at the railway station. Wait, what is that?"

Suddenly someone called from above and the quick patter of feet on the stairs could be heard. Robert stood up, he was sure he recognised the voice, but the girl who ran into the room was not Zeena. It was a girl unknown to him, but known to Rabindra.

"Mohini! What has happened?"

"Your pardon lord, I was sent by Chuni Ayah. I am to tell you that Chunia has awakened and spoken. Chuni Ayah asks that the hakim Sahib come."

Robert went to the door at once. Rabindra sighed and sat down. Until Robert understood the dangers of Zeena's presence here, there was little Rabindra could do, except double the guards all round the house and send a man to the station to intercept Alan and warn him not to believe the rumours of Zeena's death and, above all, to keep away from the House of Pomegranates.

Fifteen

Alan's return journey took three days. In the early evening of the third day, the mail from Bombay drew into Madore station. With so little baggage it was only minutes before Alan and Iqbal were standing outside the station looking for transport.

Rabindra's man who was watching for Alan missed him completely and was still searching the carriages when Alan, knowing Iqbal's tendency to waste precious time bargaining with tonga drivers, took the precaution of saying, "Never mind what it costs Iqbal, there is no time to argue. Just get me a tonga. I want to go at once to the Chikor Mahal."

Alan thought he saw for the first time a flicker of surprise – or perhaps shock, in Iqbal's usually expressionless face. Alan suspected that the bearer knew more about his affairs than he had admitted. Now Iqbal hesitated, pulling out a large silver watch from his waistcoat pocket. He looked at the watch ostentatiously. "Sahib, it is a late hour to call at the palace – unless they are expecting you?"

"Late or early, expected or not, that is where we are going. Will you get me a carriage of some sort, or shall I do it myself?"

Iqbal vanished into the line of waiting carriages and tongas.

He obviously felt that to call on the ruler of Chikor, something better than a one-horse tonga was necessary, for he came back with a Victoria, the two horses bedizened with collars of blue beads, and with plumes on their harnesses. The baggage was loaded, Iqbal climbed up beside the driver, and Alan sat alone in the back. The driver waved his whip and the horses broke into a tired trot.

It was a twenty-minute drive, and this meant that Alan had time to think again of what he was doing. He had some qualms, remembering what Rabindra had said, but he was tired of waiting for news, and was now determined to deal with the affair himself.

Three long days of train travel had given him time to think calmly. He could not understand how he had been so foolish to allow himself to take the dishonourable course of spending days with Sadik Khan, growing close to him and not telling him about his desire to marry Zeena. He could not continue with this. He knew exactly what he wanted, and thought he had discovered the best way of getting it. He was determined that Zeena should be his wife, with or without her father's permission, but he wanted to tell Sadik Khan of his intentions and at least ask for his approval. He would not break Sadik's trust. It was likely that there would be a terrible scene, but he felt that the happiness he could find with the woman he loved was more important than avoiding confrontation – and he felt sure that Sadik Khan would come round. *After all*, thought Alan, *I am not a beggar, and my family is certainly a good one. Sadik Khan held out his hand in friendship – and I will not behave in a dishonourable manner towards him.*

Leaning back in the Victoria, looking out at the coloured sky, he knew that his love of India was one reason why he wished to do the honourable thing. This beautiful, mysterious, dangerous and yet welcoming country – where so many of the men is his family had lived out their lives – would be so difficult to leave forever. But the thought of losing Zeena was equally terrible. His love for her and for her country were intermingled. This would be a long love, a love that would endure.

Iqbal and the driver were chatting together as the horses ambled along. He could hear them but only registered their words when he heard Iqbal say, "No, we have heard nothing of this. When did this happen?"

"The death took place before dawn. I myself heard the wailing begin. The funeral was at noon."

"Allah yarham! How terrible this news is! They did not wait until sunset to hold the funeral?"

"No. Everything had to be done in great haste because of the danger of the disease spreading."

Listening idly, Alan assumed the men were talking about cholera? Surely not a cholera outbreak now? It was late in the year for that. The dreaded disease! Cholera in the city, in those narrow streets, spreading to the lines – he shuddered at the thought. He began to listen properly. Iqbal was asking the driver if it was cholera.

"Only the gods know," said the driver. "It may have been cholera. The hakim said that the body should be burned, but the old Begum refused and, of course, as it was the daughter of the ruler she was able to insist. The girl was buried in the garden of one of their houses – the old Pila Ghar. Eh, sorrow! The father did not get back from his *Shikar* in time to walk with the bier. May the gods protect us from such grief! The father is said to be half mad with anguish."

Alan heard every word clearly, and tried not to leap in conclusions about what he had heard. They were nearing the palace, he could see the great gates with the carved leopards on them. They were drawing up before he had finished telling himself that of course it was nothing to do with Chikor. But he felt cold and sick, and his voice was shaking. "What do you speak of? What death is this?"

Iqbal looked horrified. "Alas, alas, you heard, Sahib! Do not believe it, it is only bazaar gossip. I will ask here – there are not true words, Sahib, only a tale from the bazaar."

But the gates were closed, and the two men on guard were quick to warn Iqbal. "This is a dark house, we have been visited by a plague. Now, even now, the hakim has been called back. Stand away from us, bhai, no one enters here."

They stood back themselves, and said nothing more, although Iqbal called to them, asking them to tell him who had died. Alan, his face grey with horror when he heard the news called him back, and the driver, offended, said loudly, "Arree bhai! I do not speak lies! It is not baazar gossip, I tell you. I saw the mourners coming back from the burial and with these eyes I saw the two rulers arrive. Their faces were the faces of men bowed with grief. Women were hired to wail, and the bier was carried down the river road to the Pila Ghar. This is a true word that I give you."

He glared at Iqbal and added, "It is no good to wait here with the Sahib. They will not let you in. It is said that the old one, worn out with nursing the girl, has fallen sick herself, and that the ruler of Pakodi, Atlar Khan Bahadur, has gone to his own residence and taken his daughter and her maid with him. Such a visitation on such a family – truly, there is no knowing where the gods will send their inflictions. Let us go from here."

Alan, in a complete daze heard of all this, only the words about Atlar Khan. Atlar Khan had gone to his own place. *Very well, let me go there, and find out what has happened.*

"We will go now to the Pakodi Mahal," Alan ordered, and Iqbal looked at his master with distress and told the driver to take them at once to the Pakodi Mahal.

It was growing dark, the golden afterglow was fading from the sky. The driver, grumbling, struck flint and steel, and lit the two lamps on each side of the Victoria.

"The Pakodi Mahal is without the wall, through the gate of the north," said the driver. "Do you keep me for the return journey, bhai, or do you stay at the Pakodi Mahal? It is also a place of mourning today. You see," said the driver – a fount of information, still offended because he had been accused of producing gossip – "you understand: the Chikor family and the Pakodi family, the young ruler of Panchghar and even the great ones of Lambagh – they are all of one blood line, though of course it is *said* by some—"

"Yes, it is *said* – you are never the one who repeats gossip! Your tongue is hung in the middle like a wooden clapper in the wind. Will you get in and let us go on our way?" Iqbal's voice, though quiet, was venomous. The driver climbed into his seat without another word, whipped up the horses and set off at a fast and shaking canter for the gate of the north.

Pagodighar, the town palace of the ruler of Pakodi state, lay about a quarter of a mile outside the red walls of Madore. The four men at the gates of the palace did not turn the carriage away when they saw Alan sitting in the back. They opened the gates and stood back saluting. When the carriage

175

drew up with a clatter of hooves and a loud ringing of the bell, a tall grey-haired servant came down the steps at once. Alan recognised him. He had been on the *Shikar* with Atlar Khan, he was the principal servant of the family. He came forward salaaming when he saw Alan. Alan could see no sign of mourning, the man was wearing his usual bright-green cummerbund and the silver insignia in his turban was brightly polished as usual. Perhaps it was all a lie! Alan asked for Atlar Khan, and the man led him up the steps and into the big receiving room, the Durbarkhana. He offered Alan a drink.

"No, thank you – but if I could speak with the Nawab Sahib."

The old servant, Amin-ud-Din, looked into Alan's face, shook his head and went out, leaving Alan burning with impatience. Amin came back almost at once with a glass, a very small jug of water and a bottle of whisky. He arranged these things carefully on a table and, pouring a double peg into the glass, put the table beside one of the divans, saying, "The Nawab Sahib Bahadur comes. But if he finds you here with no drink in your hand, he will no doubt dismiss me. Sit, Huzoor, and be comfortable while you wait – it will not be long."

Alan was standing, glass in hand, looking into the darkening garden when he heard Atlar Khan come in. He turned from the window, unsure of how he would be received on such a day, and saw that a girl had come in with Atlar Khan. She was veiled from head to foot in a heavy white *burkah*. She walked in behind Atlar Khan and went over to one of the many divans in the room and sank down among the cushions. Alan watched her, a wild hope in his heart that this was his love.

Atlar Khan came over to him, embraced him and explained,
"My daughter, Gulrukh, and I welcome you. But I am
surprised to see you – I thought you would be at sea by
this time. Instead you came back here?"

The two men, eye to eye in height, looked at each other
for a moment, then Alan decided to speak. "Forgive me for
disturbing you at such a time, Atlar Khan. I had to come. I
have been in Bombay, I was waiting – I was waiting for news,
but no one came, so I decided to come back, and speak with
Sadik Khan. I took a carriage from the station and the driver
told me some terrible news."

He could not continue, his voice failed him. He was
mortified, ashamed to feel his eyes sting and fill with tears.
He was helpless against this strong surge of emotion, and
stood staring through blurred eyes at Atlar Khan. Behind
him, from across the room, he heard the sound of ringing
bracelets, and the girl stood up.

"Baba-ji, tell him quickly. He has heard that Zeena is dead
– tell him, he is in pain."

Atlar Khan at once put his arm round Alan's stiffly held
shoulders. "My dear Alan – I am sorry, I did not understand.
Nothing has happened to Zeena – as far as we know. She
is alive – she got away from the Chikor Mahal, but we do
not know where she is. God knows who was buried in that
grave, but it was not Zeena."

Atlar Khan was just in time to put his other arm out and
support Alan who needed to be held upright as the world took
a turn into darkness and came back whirling. Alan was guided
to a divan and, sitting, put his head on his knees until the room
steadied. Then he sat up and the young girl came forward to
stand beside Atlar Khan.

"Baba-ji, do you allow me to remove this?" She pulled at the stiff folds of white silk that muffled her.

"Yes, yes – take it off. Alan is a brother, or soon will be, I imagine. You speak with him, poor fellow. What a terrible shock he must have had."

Gulrukh unwound herself from the fold of material and went to sit at the extreme end of the divan, away from Alan. She stared at Alan with deep interest, half smiling and half in tears.

"Oh, what trouble my cousin has caused us all! But she is alive, we are sure – only we don't know where she is. I was very much hoping that you would know and had come to tell us – but that is not so, I think?" Her English was good, heavily accented like Zeena's, he remembered, but very fluent. It was Zeena's voice and intonation that he heard when she spoke, and he sat, still stunned, and smiled at her foolishly, longing for her to speak again. She waited, looking at him, but he said nothing.

"Tst, tst – Baba-ji, his wits have gone, he says nothing – what shall we do, should we call the Angreze doctor?" Alan got himself under control. "No need for a doctor, Begum Sahiba, the news you have given me has cured all my ills."

Atlar Khan had returned with a drink in his hand and seated himself between them. "Alan, tell me, were you waiting in Bombay to meet Zeena? And she did not come?"

"Yes – you are right. No one came."

"Alan, I am sorry, you have been very distressed. I wish I had allowed you to confide in me that night – I could have told you so much! Saved you so much trouble and anxiety."

Alan said quickly, "Nothing you could have told me would

178

have made any difference to my determination to have Zeena for my wife."

"I see. But at least I could have explained some things to you. How did you imagine that Zeena would come to you? That girl has never taken a step alone in her life, and all of her seventeen years have been spent either up in the mountains of Chikor, or down here. Did you not realise that?"

"I had a friend – at least, I thought he was a friend, who helped me with advice and told me that he would bring Zeena to me. I was wrong to listen to him, I should have followed my instincts and gone to Sadik Khan when I first knew that I could not live without Zeena."

Gulrukh drew in her breath sharply as if she would speak, but instead it was Atlar Khan who spoke, "My God, Alan, I would have been visiting you in Chikor jail if you had – or worse, Tariq Khan might have been allowed to deal with you. And what would have become of Zeena? I dare not think."

"I cannot believe that such behaviour exists in these days. You are harking back to the bad old days, when the Mogul hordes ruled the land."

"Just think for one minute, my friend – you are speaking to a member of the Mogul hordes. Our blood is theirs. And what do you think of the events that have caused me to take my daughter from her uncle's house, where she has been staying in her mother's care? Have you so quickly forgotten that Zeena was declared dead and buried? Before that she and her maid were hunted like criminals. My daughter, who carries in her belly the hope of my house, was frightened almost to death. Make no mistake about it, Sadik Khan, dear to me, beloved of his subjects and of his daughter,

179

will not have his family name blackened just for the sake of his daughter's happiness."

"And mine is the sorrow to bear – my wife, Zurah Begum, has suffered with her head for most of her life – she does not always live in reality and some days are worse than others. She is most certainly insane."

Alan looked at this man he admired so much, and knew that he was speaking the truth, speaking with shame and sorrow. He saw Gulrukh lean forward to take her father's hand, and heard her say, "Baba-ji, do not grieve, it is not your fault – and my mother will be better soon. It is the moon that rules her."

"Beloved girl – you are my comfort and my pleasure. Thank God that your marriage was to your liking and that you bear happily the child of your love. But I think your mother has stepped over the edge of sanity now, into a dark place – and I did not take care to avoid this happening." Atlar Khan, anxious yet pragmatic, turned to his English brother, "Tell me, Alan, who is this friend whose advice you trusted?"

"A man called Rabindra. He told me that Zeena Begum would escape from the Chikor Mahal and that she would leave the palace with the dancers of the House of Pomegranates."

He expected an outcry of horror, but instead Atlar Khan said, "Ah. You enlisted the help of Rabindra. I would have gone to see him tomorrow anyway. He always knows everything, and is also a close friend of mine. You did well. Rabindra has a private army of his own, and also a great many contacts – spies, thieves and murderers. A great many rulers would like to have him for a friend, but my family is fortunate. We have his sole allegiance. Indeed, I should have allowed you to give me your confidence that night by the camp fire. Now, I think I know how to carry out this campaign. Gulrukh, I need a hot bath and clean clothes for my guest. Punjabi, I think. I also need one of your thicker *burkahs*."

With a jingle of bracelets, Gulrukh hurried away.

"Alan – we will do it this way." Atlar Khan was quick to make a plan. "The story is that you, my dear friend, have called on me at a sad time but, as a good host, I am anxious to entertain you and keep your heart – and mine – from sorrow. I will take you, of course, to the best entertainment that I can think of – a place that I know well, where I have been going for many years. We will go to this famous place, the House of Pomegranates, and I will introduce you to the charming Lara, the owner of the house. We will take a glass with her, watch the dancers for a while, then excuse ourselves and return to the carriage, cheered and rested. There will be a third passenger for the return journey. Do you understand me, Alan?"

Alan, hoping that he had not misunderstood, nodded.

"Good," said Atlar Khan. "Go now, Alan. By this time there will be a bath for you, and a change of clothing and identity. Please wear whatever clothing they have arranged for you. Your man will accept the orders of Amin without question. Amin-ud-Din is a close senior relative of your servant Iqbal."

Things seemed to move very fast after that. Alan bathed and was shaved by Iqbal and, under the minatory eye of Amin, he dressed himself in some of Atlar Khan's clothes. They fitted well. As the two men folded the turban round its conical-shaped *kulla* and placed it on his head, he glanced into the mirror and saw a man of the northern hill states

181

looking back at him. He wore the clothes easily and, putting up his hand, tilted the turban to a more rakish angle. Ignoring the smiles of the two servants, he went out to join Atlar Khan. As he walked into the big receiving room Atlar Khan rose from a divan and stood looking at him.

"Wah, bhai, what blood courses in your veins? You are one of us, you masquerade when you wear Angreze clothing! What lady of the past has left her mark on you? Some princess of the north who loved and lived with one of your ancestors – and bore him his heir? Welcome to our family again, Sirdar Sahib! Your name is Mirza Khan, I will call you that from now on, you are my cousin brother who has spent some years travelling in Europe."

"Atlar Khan – this is not the first time I have worn clothing like this. As you must know, in my Regiment, outside the towns and up among the hills, we all dress alike, Indian and British officers. I could be recognised—"

"If you are, it will not matter. You are here to collect some of your kit – see friends – Mirza, think of nothing but pleasure and good fortune. Come."

When the carriage drew up in the courtyard of the House of Pomegranates, the first person to come out was Rabindra. As usual he showed no surprise, holding the door of the carriage open for them. Atlar Khan stepped out first, followed by the disguised Alan.

"Greetings, Rabindra. You remember Mirza Khan, my cousin brother?"

"Of course. Welcome to you both – but this is a sad day for your family surely?"

"Ah, of course, you have heard the news that is being called from the mosques. Terrible. We have come to ease our sore hearts in the warmth of this House of Many Pleasures. Life must go on, however many beauties go to dust. They say that the brave and the beautiful are always young – even when they die. But let us not think of that. Can I send my man round to the back with the carriage – I think you may have a package for me? Meanwhile, I will take my dear Mirza in and find Lara – and perhaps you will call on me tomorrow?"

Not by the flicker of an eyelash did Rabindra show any sign of surprise. He moved forward to lead the way to the part of the house which was public. "Come and let us find Lara – she will seat you and make sure that you are comfortable and well entertained. The dancers will be in again soon – come and be welcome."

"And you will send my man and the carriage round so that they may stow the beautiful 'package'?" asked Atlar Khan smoothly.

Alan, his shoulders braced, found that he was feeling exactly as he always did before an attack, or when he was in countryside where an ambush could take place around every corner, every slope of hillside could suddenly boil with a well-armed enemy. He choked as Rabindra said, "I will certainly send your carriage round to the back but, as to the 'package', it will be necessary to check it, and be sure that all is well. It may be, in fact that it will be some few days before we can deliver the 'package' – you will understand how delicate the goods are."

"I trust it will not be delayed – I will be leaving for Pakodi tomorrow. You know the passes will be closed if the weather breaks, and I wish to get my goods up to Pakodi before the winter sets in. There is talk of snow." Atlar Khan's voice held ice in it, thought Alan – let alone talk of snow.

He found himself in the room without knowing it, crossing the threshold without seeing anything.

The room was large, with a scattering of divans and cushions tossed at random on the floor. Against the walls were cushioned seats, and heavy velvet curtains that could have been drawn for privacy were swagged back. The place was crowded. The babble of voices beat on his ears, drowning out every other sound. An enormous charcoal brazier glowed red in one corner and several cooks were working over it preparing skewers laden with chunks of meat. The smoke and smell of grilled meat mixed with all the other smells, and a blue haze shivered over the cooks as they worked. Rabindra led Atlar Khan and Alan towards the back of the room and seated them in an alcove, cushioned and curtained, with a window opening on a garden where moonlight laid cool silver on the plume of a fountain. The air was fresh in this small nook and the noise diminished as Rabindra pulled the curtains, dividing them from the hall.

Before they had seated themselves, a boy wearing a beaded brocade coat and a scarlet gauze turban came in. His eyes were lined with antimony, and he smiled with practised charm, asking them what their pleasure was. Rabindra waved him away. "There is nothing here for you, Amar. Tell Lara-ji we need a bottle of whisky some glasses and ice." The boy, with a speaking look of regret, vanished on a waft of scent as he dropped the curtain behind him.

"Pfui – is it not strange that what smells good on a woman does not please if a man wears it." Atlar Khan crinkled his nose with distaste. "It depends on what your pleasure is and where you find it." Rabindra said in response. "Amar is much sought after in some quarters." Rabindra turned to his other guest. "Now, Alan."

Atlar Khan interrupted. "Rabindra, the name is Mirza."

"Ah – of course. Mirza, I sent a man to the station, telling you not to believe any stories and to avoid going near the Chikor Mahal or this house."

"I saw no one at the station," said Alan, "I was in a hurry. I went straight to the Chikor Mahal, where the gates were locked – it was the most devastating shock, but thank God I thought of my friend Atlar Khan."

"We should not stay here too long. Could we take the 'package' you have and go?" Atlar Khan's words were almost inaudible.

Rabindra leaned across to speak close to Atlar Khan's ear.

"I am happy to see you. This would be the perfect way to get it away from here – but at present we have a difficulty. Your honoured Begum, the lady of your house, is anxious to lay her hands on your 'package' too. This place is watched and we need to be careful."

Atlar Khan nodded, but Alan said impatiently, "Watched, although there has been a funeral – I do not understand."

Atlar Khan intervened, for Alan was glaring at Rabindra. Alan was losing his temper and was strung tightly, the earlier shock had left a good deal of tension behind.

"Wait, Alan. There must be a reason for all this, we do not know what has been happening here. Wait, let Rabindra speak."

"Your cousin brother is angry with me – and he has good reason. But there have been such disasters here. And I cannot really speak of them without invading the privacy of your house, Atlar Khan."

185

Atlar Khan raised his hand. "My daughter is with me, Rabindra. She has told me all she knows, but that is not everything. The girl Chunia and her whereabouts is one thing we do not know. Do you?"

"She is here in this house – she will survive. She has been taken from the hand of Yama, though indeed she almost crossed the threshold of death. This evening she woke, and spoke – Zeena Begum has been sitting with her, night and day, and is determined not to leave her. That is why I say it may take two or three days to get her away. And, as you will understand, being already dead to her family, Zeena Begum is in great danger. The funeral is over but Zurah Begum will not be pleased if Zeena is discovered alive."

Atlar Khan obviously understood, but Alan did not. "Surely you must tell Sadik Khan that his daughter still lives – then no harm will come to her."

"Mirza, you are thinking like an Angreze. You have lived among them for too long. Understand this. Zeena's death has saved the family from terrible disgrace. Tragic, yes, and something to weep over each time her charm, beauty, and her promise are remembered. But it would be more tragic still if we were to tell Sadik Khan that his daughter was here, alive. Such a man, ruler of Chikor, would not receive this news with joy. His anger would be felt throughout all the states of India: a marriage contract broken, shame brought to his family's name and, worse still, the embarrassment of his beloved daughter eloping with an Angreze. I know my brother, Mirza, and I know him enraged. I will not tell him anything. Let him mourn his daughter and cherish her memory.

"Myself, I am sure that he must suspect something – he

is not a fool. But dead, Zeena can remain a source of pride and sorrow. Alive, and running from her father's house to the arms of an Angreze who has eaten her father's salt and been received as a brother, Zeena will be hunted. Try to see it as we see it – you are going to *have* to try to understand our world otherwise you will make yourself and Zeena very unhappy. That is one of the reasons why I do not like mixed marriages. They often founder. Thought processes and attitudes differ widely on many things, and patience and understanding are important. Allah! You and Zeena have a great deal to learn."

Rabindra, who had been listening to Atlar Khan and watching Alan, was interested to see that the younger man was listening keenly. Atlar Khan was a man of wisdom and experience and Rabindra, remembering the weakly child that Atlar had been, thought how well he had conquered illness had become the strong man he was.

He heard Alan say, "I will try – if love can aid understanding, it should be easy."

Love, thought Rabindra, *what an important part that dangerous emotion played in the hearts of the young – and what havoc it created.* Suddenly, he saw Robert making his way through the crowded tables and realised his thoughts had been too vague – for Robert was another whose heart was troubled and he was not young.

Atlar Khan and Alan had both seen him too. Alan turned his back quickly. "Rabindra, I see Colonel Maclaren coming towards us. He knows me well, his people have a house just across the loch from my home. He will certainly recognise me – should I leave?"

"There is no need. He has been seeing Chunia, Zeena's

187

maid." Quickly he explained to Alan what had happened after Zeena had left the Chikor Mahal, ending his account by. "We were discussing how he might help me to get Zeena safely away to the station to start her journey to Bombay, when you drove up."

Atlar Khan, who had listened to Rabindra's version of events in the Chikor Mahal with suppressed anger and with dismay, turned to greet Robert as he joined them. "You remember Mirza Khan, my cousin brother, of course?"

Robert blinked a few times but felt he should play the game. "Mirza Khan – yes, of course, I know him well. I thought you were awaiting events in Bombay?" There was a note of uncertainty and sadness in his voice as he looked at the handsome young man in front of him. Alan picked it up at once. Contempt or perhaps jealousy? Whatever it was it annoyed Alan and he bowed coldly and turned away without answering. He spoke instead to Rabindra, in faultless Urdu.

"Rabindra, this delay you spoke of – may I perhaps see the 'package' we came to collect. Perhaps I can help to prepare it."

Rabindra smiled. "Indeed Mirza Khan, that is possible. As soon as Lara comes she will take you and allow you to advise how best this very valuable thing may be arranged."

Alan understood that there was still a delay and was perturbed by it. *Am I never to see Zeena – and why is she lingering, does she not know that we are here for her, and what is this fellow Robert turning his disdaining eyes on me for? What was* he – *a man surely on the verge of retirement – going to do to help?*

He felt a wild impatience rising in him. He could not bear this waiting any longer. He was about to tell Atlar Khan that immediate action needed to be taken, when the curtains were pulled open and Lara, the owner of the house, slipped in. Everyone had heard of Lara. She had taken her place in the legends of the beautiful dancers of the north. She stood smiling at Alan and, aged as she was, he could for a moment see the golden girl she must once have been. She looked then at Atlar Khan, and gave them both the sweeping dancer's salaam, moving with as much grace and agility as she always had – Atlar Khan and Rabindra were the only two men present who remembered Lara as a young woman. Atlar Khan smiled. "I must present to you Mirza Khan, my cousin brother – I think this is his first visit here and, although he will not come again for some time, I feel sure you will remember him and make him welcome for my sake – if not for his own."

"He is welcome, indeed. I look forward to many meetings – perhaps." Her voice was husky, and as the light fell across her face Alan saw that she was in fact very old. Behind Lara stood an unkind contrast: a young woman who did not need to speak to show her hospitality, her eyes said it for her. She was unusually tall for a dancer – her hair, thick and shining, was drawn back and pinned to fall down her back to her waist. It was a brilliant spread of curling red hair. Lara smiled, seeing that of the men whose eyes lingered, only Alan and Rabindra looked with momentary admiration. "I have brought Rukmini to care for your wants – please tell her what you would like to eat and drink, and if you wish to see the dancers – or a particular dance – she will arrange that for you."

Atlar Khan murmured his thanks, Robert remained silent, but Alan thanked Lara. "We are most fortunate to be so attended. But for a moment, may I speak with you, Lara-ji?

189

I understand that you will take me to look at the 'package' we are to collect – if I could come with you now?"

Before Lara answered she looked across at Rabindra, who nodded.

"I have taken the lady who has the package into the garden – I will take you to her now."

Robert had been listening to this interchange and said, abruptly, "Rabindra – I trust that my patient and her attendant are not about to be disturbed. In fact, I forbid it. The patient has only just awakened. She is still in a very delicate state – as for her attendant, she needs rest and peace, not company. There is no question of any meeting at present."

He spoke with authority, as if expected to be obeyed. Alan, who had stepped forward to follow Lara, stopped, and looked at Robert with an unfriendly eye. Lara also hesitated, but Atlar Khan moved smoothly forward to stand beside Robert, at the same time nodding to Alan to go. A confrontation between Alan and Colonel Maclaren would not help matters, thought Atlar Khan wisely.

Rabindra, though, was standing back and watching with interest, a slight smile on his face. *My poor friend Robert,* he thought, *you are in a parlous state if you are willing to ignore all the implications of this meeting. This is what we were looking for this evening – a way of getting Zeena into Alan's keeping – but your heart has conquered every other sense you have. You should have married some good sensible woman years ago and raised sons with your name. Well, let us see how this King of Hearts, Atlar Khan, handles this difficult passage.*

"Colonel Maclaren, I believe that you know all about the Chikor Mahal situation. It is an unhappy one, but at least what must have been a very embarrassing complication for you will be safely removed very shortly – we are here now and I can take over my niece's affairs. You were noble indeed to risk your life by offering to assist Zeena. Thank God all is almost arranged, and you are saved from losing, at the very least, your good name and position here."

Rabindra was impressed: *you are indeed a prince of diplomacy, Atlar Khan Bahadur, – I see your father's courage and charm in you so often. Ah Dil Bahadur, you have left a son to be proud of, even though we can none of us acknowledge him as yours.* Rabindra looked back down the years and felt the ache of loss. *It is time I too left this earth, I will have fulfilled my vow to the Lambagh family if this girl gets safely away – and perhaps a son of hers will come back, to live here as his grandfather did.*

For some reason this thought brought with it a feeling of sorrow, stranger than he had ever felt. He gasped and for a moment some new grief darkened his eyes. Robert's offended voice brought him out of this dark place of depression. "Well, I am delighted of course that everything is working out so well, but there can be no question of the maid being taken from my care. She will have to stay here for weeks yet, and I think you may find that the lady who has been caring for her is most reluctant to leave her."

Atlar Khan smiled. "Oh I believe that she may be persuaded." And Robert turned away frowning.

Rabindra forced his mind back from these disquieting thoughts of the past – or were they of the future? – and took over the soothing of Robert's hurt feelings.

Alan followed Lara through a series of passages, all of which were shadowy with small oil lamps as the only light.

They stopped before an high-arched door, and Lara said over her shoulder, "Sahib, she is sitting on the lawn beside the fountain. It is not dark, the moon is high and you will see the fountain's spray."

Alan forgot to thank her. He saw ahead of him the plume of the fountain, clear in the white light of the moon. He walked quietly across the lawn and at last stood beside the fountain, looking down at Zeena.

Sixteen

The splash of the fountain and the thick turf under his feet had muffled his footsteps. She had not heard him approach.

She was holding a spray of jasmine. In the brilliant light of the moon she was a study in silver. Unveiled and in a airy robe she was displayed to him for the first time. He looked at her in silence, afraid to move closer or speak, in case the vision vanished.

She looked so different. He had not seen her in anything but thick silken robes, and veiled. Now she wore weightless silks, lifting and blowing in the night breeze. She was deep in thought, twisting the spray of jasmine in her fingers, lifting it to her face to sniff it. The scent of the flowers was all about her. This picture of her, he would remember all his life. What was she dreaming about? Could she be thinking of him? He thought she looked melancholy and could not bear the thought that sorrow should have touched her. He moved closer.

"Zeena."

The spell was broken. She started to her feet and turned, staring. "Who is it? What do you want?"

He saw that she was pulling a light veil down over her face. She had forgotten him, it seemed. This could not be.

Surely she had not recognised him. He took off his turban. "Zeena, it is me – Alan. I forgot that I am wearing Atlar Khan's clothes – I did not mean to startle you. Zeena, have you forgotten me completely?"

Yes – for a short time in the garden he had not disturbed her thoughts. She had been thinking of Chunia, glad that she was conscious, had recognised her mistress and was recovering, taking the first important steps away from death. Zeena had been overjoyed at first, and then reality had broken into her joy. What were she and Chunia to do now? Where could they go?

Chunia was too weak and shaken to be moved, and Chini Ayah had said that to move her would be dangerous. Lara had said at once that Chunia could stay as long as was necessary, but that "You, Begum must go, The searchers are still out, Madore is not a safe place for you." Zeena had stopped Lara speaking before Chunia, had drawn her away from the bed and had then said in a quiet and final tone that she would not leave without her maidservant. Lara had folded her arms and turned away, saying, "As you wish, Begum Sahiba. Then you will be found and taken either back to the Chikor Mahal or to Tariq Khan, and Chunia and all she has suffered will have been for nothing. Listen to me, child of princes. If you are found – which you will be, then Chunia's life and your life will not be worth a handful of dust – not even the dust that was thrown into the empty grave of the Pila Ghar where your mother's tomb was built."

The empty grave! The words chilled Zeena's heart.

"What do you mean, a grave beside my mother's tomb? There is no grave there!"

"There is now. Listen while I tell you what Zurah Begum has plotted."

Lara then told Zeena of the latest happenings in the Chikor Mahal, of the false funeral and her father's return. Zeena's first thought was that she must go at once to comfort his grief. Lara looked at the young Begum with pity.

"You think so?" said Lara, "You think your re-appearance will comfort your father? Have sense, child of love. Think a little."

The knowledge that she could never go back had been lurking in the shadows of Zeena's mind, and Lara's question made her see clearly. Her father, proud head of an ancient family, would not be happy and comforted to see his daughter now. By merely being alive, Zeena would prove to the world, *his* world, that she had flouted customs, and had broken her marriage contract. Soon he would discover that she had run away and spent time in a famous house of pleasure and that she was the mistress – as her father would see it – of an Angreze. As far as her father was concerned his daughter was dead, dying as she had lived, the beloved virgin daughter of the ruler of Chikor, and it was better so.

She would never be alive to him again, she could never go back.

It was a puzzling feeling. She belonged nowhere now. She tried to cling to the idea of Chunia, still alive and with her. That at least gave her an identity. But even the thought of Chunia was not enough to fill this emptiness. *Who am I? Who will I be now?* She stared at Alan, not really seeing him. *Who is this man to me?*

Alan saw her clearly and sensed her misery as she looked at him.

"Zeena, *have* you forgotten me?" Alan asked, desperate for an answer.

"No. I have not forgotten you. But I have not thought of you. There have been many happenings, changes." She was speaking in Urdu, her command of his language seemed to have deserted her.

"I know. I waited for you in Bombay, this was foolish of me. I should have stayed here to help you." He could think of no way of explaining why he had deserted her, had left her to face this nightmare scenario alone. She looked up at him, but he could not read her expression now that her face was once again behind the veil.

"There was no way for me to come to you. Many terrible things have happened. My girl Chunia was beaten almost to death because she would not tell those in the Chikor Mahal where I was. After I saw how she was I could think of nothing but her. What there was between us seemed of so little value set against how she had borne pain and shame for me. But, she lives – and I am supposed to be dead. It seems so unbelievable, unreal."

If only he could take her in his arms, comfort her somehow – her light veil was like a wall between them, symbolising a barrier that seemed impossible to cross. Alan knew he must reach her, every word she said seemed to build the wall higher.

"You are not dead, Zeena, and now I am here with you, I will look after you. Will you try to remember how much I love you, how long I have loved you – we are together now, soul of my soul, and I will never leave you again. I have come to take you away from this place, as I promised. And look, I still have your promise, the rose you threw to me, remember? Zeena, I cannot see your eyes, please unveil beloved, do not hide from me."

His words, spoken with such passion, aroused feeling in her, memories, echoes of a time past: "a long love that never dies. A white rose, a journey—"

She looked down at the crushed rose in his hand. The words reverberated in her mind: "a long love . . . a grave that is not a grave." Had a cloud come over the moon so that all she saw was darkness ahead of her? With a sob of fear, she snatched off her veil and fell forward into his arms.

"I am no one," she said. "I have nothing. I do not know where I go."

"You are my love. You are coming home with me, you have my heart and all that I am. I shall take you home."

"Home? Where is home for me? Will your home become mine? How can that be? They say it will be alien to me, Alan, so far across the dark water."

He tightened his arms round her. "Yes you will be disorientated for a little time, but not for long. I shall be with you, you are taking part of your life with you, in me. I know and love your country, you will teach me more about it, and I will teach you about my land. Have no fears, my soul, my home will be yours."

Wrapped in the strength of his arms, her head on his breast, hearing the steady beat of his heart, she rested, silent. He longed to kiss her but battled against his desire – she was shocked and shaken and he could wait until she was at peace with herself.

His arms are strong, she thought, *they hold back the dark*. But the picture of the empty grave still haunted her. She shivered.

197

"What is it Zeena?" Are you cold? Would you like to come into the house?"

"I am not cold but I am full of fear," she said. "I can see an empty grave – I remember the old man said he saw 'a grave that is not a grave'—"

"What old man?" demanded Alan, suddenly annoyed and jumping to conclusions. "Is it that old doctor who has frightened you? Do not think of empty graves, put such thoughts from your mind. We will be away from this place soon, away from all of it and everyone in it."

"And Chunia also? She comes too?" Zeena asked.

Robert, who had been approaching silently over the grass, heard all this and was annoyed in his turn. Old doctor indeed! He heard Zeena's question about Chunia, too, and answered it before Alan could speak. "There is no question of Chunia going anywhere at present, Zeena. She is not well enough to be moved. Nothing can be done in haste. You are safe enough here for the present. News has come from the Chikor Mahal. Zurah Begum is said to be gravely ill, so there will be no searchers out for you. It is possible for you to return home, I should say. I can drive you there, my carriage is in the stables. You could stay in the Chikor Mahal for a few weeks until Chunia is well enough to be moved, then you can decide what you wish to do."

Zeena felt Alan's arms tighten around her as if he would never let her go, and when he spoke she knew he was angry. "Colonel Maclaren, there may be no question of Chunia being moved, but I do not think you have considered all the dangers of Zeena staying here, or worse, of returning to the Chikor Mahal." Was the man mad, he wondered, suggesting that the search would be called off because the old Begum was ill? Or was there another reason for his desire to keep Zeena here.

"The Begum Sahiba is coming with me to the Pakodi Ghar, at Atlar Khan's invitation." Alan could feel his anger growing. "There we will spend several days before setting off on our journey to England." His voice, decisive and hard – as she had never heard it before – was comforting to Zeena. Her father had that tone in his voice when he was angered. It now gave her a feeling of security that she had thought she'd lost. She did not attempt to leave the shelter of Alan's arms.

Robert could not look at her, held in Alan's embrace, obviously glad to be there, and feeling no shame in front of him. It hurt, and the hurt enraged him. Keeping his voice steady with an effort, he said, "I do not consider two or three days long enough to think before making such a decision. It is a very big decision for a girl to make, to leave her home, a loving family, and her own country to go far away to another land and a different world. I think the Begum Sahiba needs more time. Also, there is another matter. Do you not feel that it is necessary that the truth be told to the ruler? I cannot bear to think of the pain he must be enduring, thinking that his daughter, his only child, is dead. It is a very cruel way to behave to my friend, Sadik Khan."

Alan felt Zeena pull against his arms. *If she agrees and says that she must return to her father, knowing what I know now about the dangers she has escaped, I shall attempt to kill this stupid fellow.*

But Zeena's voice, as she moved out of his arms, was clear and strong. "I have heard all these reasons before, and have myself thought deeply before making a decision. I will never return to my father and, if I did, it would be no comfort to him. You know nothing of our customs. Ask your friend Rabindra, and believe what he says. My decision is mine to make and I am going with my lord and, Chunia, when she is well, will come to us. We will wait to hear what she would wish to do. Crossing the seas will be hard for her, perhaps she will wait for our return."

What a queen, thought Alan, *what a girl I have found.* And those words "wait for our return" – she said them so confidently that he almost believed that they *would* return, though in his heart he was sure that that would impossible. Once this wretched, interfering fellow left them and he was alone with Zeena, he would explain to her that they would not be returning – or at best, not for a very long time. Now what was this foolish man saying.

Robert was sick at heart. He, too, had fallen in love with this young beauty. "Zeena, it will probably be at least six months before Chunia is fit to travel, and you will remember how your presence revives her. It might be fatal to desert her now. Have you somewhere you can go and stay while she is recovering? I may not know much about your customs, but I do know that the hill rulers take their families back to the mountains when the Durbar season is over. Your uncle, Atlar Khan, will be leaving shortly – where will you stay? I understand there is a women's hostel near the flower market, where it might be possible for me to make arrangements for you."

Alan broke in sharply, his patience gone. "Can you not understand, Colonel Maclaren, Zeena Begum is my affianced bride. She will be with me. You are correct in saying she cannot stay here. She is not going to stay here, we will leave ahead of Chunia and she can follow, if she wishes, as soon as she is well enough to make the voyage. We will be leaving in a fortnight at the latest." He looked at Zeena to see if she had understood. He wondered if shock had driven the English language from her mind. But he need not have worried, she had understood most of what he said. Only two words had bewildered her.

"Fortnight? Voyage?" she said doubtfully. "What are these?" She was looking at Alan, asking *him*. The doctor might have been invisible. Alan was deeply relieved. She was not enthralled by Robert Maclaren – and she had not forgotten all her English.

"A fortnight is fourteen days and voyage means a journey by sea. We will take a ship from Karachi – Atlar Khan suggests that is easier and better than going to Bombay or Calcutta. As to Chunia – Zeena, you do understand, it will be better for her to follow us, as soon as she is well? As she wishes of course. Do you agree?"

To his relief she nodded and answered him in English. "Yes, I understand. But can we not wait a little time. She is very strong, she might heal more quickly."

Both men spoke.

"There is no question of her travelling for at least six months." Robert was adamant.

'I think it will take time." Alan wanted to offer her same choice. "But if you want to wait—" He looked at Zeena, praying she would be firm and say she wanted to leave at once, but again Robert rudely interrupted.

"Why don't we sit down and discuss this. See – the moon is down. It will be dawn soon and, you, Zeena, have been without sleep – we also! Our brains are fogged. Go to sleep

201

now Zeena Begum and we will meet later, after you are rested when we can talk about what is best."

The fellow was doing everything he could to hold her here. Alan was becoming infuriated but, before he had a chance to tell the doctor to mind his own business, Rabindra, followed by a girl, came across the grass towards them.

"Alan Sahib, you must take Zeena and go at once. Mohini will show you where to go. Do not wait to talk now, make no argument. Tariq Khan and some of his followers are in the house. They are calling for wine and music and the dancers, and their eyes are sharp and searching."

"Chunia—" It was half gasped by Zeena.

"Chunia is safe, but the Sahib and you are not. Zeena, you risk his life if you delay now and he is seen."

The girl, Mohini, who had come with him hurried forward and, snatching Zeena's veil, wrapped her into the draping folds of a cotton *burkah*, that clung and hid everything. Over Alan's head, Rabindra pulled a loose white shirt that fell below his knees, and then added a velvet waistcoat and an untidily tied turban. Mohini had already pulled Zeena's gauze veil over her own head and in answer to her urgent whisper – "Begum Sahiba walk like an old one. Bow your shoulders" – Zeena bent her back and began to stumble after the girl. Alan followed and Mohini trotted ahead of them, talking, laughing and humming to herself. Looking at the threesome Robert thought at a distance the disguise would pass – a Pathan, an old woman and a girl of the streets, setting off for home, the day's work over. He prayed that no one would come close to them. It was impossible for Alan to disguise a firm soldierly stance and stride, but Zeena – well Zeena was well disguised – stumbling under the folds of the *burkah*. Mohini was too well dressed to be a girl of the streets – but close up her painted mouth and tinsel ornaments proclaimed her for what she was. He was momentarily amused, watching them as they vanished into the shadows but then remembered what Rabindra had said.

"Is it true, Rabindra? Is that man really in the house?"

"Yes. He is in the *selamlik* and he has two of his guards with him and several other followers. As long as we can keep them all together – the singers are entertaining them and the dancers – all will be well. If you will come with me and converse with me, and with him. Express no sorrow about the death of his betrothed unless he mentions it to you. You would not be expected to know anything about his private life and, Sadik Khan, however close your friendship, would be unlikely to have spoken with you about the marriage plans for his daughter. But talk – talk about anything and be sure his glass is always full. Come my friend and help me make time for the others to leave unseen."

Seventeen

The drive from the House of Pomegranates to the main road was long and winding. It had not seemed as tortuous when Alan had driven with Atlar Khan in the carriage – when he had been full of excitement at the thought that he would at last see Zeena. Now he had Zeena stumbling beside him, and the shadowed drive seemed menacing – every shadow hid danger, and the trees were full of whispers.

Sakhi Mohammed walked in front, Zeena and the girl Mohini, hand in hand, followed him and, Alan, holding his pistol, was behind them. He had seen the drawn sword in Sakhi Mohammed's hand, and was at once filled with alarm. Had Sakhi Mohammed seen anything, or was he just getting ready in case they were attacked. Two men against how many of Tariq's assassins? It seemed small protection for Zeena. He did not think of protecting the other girl – all his fear was for his beloved. Then he saw a glint of metal in Mohini's free hand – so she was armed and ready to fight, which shortened the odds a little. He suddenly remembered a historical fact – the women of the Scottish Highlands had, long ago, fought beside their husbands. He hoped that if anyone jumped out of the bushes at them, Mohini would not get in the way of his bullets or Sakhi Mohammed's sword arm. This girl, lightly dressed in veils and muslins, bore no resemblance at all to the brawny women of the clan battles.

Fortunately they did not have long to hurry through the menacing shadows. Atlar Khan had brought the carriage as far up the drive as he had dared, and was standing beside the open door waiting for them. "I have seen no one – let us go."

Still holding Mohini's hand, Zeena stepped forward but, as they came together to the door of the carriage, Mohini stopped and raised Zeena's hand to her forehead and then to her lips, and whispered, "Go safely, Khanum. My life for yours, now and always." She released her hand from Zeena's, stepped back and vanished into the shadows of the drive, back the way they had come.

Zeena did not dare to call out, but would have run after Mohini to stop her, but Alan caught her arm and held her back.

"No Zeena, let her go," said Atlar Khan. "She will bring us news of Chunia tomorrow. Get into the carriage and let us get home. I do not care for the stillness round here – I hope that Rabindra has thought of some way to hold Tariq's attention, the man was certainly suspicious and will send searchers after us if he is not distracted."

Sakhi Mohammed did not come in the carriage with them, he turned his horse and followed Mohini. Alan helped Zeena up the steps, and took the seat beside her, and Atlar Khan sat opposite. He leaned across to speak to Zeena.

"That girl – do you know her?"

"She was with the dancers who helped me leave the Chikor Mahal – and she also helped to nurse Chunia. Why?"

"She must be from Lambagh. She used the old words: 'My

life for yours, now and always.' It is the old oath, given and taken – the oath of fealty to the ruler."

"Lambagh? Where my great-grandfather Dil Bahadur lived?"

"Your great-grandfather? Who told you that? Dil Bahadur was your grandfather. He was your mother's father – and mine."

"Zurah Begum told me one day that I came from the family of Lambagh and that I was the cause of great scandal – but she often said such things to bring me down, so I did not listen." As soon as she had spoken, she bit her lip and glanced sideways at Alan beside her. *Scandal* – she frowned at her own words. There was so much that Alan did not know about her – she wondered if his love would still be hers now that she was no longer part of a good family. All she had now were more scandalous stories, a lost reputation, and a sojourn in a brothel. Alan must knew it well. Did he still want her as his wife? Atlar Khan was talking to her and she was not listening. "I am sorry uncle, what did you say?"

"I said that you were wise not to listen to the stories of an old long-forgotten scandal. It was only ever repeated out of jealousy. My poor Zurah, her envy has driven her mad. My fault. I did not realise how it tormented her. She was always green with envy. Forget all that she said or did – it is all over now. You are entering a new life, and we must think only of that. Forget the false funeral, the empty grave – Zurah, too, will be sorry for the harm she has caused when she comes to her senses."

It does not matter if she is sorry or not, thought Zeena, *I hope I will never see her again. And I shall hate her always for what she has done to Chunia – and would have done to me.*

The sky was growing light – through the dark trees that

bordered the road it glistened like silver, but Zeena did not see the light. There was nothing but a cold darkness in her heart. The false funeral and the empty grave haunted her. *If Zurah, envious, mean-spirited Zurah, had had her way,* thought Zeena, *I would be lying in that grave beside my mother's tomb – my mother so loved by all who knew her that this bitter woman who was supposed to be her friend would have killed her daughter. Was it love that caused jealousy so cruel? If so, was love so cruel?* But something stirred in Zeena and emerging from such sombre thoughts were the words: "Love is all. Love conquers all. Love is everlasting, stronger than death." This was voice so clear and yet so quiet. A voice she had never heard and yet knew well. *I am dreaming,* thought Zeena, *there is no one speaking such words here – I must be dreaming.*

She *was* dreaming. The broken nights, the long days of anxious thought had taken their toll. Her head was resting on Alan's shoulder, his arm was around her, holding her close, trying to shield her sleep from the bumps and jolts of the carriage.

"My love," said Alan softly, "my dearest love." The words sounded in Zeena's dreams, she smiled and slept soundly at last, and did not wake even when they arrived at the Pakodi Ghar. She was carried into the palace in Alan's arms.

While Zeena and her party were hurrying down the drive towards the main road, Robert, reluctant, his heart burning with jealousy, walked back into the roaring, bustling crowds of the *selamlik*. It maddened him that he had not been able to persuade Zeena to postpone her departure with Alan. He told himself that he knew that it was wrong for her, that she would be miserable living in the north of Scotland with that young man, who really knew nothing about the habits and customs which had ruled her life so far. She was making a terrible mistake. Why would she not listen to him? He would not admit to himself that he knew well why she had refused to listen to him. He could not bear what he had seen in her eyes when she looked up at Alan Lyall. It was love he had seen, clearly. She loved that young man.

Robert was in pain. In love. This was the first time in his life that he had fallen in love, and it hurt him to think that he had even played his strongest card to stop Zeena leaving: he had spoken of Chunia's need of Zeena and yet it had not altered her decision to go. He remembered her eyes when she had looked at Alan! The way she had said, "I am going with my lord." Her lord! That young puppy, Alan Lyall – he could remember him as a long-legged boy of ten, riding like a maniac along the shores of the loch, racing the wind. *Then*, he had thought him a pleasant, courageous child, but now – here he was, a grown man, taking away the only girl Robert had ever wanted, and Robert could find nothing good to say about him. Well, the girl had made her choice and there was no place for him in her life. The loss would haunt him forever.

He saw Tariq Khan across the room, a bejewelled toad, seated cross-legged on a divan. The toad waved to him and beckoned him over. I shall have to go and join him and his circle of sychophants. At least I am doing something to assist in Zeena's escape. He started to drink seriously, buying drinks for anyone in Tariq Khan's circle who had an empty glass, and drinking glass for glass with them, laughing at jokes that were more lewd than amusing. He observed the way Tariq's black eyes shifted from girl to girl, among the singers, and musicians and the girls serving the wine. The vulgar Tariq was always looking to make his choice for what was left of the night? Or was he searching for a disguised Zeena among the tinsel beauties? The thought was nauseating and frightening.

Robert poured whisky down his throat, trying to deaden his feelings, and regretted what he had always been proud of – his hard head. The noise in the room had risen and the beautiful girl, whose singing voice was like honey, could not compete against the noise. The dancers had come in, a whirl of slender arms and legs, and floating skirts. Robert saw, among the scarlet-skirted dancers, the girl Mohini, whom he had last seen hurrying away with Zeena. She was dancing close by and, for a moment, her gleaming, khol-ringed eyes met his, and seemed to flash a message. Then she was looking away from him, her head moving from side to side in the ritualistic posturing of the dance. *So*, thought Robert, relieved, *they got away safely or Mohini would not be here. Atlar Khan and his carriage must have picked them up. Zeena will leave India in the next few days – my golden dreams must fade now. I must pick up my life, unchanged.*

He held his glass up and drank a silent toast to a dream, and saw that Tariq Khan's black eyes were watching him, a steady stare, his expression unreadable. Robert ignored him, no need to pretend he had an interest in this man any longer. He watched the dancers instead, following Mohini's fluid gestures, her hands and arms rippling in movements so slight that they might have been blown by a wind, as a bird's feather's move in a breeze.

Tariq's eyes grew keen. He spoke to Robert suddenly. "Eh,

Sahib! You watch the dancers so closely! Is it the dancers or
the dance that you admire?"

Robert found it hard to look at him without showing both
his fear and revulsion. "But the dancers are the dance, surely?
I enjoy watching both."

"Yes indeed, I see you do. Have you chosen a girl, Colonel
Sahib? A girl for the short sweet hours before dawn? This
is the dance of love – each movement designed to rouse the
passions of a man. Who will you take to pleasure you in an
upper room? Their price is high, but they are well trained.
Sweet and soft and made for pleasure. Have you chosen,
Colonel Sahib? Or do you prefer other pleasures – they cater
for all tastes here. It is known as a place for rich men and
maharajas only, Colonel Sahib."

On his lips the title was an insult, his manner was revolting.
Robert realised that one of these girls, so young and gracefully
appealing, would tonight be the prey of a man like Tariq.
This man was what Sadik Khan had been prepared to give
his daughter to in marriage – this creature of darkness here
beside him. It was difficult to believe.

Robert had known Sadik Khan for some years and had
always liked him. He had appeared an honest, kind-hearted
man, who, rare among the very wealthy princes, had seemed
to have the welfare of his people at heart. He had given
generously to the mission hospital, and to other charities,
and had used his wealth to do what he saw as good. He had
built and endowed two schools, one up in Chikor State, and
one here in Madore. Robert had respected Sadik Khan and
had thought of him as a friend. He could not understand how
the man could accept Tariq Khan as a son-in-law. *Rabindra
was right*, Robert thought, *I do not know the people of this*

country that I love, I have not learned as much about them as I thought I had.

The dancers were now taking it in turns to perform alone. There were six girls and a leader, a tall flashing-eyed creature with long red hair. She danced alone, her arms raised and the rest of her body undulating like a snake coiling, her breasts quivered and jumped in time with the muscles of her belly and the beat of a drum. Her audience shouted and clapped and Robert heard bids being offered for Kairne. Tariq Khan was not bidding. He had removed his unpleasant stare from Robert and was watching the line of girls. The leader had moved to one side and it was now Mohini who stood alone. Her dance was different – a matter of graceful posturing, gesturing of the hands and arms – more delicate and seductive, to Robert, than the leader's had been. He noticed a great many of the older men were bidding for her, including Tariq. He had signalled to one of his companions: "This one," he had said, and had handed the man a handful of notes. As Mohini's dance ended the man stepped forward and tucked the notes into the waistband of her skirt, indicating Tariq Khan as he did so. Mohini was to be Tariq's companion when the dance ended.

Suddenly, Robert felt revulsion. He could not bear this situation. He looked at Tariq Khan and saw that the man was smiling at him, a smile of triumph. Robert got up and went out of the room to look for Rabindra. He found him outside, sitting beside the fountain talking with Sakhi Mohammed. They both stood up as Robert came to them.

"Robert," said Rabindra kindly, "I owe you much money for all the drinks you bought those goats. I was just coming to get you away from them. Atlar Khan and his party escaped.

211

There is no need for you to endure any more of that company. It has been a long night for you, you will be glad to get home to your bed. My thanks for all you have done tonight."

Robert felt he had done very little and said. "All I seem to have done is to turn Tariq Khan's interest towards Mohini. I wish it was possible to save her from him. She does not deserve to have to spend any time with such a man."

Rabindra was alert at once. "What do you mean, Robert?"

"You must know what happens after the Dance of Love – Tariq has bought the services of Mohini, that girl who helped Zeena get away. It seems a poor reward for her services to now have to amuse that devil."

"Mohini!" said Rabindra, "That must be stopped at once. He has no real interest in girls. He has chosen her for other reasons. He wants to question her, he must have guessed that she has danced many times for the Chikor ruler, and might know where Zeena is likely to be hidden.

"Robert, you can do me one more service if you will. There is still time for Mohini to be saved from Tariq. Stay here, I will go and get the girl."

A streak of yellow light suddenly lay across the shadows around the fountain. Someone had opened a door or a window and was standing there, listening or looking out. Rabindra followed the line of light with his eyes and unexpectedly laughed out loud. "Well Robert, you can take her with you – I was surprised when Lara told me that you wished to have a presence in the *bibighar* of your house. It has been empty far too long. But there was no need for you to pay! I will see you get your money back, and Mohini will be happy to serve you. You may have her services for a month, and you may find –

aha, that you wish to keep her for longer. Sakhi Mohammed will find her, and bring her round if you will have patience – I will go and arrange another entertainment for Khan Sahib Tariq Khan. I have just the person for a man of discernment like him."

Rabindra, still chuckling to himself, walked towards the line of light. Sakhi Mohammed said softly, "The one who listened has gone – have a care Sahib when you ride out tonight. I will accompany you if Rabindra will give me leave." He followed Rabindra and Robert was left alone to work out what plan Rabindra had. To him it did not seem to be wise, Tariq would be more determined than ever to take Mohini. He thought of Chunia, his patient in the upper room – how much had Tariq had to do with that attack? Left alone in the pre-dawn darkness beside the fountain, Robert began to tremble. The falling water of the fountain's spray seemed to be whispering a message: "Love, love is life, and life passes swiftly. Take love while you can. A tomb is a lonely place. Take love."

The sound of horses on the paving of the courtyard blotted out the fountain's words, and Robert was glad to see Sakhi Mohammed mounted and leading Robert's own beast. Behind him was another horse and rider. A heavily veiled woman – Mohini? There was no way of telling, until she lifted her hand and held the veil aside for a second. It was her. Robert rode off, and heard the other horses move up behind him.

Riding down the dark roads and through the gate of the North, Robert was glad to see the city streets but, at the same time, he wondered how much gossip would follow if the presence of a woman in his retinue was noticed. But the streets were quiet, all the houses were in darkness.

213

It was so early, the sky was just beginning to show a line of light on the horizon. They would be home before the city awoke.

They crossed the city, and came at last to the civil lines where Robert's bungalow was hidden behind high walls. Sakhi Mohammed called to the gateman, who came out still half asleep to let them in. They rode up the drive to the portico where Robert's bearer, Sheffi, the chief servant of his household, waited for his master as he always did, no matter what time Robert returned. There was a syce waiting, too, to take Robert's horse.

Robert had been dreading this arrival. What would Sheffi make of his master arriving with a woman – in all his twenty-five years in Madore, Robert had never brought a lone woman into his house – and certainly never a woman from a house of pleasure. He saw with dismay that Mohini had unveiled, there was no disguising where she came from now. But Sheffi showed no surprise. As usual he moved forward to hold Robert's horse while he dismounted. The syce took the reins from him and went to attend to Mohini's horse.

She had dismounted without help and stood quietly waiting. Robert was beset with the necessity of making a decision. Should he tell Mohini to come into the house with him, or should she go straight to the small building, just to the left of the house. This was the *bibighar*, the women's house. The question was answered by Mohini herself, who asked if a lantern could be brought to her, and then she walked away towards the *bibighar* with no more words. Robert was about to order a lantern but Sheffi told him, "The lamps are already there, Sahib. I had a message."

Robert knew that Rabindra had sent word. He saw four

men standing in the shadows. one came forward and saluted Robert. "I have orders, Sahib, to post my men round the house."

His bungalow had become an armed camp but, remembering the expression of Tariq's face, Robert was grateful to have guards. The drink he had taken during the long night was beginning to make itself felt. He asked Sheffi for tea and, then, when Sheffi brought the tea, he dismissed him and, undressing, went into his bathroom and took the cold bath waiting for him, glad to feel his head clearing a little. He would sleep, then be ready for whatever the new day brought. At least Zeena was safe from Tariq Khan – but close on the heels of that thought he imagined her in the arms of Alan Lyall and lost all hope of sleep. Work, that was all that would help him now.

He tried to plan his day, hoping this would send him to sleep. He would have to go back to the House of Pomegranates and see how his patient, Chunia, was getting on. Chunia, now bereft of Zeena's presence, as he was. Perhaps he would get some news of Zeena there – oh, was she never going to leave his mind? Did he truly *want* to forget her? He could not say truthfully that he did. Tomorrow, he thought, tomorrow I will pull myself together, rid her from my mind, and be myself again. Here I am, behaving like a lovesick boy over a girl young enough to be my daughter. I am fifty-two, and she is seventeen. I am an old fool. He turned over, determined to sleep but now he saw the pale sky through the open veranda door. It was almost day.

A few minutes later he realised that the veranda door should not have been open, and that there was a figure standing against the pale light. For a moment he was terrified. They had followed him – here was one of Tariq Khan's thugs come to end his life with a sharp knife or a cord. Robert opened his mouth to shout and then his eyes registered the shape of the figure in the doorway. It was certainly female.

Robert pulled the mosquito curtains aside and saw her move towards him. He had been thinking of Zeena, longing for her – and she had come to him? It was a dream, though, and did not last as the woman came closer and spoke. "Lord, you are awake? Did I wake you?"

A drift of scent, sweet and heavy, sandalwood and roses, came to him. Mohini was standing beside his bed, dressed, in a long muslin shirt. With the light behind her, the shirt was totally transparent. He looked away from her revealed figure.

"No, I was awake, Mohini." Robert spoke gently. "You did not sleep? Are your quarters comfortable, or is there something you need. You were not frightened, were you? There are guards sent by Rabindra, so do not be afraid."

"I thank you, Sahib, all is well in the house, and I have no fears. I did not sleep because I thought of you, I thought you would be lying wakeful, and I longed to come and bring you sleep."

The shirt she wore had no fastener and now, as she moved her arm to lift more of the mosquito net aside, the shirt fell open, and he saw her breasts, round and full, like the breasts of the sculptured girls he had seen on the walls of Hindu temples. He tried to close his eyes or look away, but could not. She was studying his face, her gaze direct, and as she looked into his eyes she slowly removed her shirt and let it fall to the floor. Each movement was graceful and seductive. Her naked body was beautiful. How long was it since he had passionately held

216

a woman in his arms? He had never felt flesh like this. She was in his bed and he could not withstand her, his body took over his mind and he no longer wanted to push her away.

Mohini's hands – and words – caressed him. "I bring you sleep, lord." She spoke so softly and with every practised touch she brought him to a fiery awakening, until thought and memory were all burned away in the flames of his body, the furnace of desire, too long unslaked.

Dawn flooded the sky, birds, chirpily, greeted the coming of the day, but the two naked lovers on the bed in the shaded room neither heard nor saw anything but themselves, until sleep came and took them both.

It was late in the morning when Robert stirred. He turned his head and saw Mohini lying beside him, her long hair tangling over his body and her eyes open, smiling into his. She sat up as soon as she saw he was awake, and reached to pick up her shirt. How beautiful she was, her every movement seemed designed to send his thoughts into channels of desire he was trying not to follow. He had to send her away – there was no place in his life for her.

While he was trying to think of a way to tell her this – words that would not hurt her – she turned to smile at him, and he could think of nothing but her gentle grace. He watched her take up his comb and bring order to her long hair. Her hair was golden in the morning light. She was very fair, her skin was paler than Zeena's, and her eyes were delicate too, long tilted eyes, turquoise eyes, the same blue-green as the stone she wore on a cord round her neck. He did not say anything about sending her away when he finally spoke.

"Where do you get your bright hair, Mohini? Where is your country?"

"I have no country, lord. My mother came from Turkey, from the hills beyond Lake Van. She was light haired, I think. I do not remember her very clearly. She left me when I was in my second year."

"And your father."

She shrugged and shook her head. "My father? I do not know. I was born in the House of Janki in Lambagh. My mother left me there when she went to Madore with a man who bought her for a month. He was a camel drover, but I do not think he was my father. My mother did not return. I stayed in the House of Janki in Lambagh until I was fully grown and had entered womanhood, then the woman who was in charge of the girls sent me down to Lara in the House of Pomegranates. I was trained by Lara, lord. I pleased you? You slept in happiness?"

What could he say, looking into those eyes, with the feeling of her close to him still lively in his memory? He smiled. "You pleased me, Mohini." It was her reward, it seemed, she beamed with pleasure.

"I am yours, lord. You are a king among men. I am here to serve you. It is permitted to wear your robe? It would not be seemly to go out from your room in this shirt. I came in haste, with no clothes of my own, but they will be sent to me today. I go now, before the house wakes."

Robert could not stop grinning to himself. He watched her wrap herself in his dressing gown and slip through the open door and vanish. As she did so, he heard Sheffi's knock on the door, and the rattle of his early morning tea tray. So life was to go on as usual – with the addition of Mohini living a

218

hundred yards away. His to command – what had she said: "You are a king among men – I am here to serve you."

While Sheffi shaved him, Robert sat thinking. This way of life seemed remarkably pleasant. He could not tell Mohini that she had to go. After all, he had to wait until Rabindra said that it was safe. But it was his heart that ruled him now. He would refuse to send her back to the life she was leading in the House of Pomegranates. What a ghastly life for a girl so gentle and loving. He could not do it. She was a special creature, and she had stopped him from thinking of Zeena. The spell that had held him, the longing for her, had gone. Zeena was still a beautiful dream, but he had held a warm reality in his arms – a girl who looked at him as Zeena had looked at Alan. Mohini called *him* "lord". He had no envy in his heart now. Rabindra was quite right. He had lived alone too long.

He dressed and ordered his horse to be brought round. He thought of the day ahead of him with great happiness. He would pay his usual visit to the civil hospital, call at the mission hospital, and then go to the House of Pomegranates to see how the girl Chunia was.

Sheffi came to ask him if he would be back for tiffin, his usual question at this time in the morning. "Yes," said Robert, and thought again that his morning routine had not been changed in any awkward way. But the night – Robert hoped with a lift of the heart – that his nights were going to be delightfully different.

As he rode past the *bibighar* he saw that the curtains over the door moved aside a little, and smiled to think that there was, at last, someone other than his servants to watch him leave, and wait for his return. He was still smiling as he came up to the gate, and the day began to change.

Eighteen

There were two men talking to the guards at the gate: two men in uniform, mounted on splendid horses. The pale blue turbans cocked aslant on their heads were marked with the crest of the rampant leopard that told Robert where they came from. They were Chikor troopers, and senior at that. One of them was a *risaldar*. What could they be doing at his gate? Searching for Zeena? His heart sank at the thought – not more trouble, more danger for that unfortunate girl? It was a relief to him to see Sakhi Mohammed come from the gate house – particularly as there was no sign of anxiety on his face. Robert saw him pause to speak to the *risaldar*, who dismounted at once and came to stand at Robert's stirrup, saluting.

"Salaam Sahib. I bring you an urgent message from His Highness Sadik Khan."

Robert took the paper, and unfolded it, to see Sadik Khan's characteristic black scrawl.

Robert, there is trouble in the Zenana: my sister, Zurah Begum, is ill. I think, very ill. I know you do not attend my womenfolk as a rule, but Zurah Begum will see no one else – one of the women here will act as a nurse. Please come in haste.

220

Robert looked up from the paper to meet the eyes of the *risaldar*, and of Sakhi Mohammed who was standing at his shoulder. The *risaldar* spoke first.

"There is a cloud over the palace of Chikor, Sahib. The death of the Choti Begum was an evil stroke of fate. But now, Fate has struck again. His Highness is in great distress."

Robert had never attended any of the royal ladies of the princely families. The two lady doctors at the mission hospital undertook that duty. Normally, if Robert received a call to one of the Zenanas he merely sent a message to either Doctor Helen Vibert or Doctor Doris Fuller. Those ladies dealt with a variety of emergencies, with experience and skill. But this call from Sadik Khan was different. The fact that he had said the Zurah Begum would see no one else, and that one of the women of his Zenana would act as a nurse, was a plea for privacy.

Robert said at once, "I will come," then turning to Sakhi Mohammed he said, "I shall need my bag – will you come back to the house with me and tell me exactly what I shall need?"

This was merely another way of asking for information about what was happening in the Chikor palace. Sakhi Mohammed, as a household servant, could be asked questions that could not be asked of a member of the ruler's guard. As soon as they were out of earshot, Sakhi Mohammed did not wait to be questioned.

"Zurah Begum is sick. We know Sahib, thou and I, that there has been no plague to infect her – but she is in truth, very ill. It seems that her mind has been badly affected, and she is convinced that she is being punished, that she is in

221

the very hand of death. She called the ruler to her bedside
to hear the truth."

"The truth? You tell me that the Begum has told all, that
she has confessed that she had one girl beaten almost to death,
that she announced the death of the Choti Begum and held a
false funeral?"

"Yes. She has told all that, and also more."

But Robert could only think of one thing – Zeena's
safety, that was all that mattered. "Sakhi Mohammed, are
they searching again for the Choti Begum? We must go at
once to warn Atlar Khan."

"Wait, Sahib. Listen to me. The old Begum has poured out
all her sins and has gained no relief to ease her way into death.
The ruler does not believe a word – or so it appears. Perhaps
he does not want to believe. He says that Zurah Begum's brain
is turned by her sickness and that she is babbling in delirium
before she dies. The ruler himself is destroyed by grief. He
has been twice to the Pila Ghar to visit the supposed grave of
his daughter. He has ordered builders and two architects to
come and build a tomb above her grave – it does not matter
what Zurah Begum whispers to him in her distress. He does
not believe her."

"For God's sake! Is he *mad*?"

Sakhi Mohammed shrugged. "Indeed Sahib, you may well
ask in the name of God. Is the ruler's mind destroyed? Who
can say?"

While Robert stared at him in dismay, Sakhi Mohammed
shouted to a syce to fetch his horse who was standing
outside the stables staring at them. As the man ran to
obey him, Sakhi Mohammed walked into the house calling
to Sheffi to bring the Sahib's *jado* bag – the wonderful bag of

instruments and drugs that Robert used in his work. A magic bag to all.

Holding the bag in one hand Sakhi Mohammed mounted his horse. The two men rode down the drive and Robert made up his mind where to go.

"We will go first to the Pakodi Ghar. We will go from there with Atlar Khan." He admitted to himself that events had got away from him. He could not imagine what he was going to find when he reached the Chikor palace, and felt that he must have the help of Atlar Khan who was, after all, the husband of this unfortunate woman, Zurah Begum. He wished that he could have stopped to call in one of the lady doctors, as he had never met Zurah, but Sadik Khan had made it clear that he only wanted Robert.

As they rode up to the Gate of the North – the first time Robert had seen it since he had come to India and had decided to spend his life there – Robert felt himself a stranger and, riding under the arch of the great gate, he was suddenly very conscious that he had crossed a line. He had left British India behind. Here was the free India, an India under the rule of the native states. The laws of Great Britain lay very lightly on the men who ruled here. He wondered if the white men who lived in such pomp in Delhi realised how little they mattered here. But he was being disloyal – this was his government that he was criticising. Or was he seeing things as his Indian friends must see them? He, who lived in an out-station, thought he knew so much about India because he had troubled himself to learn the language properly, and make many Indian friends. He was welcomed in many Indian houses and also by the native princes, but now he felt that he knew very little, that he had been living all these years on the edge of knowledge, without really learning anything. How could the government of India have allowed Tariq Khan to continue as a ruler – with his reputation? Or had no rumours of his behaviour reached Delhi? What was it he had heard some of his Indian friends saying: "Delhi is a far cry."

He was still deep in thought when they reached the gates of the Pakodi Ghar, and spotted Atlar Khan with a retinue waiting at the gate. Atlar Khan was accompanied by Alan Lyall and, also, Rabindra. Alan no longer dressed as a Punjabi princeling, but wore his own clothes.

"I must thank you for your kind assistance last night." Alan thanked the doctor who, not long before, had made his blood boil. "I believe you held Tariq and his men back from us, and we left in safety – it was a brilliant performance on your part."

Robert wondered what Rabindra had said, and was embarrassed by Alan's genuine gratitude. "I do not think I did anything except pour alcohol down their throats and attempt to be sure none of them left the hall – it was nothing, really."

Atlar Khan added to Alan's words of appreciation. "My dear Robert, you are too modest, and the results of your plan have worked out so well. You may not have heard all this, but when the Choti Begum was seen riding with you, surrounded by some of Sadik Khan's best men, Tariq Khan left Madore. Once my niece was seen going into your grounds, Tariq became afraid of what Sadik Khan might have discovered about his behaviour at the House of pomegranates. Tariq was seen leaving the city early this morning."

Robert, with memories of the previous night fresh in his mind, was confused. Zeena riding with him? "I do not understand – what plan is this that you speak of?"

"All you British are the same – always modest about your successes," said Atlar Khan, with a friendly yet mocking smile. "I speak of the plan to dress a girl in Zeena's *burkah* and ride into your grounds with her! My dear Robert, Tariq did follow you, of course. We knew he would. But he would not have dared to send his men into your house to take Zeena, thus invading British territory! Rumours about his conduct have already started on their way to Delhi – Tariq's seat on the throne of Sagpurna is far from secure, as it is, with a Hindu majority in his state clamouring for his removal. You did brilliantly, thinking the plan out so quickly, and Mohini acted her part very well. She will be suitably rewarded."

A plot? A plan? Mohini acting her part? Robert thought of the hours he had spent in the arms of this sensuous dancing girl. Had she been party to this plot, was that all it had meant to her – acting her part well for a reward? His pain was acute. The new way of life he had envisaged was nothing more than part of a plan, thought up by Rabindra – it could be no one else. Pain turned to anger. He felt he had been used in a way that was devious and cruel.

He turned his head to look at Rabindra, his old friend. "Well, it may have been a clever plot. I did not devise it – and in any case it is pointless now. I understand that Zurah Begum has told Sadik Khan the truth – so the way is open for Zeena to return home in safety, and you Captain Lyall will be able to pay court to the Choti Begum with her father's permission. After all Sadik Khan will have heard about Tariq Khan, he cannot accept him as a suitable son-in-law."

His words fell into an extraordinary silence – Rabindra was slowly shaking his head, and Atlar Khan seemed to be looking at him with pity. He waited for someone to speak. But it was

Alan who spoke. "Is this true? Does Sadik Khan know the truth now? Why then are we waiting – I will go at once and speak with him."

Atlar Khan sighed and said heavily, "Things are not always what they seem. Colonel Maclaren has not been told everything, I believe."

Robert heard Sakhi Mohammed make a sudden movement and turned to look at him. The old man met his eyes and gave a slight shake of his head and, Robert, who had been going to repeat all that he had been told, knew that he was being asked to be quiet.

"Robert, my wife is very ill." Atlar Khan voiced his concern. "Before we speak any more of these matters, I think we must answer Sadik Khan's call. We can speak on the way.

"Alan, it is better that you stay here. There is, I assure you, no sense in your attempting to speak with Sadik Khan at present. He is overcome with anxieties, and grief."

"But Atlar Khan – we know that we can at least lift his grief from him, tell him that Zeena is alive and well, and here, in safety at your palace. I am sure that on hearing this joyous news, he will listen to me, and accept my offer to marry Zeena."

Atlar Khan who had turned away, gathering his reins and preparing to mount, said briefly, "You do not understand how things are, Alan. You stay here. We will talk later about our plan for you to go up to Faridkote with the two girls. Leave us now, we must go."

Alan Lyall was not known to his brother officers as a man of wild passions, or of quick temper. He was reckoned to be a quiet man, patient of nature, a man of cool courage and discipline, a man who had command over all his feelings.

This was how everyone had thought of him. But that was before he had met Zeena.

His feelings for Zeena had transformed his nature. His love for her was all-consuming, and he had waited long enough.

Atlar Khan's careless speech had been the final spark to light his impatience. He was furious with himself for having listened to Rabindra's advice: "Wait, Sahib, be patient – everything will come right." It seemed to Alan that he was doing nothing but waiting. Now, standing on the outskirts of this group of men and being told to wait once more, his temper snapped.

Atlar Khan had just mounted, saying, "Let us go – we can decide on how Zeena travels later," when Alan lost control, lost his good manners and, stepping forward, took hold of the bridle of Atlar Khan's animal and halted it.

"*I* will decide how my future wife and I will travel. I am coming with you, and I am going to speak with Sadik Khan. I shall tell him the truth, and ask him for his permission to marry Zeena. Hiding everything is ridiculous and is not necessary any longer." He looked up into Atlar Khan's astounded face and spoke directly to him.

"Your Highness, you heard what your brother said to me on the day of the first tiger hunt. He told me then that I was a member of his family, that my name would never be forgotten. I will come with you and remind him of what he said then, he will, I am sure, welcome me, and give me a fair hearing."

His faultless Urdu, his carriage and the mounting passion in his voice, surprised all the men who heard him.

Atlar Khan, looking down at Alan considered this. *He*

227

could indeed be a member of our family. He is one of us in every way – except in blood and in understanding. He has no idea how our past is built into us, immutable. Our habits and our customs come down to us from the dawn of our race – will he ever learn this? If not, he and Zeena will have a hard life. Unless their love is strong and enduring.

"Love conquers all," said a voice that sounded like the ring of a crystal goblet flicked by a finger. Had he heard it, or was his imagination stirred by the romance of Alan's burning love for Zeena? Aloud he said, smiling, "Lalla and Majnun – a love story indeed. Of course you can come with us my dear Alan, if it seems so important to you. But I must ask you to hold back from speaking with Sadik Khan until we have heard what he has to say to us – and have had the doctor's opinion on my wife's condition."

A wave of shame washed away all Alan's rage. He had completely forgotten that Zurah Begum, who had become a nightmare figure in his mind, was the wife of this kindly, understanding man who had already helped him and Zeena. He bowed his head. "I am ashamed before you all. Please forgive my ill manners – I will of course wait until you tell me that I may speak."

A syce was already bringing up one of Atlar Khan's horses, and presently the cavalcade set off. Atlar Khan and Robert rode ahead of the others. Rabindra rode beside Alan, and after a few minutes Alan heard him say, "Sahib. I would ask you to listen to me. There are some things that you should be told before you speak with Sadik Khan. May I speak?"

"Of course you may, Rabindra-ji, but please do not tell me to be patient."

"No. I will not, though patience is something that is needed.

"Now let me explain something to you. Sadik Khan has been told that his daughter lives. The Begum Zurah is ill in her mind and in her body, but her fear of death has driven her to tell the truth of all her actions of the last weeks. Sadik Khan has listened to her, has put right most of the wrongs she has committed in his household. He has expressed the wish that the unfortunate maid Chunia be brought back and re-instated in his Zenana because of the love that his daughter bore for her – his beloved *dead* daughter, Sahib."

Alan looked at Rabindra, astonished. "But you have just said that Sadik Khan knows that his daughter is alive – Zurah Begum has told him."

"Yes. She has told him but he will not believe her. He says that the shock of Zeena Begum's death has twisted Zurah's logic. Sahib, he prefers to think that his daughter is dead than that she ran away from his house to avoid the marriage he arranged for her."

"I cannot believe this. He must know what kind of man Tariq Khan is."

"Tariq Khan was the accepted suitor. A fellow ruler, a man of wealth and importance. And the marriage contract was signed in front of the necessary witnesses. If it became known that Zeena Begum ran away, that the contract was broken – wah! How Sadik Khan would be humiliated! This is so, Sahib. I tell you. As far as Sadik is concerned his daughter is dead – gone from his palaces forever. Have a care Sahib, think deeply over what I have said before you speak with the ruler."

While Alan was still trying to accept and believe what Rabindra had said, the big gates of the Chikor Mahal rose in front of them, and Atlar Khan was waiting there with

Sakhi Mohammed and the others of the retinue. Alan saw Atlar Khan and Rabindra exchange glances, then Atlar Khan nodded as if relieved and said, "Very well, let us go in." The gates swung wide as he spoke. The two British men rode close behind the others, almost as if they were banding together to be strong against what awaited them.

"I cannot believe what I have been told – Sadik Khan does not wish to know that his daughter lives." Alan turned to Robert.

The doctor's reply gave him no help. "I am beginning to find it very difficult to understand. I can believe this because I trust Rabindra – but I cannot understand anything of these customs any more."

They reached the steps of the veranda, dismounted and walked up through the arched door into the reception room where Sadik Khan awaited them, his senior ministers seated round his gilded chair.

Within two hours, the visit to the Chikor Mahal was over. Alan had achieved his short interview with Sadik Khan, his friend – the man whose life he had saved at some risk to his own.

Sadik Khan had looked at Alan so strangely – so coldly, that Alan felt that the ruler had no idea who he was at all. Rabindra, standing beside Sadik Khan had prompted him gently, "The Angreze Captain, the man you took on the tiger shoot."

At once Sadik Khan had held out his hand, "Of course, Alan Lyall, you must forgive me, of course I could never forget you and your gallant action. But now I am in such deep grief that I find it in my heart to wish that you had left me to the tiger's mercy. My daughter, you understand, my only child is dead. I shall never see her again, she has gone into the shadows. How can I bear this loss. First her mother, my beautiful Yasmin, and now my child, the gift her dying mother left to me. Alas, alas, let my life end too."

He had turned away from Alan, his shoulders shaking. Alan was in a state of utter disbelief. The man was acting. Alan was sure of it – there was no sorrow in those eyes, only a burning anger. He could think of nothing to say. He bowed his head and stepped back. "It is finished, Sahib." Rabindra said quietly. "Better you go." But as Alan backed towards the door Sadik Khan spoke with a sense of great urgency.

"No, I owe the Sahib my life, I must say farewell to you, Alan, and I hope that when you return after your leave, you will come and see me. Then I will be able to show you the tomb that will have been raised above my treasures – my wife and my daughter will lie beneath a tomb that will reflect their beauty and virtue, and I shall lie with them when my time comes. Now, Alan, you are at liberty to go. Go in peace – Ma as Salam, until we meet again."

Such words of peace and friendship, said by a man whose eyes blazed with hatred. Looking into those eyes, Alan knew that he would never see Sadik Khan again. He was glad to reach the door and walk out into the clear air of the autumn day. Shortly after that, the horses were brought round and Robert emerged from the Zenana with Atlar Khan. They rode off together, and only Rabindra stayed in the palace.

As they rode, Alan and Robert dropped behind, allowing Atlar Khan to ride alone, out of respect for a man whose wife was dying – or was she? Dying in that palace of lies, thought Alan, who questioned Robert by whispering, "Is Zurah Begum dying?"

Robert shrugged. "I honestly don't know. I could not discover what was wrong with her – the only symptoms she shows are extreme emaciation and fear. I think she has convinced herself that she is dying, and frankly, she may very well talk herself into death. She went in and out of consciousness in a strange way – almost as if she was trying to escape from life. She said very little – little that I could understand. She spoke the word 'futwa' which is not a word I know, and she told her husband that she had to go. He said nothing to her of comfort. All he said to her was this: "Your daughter lives and carries her child. Your conscience need not carry her." Then he stood back and neither of them spoke again. I will not go to her again, one of the lady doctors must go."

When they reached the Pagodi Ghar, Robert took his leave, explaining that he had work to do. In fact, he had decided to go home, to see the beauty Mohini. He did not feel that he could go through the day without discovering whether or not she had been part of a plot to aid Zeena's escape. Surely her lovemaking had not been a sham. He had to find out. If she had been acting a part he would hand in his resignation and leave India, a country that he had come to care for.

Alan, walking in to the reception area, found Atlar Khan there, talking to a veiled girl. Alan's heart leapt, but as if he had guessed what Alan was hoping for, Atlar Khan said quickly, "Come in, my brother – I am arranging Gulrukh's journey to Faridkote, where her husband is waiting to take her home."

Alan was about to leave them, but Atlar Khan stopped him. "No, Alan, do not go. You are my brother, and this concerns you too. I think it would be good if you and Zeena

Begum travelled with Gulrukh. The mail train to Karachi goes through Faridkote. You could take the train from there – and it would be good for Gulrukh to be escorted by you. It would relieve me. I am unable to travel with her, as I must stay here until her mother recovers – or until we know how things are. If you go with Gulrukh, I will have no anxieties."

He looked at Alan, obviously expecting him to agree at once. But Alan had his own concerns. So far, he had not seen Zeena since he had carried her into her room in the early hours of the morning. He needed to see her, to be sure that this plan would be to her liking – there was Chunia to think of and, he did not believe that Zeena would leave her maid until she knew exactly what was going to happen to her. Surely he would not be kept from Zeena by the rules of the Zenana. Not now.

But when he said that he would like to talk to Zeena before agreeing to any journey, Gulrukh began to argue at once. "She is still sleeping, and I do not care to wake her. She was so tired. Colonel Robert Sahib said that she had barely slept for three days – I think perhaps it will be better if we allow her to stir in her own time, and then I can tell her what we are going to do, help her to dress, and the packing can be done by Sushi, and then—"

Atlar Khan who had been listening to his daughter, and watching Alan's expressions, half smiling to himself, said, "Gulrukh, you are leaving soon after dawn. I think your new uncle wishes to see his bride, which in these circumstances is quite permissible. Tell Sushi to wake Zeena Begum – you may go and tell her that Alan wishes to see her, but do not delay her dressing. You will have time on the journey for all the talking you will wish to do. You have little time – go, Gulrukh."

233

There had been a snap in his voice, and Gulrukh did not stay to argue. She hurried away, and Alan sighed with relief. "Thank you, I was afraid it would be forbidden – I am grateful to you."

"Indeed it would have been forbidden," Atlar Khan explained. "Usually you would not have seen her face until you raised her veil after the ceremony. But this marriage is different. What ceremony will there be? Will she become your wife by Christian rites? Must she give up her religion?"

Alan was forced to admit that he did not know. "It will be as she wishes – if it is necessary then I will become a Moslem."

This is the madness of passion, thought Atlar Khan.

"I think you must talk with someone who knows these things when you reach England. But I think there are no mosques or moulvis in your country of Scotland."

"Then, if she wishes to be married by the rites of Islam, I will delay our departure from Karachi – or perhaps we could be married by the captain of the ship." Alan had not thought of any of this, and was growing irked by what appeared to be more impediments to his marriage.

Atlar Khan sensed Alan's growing impatience. "Be calm, Alan. If only there was more time I would arrange your marriage here. But for you, time is important. To be truthful – Alan, I do not want you to be here much longer. Sadik Khan I guarantee – will know everything about the love between you and his daughter. Make no mistake about that. He knows that it was not only fear of marriage to Tariq Khan that sent Zeena running from his household – it was also love for you. He is a man of strong passions, possessive and jealous. Do not forget, he is of the same blood as my wife Zurah Begum, and it was her jealousy that sent her mad and ruined our marriage. Sadik Khan's pretence of mourning for his daughter is to save his face – but also to hide his burning jealousy of the man who has won her love. I am afraid that this jealousy may drive him to take vengence on you both. I want you on your way as soon as possible – which is dawn tomorrow.

"I will make sure you have time to speak to Zeena. The half hour I gave my daughter is up. Let us go and separate those two – take my niece into the garden, and I will keep Gulrukh with me. They can talk on the journey, but now you need time with Zeena. I understand that. Come."

Zeena had slept undisturbed throughout the day. She woke when the sky was golden with sunset, and the garden was full of sounds of birds settling for the night. It was a happy awakening. The last thing she had heard was Alan whispering words of love to her in the darkness of the carriage. She could still feel his arms around her. All the doubts and shadows that had surrounded her over the last few days seemed to have blown away, and her mind was clear and happy. Alan had promised her that his home was hers, that he would be with her, would love her forever.

Atlar Khan led Alan out into the garden, and pointed to the shuttered windows of the Zenana. "Your lady is in there. I am going to interrupt their endless chatter. When she comes, she will come out by this door here – so be patient, Alan, I will send her out to you as speedily as I can."

Walking back into the house, Atlar Khan felt envious of the ardent joy he saw on Alan's face. The joy of a man waiting for his love. There had been nothing like that in his marriage. An arranged marriage, entered into to please his mother. He had not wished to be married. As a young man he knew that

Zurah Begum had fallen in love with him. He remembered
walking through the palace so long ago. He saw Zurah as
she had been in the first days of their marriage – a young
girl, slender and lovely, her beautiful eyes fixed adoringly on
him. Those eyes had never looked away from him, but she
had smothered him with a burning love which had slowly
changed into a possessive passion. He blamed himself. He
had never given her the love she looked for. He had been too
set in his ways, too used to his freedom to bother to learn to
love a child – for that was all she had been. So young.

He had married her to get an heir. Once his two children
were born he had seldom visited her bed. She had grown, in
her search for love, so jealous and possessive that no one
could love her – and now she was dying, unlamented by her
family. Perhaps she was already dead?

For a minute, as he stood before the Zenana doors, he
seemed to see a little, slender figure vanishing ahead of him,
her eyes still turned accusingly towards him. He blinked and
shook his head, and the vision vanished. There was no one
but Sakhi Mohammed waiting to speak to him. "Highness, I
regret there is news from the Chikor Mahal. Rabindra-ji waits
for you in the receiving room."

Atlar Khan found Rabindra standing before the window in
the Gul Kamra, looking out into the evening shadows of the
garden. Atlar Khan did not wait for Rabindra to speak. He
said at once, "Zurah Begum is dead?"

"Yes. I regret to bring you such news, Nawab Sahib. She
died at sunset. His Highness Sadik Khan asks if you and
the Begum of Panchghar will come for the prayers before
the body is carried to the place of her burial. The imam is
already in the Chikor Mahal."

No mention of the Choti Begum – Sadik was going to keep the secret of Zeena's death to the bitter end, Atlar Khan realised. All the better for her chances of getting away safely. Give Sadik another day or two, and he might plot his vengeance. Atlar Khan met Rabindra's eyes. "I will come, but I will not bring my daughter, who has been much disturbed by the evil infection that hangs about the walls of the Chikor Mahal."

Rabindra said quietly, "There is no infection, lord. The Begum died."

Atlar Khan looked at him keenly. *What now*, he wondered, *murder?* Revenge could come to Zurah Begum from many quarters, old scores being settled. He sighed and said. "What are you telling me? My wife was poisoned?"

"Nay, Huzoor. The Begum looked for forgiveness and acceptance of a sin. She received neither. Sadik would not accept her confession – and so she died. It is as well that she died thus. It could have been the knife, or the strangler's *rumal*. She had many enemies."

There was nothing Atlar Khan could say to this cruel truth. To pretend he was grief stricken would be foolish, but still he felt the weight of his own neglect, sorrow for the things that might have been. Rabindra began to take his leave, and Atlar Khan told him to wait. "I am ready to come now – but I must tell my daughter first."

He found Gulrukh scolding Sushi for allowing Zeena to go to Alan in the garden, and she began to tell her father a long tarradiddle, but broke off when he told her his news.

He had not expected his daughter to insist on going with him. Without a word, she wrapped herself in a *burkah* and told

Sushi to come with her. Atlar Khan protested, but Gulrukh would not listen.

"Of course I must come! She is my mother, and I can remember how much I loved her – and she loved me before this madness seized her."

Gulrukh was right. Of course she had to make an appearance for the sake of the family. Atlar Khan heard the jingle and clatter of a carriage outside the Zenana doors. Rabindra must have ordered it up, knowing what Gulrukh would do. How could he know? Not for the first time had Atlar Khan felt the hair on his neck prickle when he thought of Rabindra's omniscience. He led the way out to the carriage and helped Gulrukh to clamber in with Sushi's help. His horse was there. He mounted and followed the carriage down the darkening road to where the long prayers and farewells for the senior Begum of two states were about to begin. A long farewell.

He turned his mind from thinking of what awaited him, and instead he imagined Alan and Zeena alone at last in the garden.

Robert rode back to his house alone, with some very unpleasant thoughts to keep him company. The worry that concerned him most was not the sick old woman he had left in the Chikor Mahal. He was unable, for the first time in his professional life, to give his thoughts to one of his patients. The memory of Atlar Khan's words, "Mohini acted her part very well," was all he could think about.

The house was quiet as he rode up the drive. No one came out to welcome him – of course, at this time, Sheffi would be praying in the mosque as he did every Friday. But if all was as it had seemed to be during the magical hours he had spent with Mohini, *surely* she would have come to see why he had returned at this unusual time?

Perhaps she had already returned to the House of Pomegranates – her duty done, she did not have to stay. There would no doubt be other duties waiting for her in the House of Many Pleasures. He had been a fool to dream about a new life based on what was only a few hours paid work for her.

He dismounted and shouted for his syce to come and take his horse. The syce came running, full of apologies. "I did not expect the Sahib at this time – I was grooming the horse of the one in the *bibighar*, Mohini ben."

Robert's heart seemed to stop for a second and then raced ahead. "The horse is still here?"

The syce looked surprised and a little confused. "Indeed it is still here, Sahib. Should it be gone? Did I do wrong? I was not told to take the horse out – Mohini ben did not give me any orders. Sheffi said that she would not ride with you today."

"She is still here?" asked Robert, who was striding down to the *bibighar* before the syce had finished saying that Mohini was still in there.

As Robert stepped onto the veranda, the reed curtain over the door was pulled aside and an old woman looked out at him. He had never seen her before. The old woman looked startled, but did not move from the door.

"She is within, Garib Parwar. She did not expect you, she is not dressed to receive you."

Robert pushed past her without ceremony. His thoughts were full of suspicion. Who could say what he was going to find. A girl who played her part well – what might she be doing? For one mad moment he imagined her entertaining

239

Sheffi in his absence. He strode to the back of the house, and pushed open the first closed door he came to, the old woman pursuing him, said, "Sahib, Sahib, wait, she is bathing," but Robert did not hear her. He was looking at Mohini, scantily wrapped in a towel, her long hair dripping over her shoulders.

"My *lord*! I did not know you would come at this time. Please give me a few minutes, I will dress, my woman will make lemon tea for you."

She had made no flurried ungraceful movements to cover herself, her smile was full of pleasure. She was already scooping up her wet hair, as the old woman stood back from the door. Robert could think of nothing to say. He could not look away from the sight of Mohini in beautiful disorder, totally unashamed. She was more beautiful like this than anything he had ever imagined. In that moment he realised that it did not matter if she had only been obeying orders when she made love with him. She had called him lord, she had smiled with warmth, and was glad to see him. All he wanted was for her to be as she was, here with him, for as long as she would stay. He ignored the old woman. He would discover who she was later – meantime, he pulled the door shut again, and stretching out his hand took Mohini's rounded wet arm and led her into the bedroom.

"To dress now would be a great waste of time," he said firmly, and heard Mohini's soft laughter as he took her into his arms. Sight and hearing were all lost in the delights of touch and sensual discoveries, in the country of passion.

Nineteen

On the other side of the city, through the Gate of the North, the Pakodi Ghar stood sheltered behind its high walls and thickly growing trees.

In the scented garden Alan waited alone. Light spilled out from shuttered windows, although it was not yet dark. The first stars were beginning to show, pale in a sky still streaked with the scarlet and gold of the sunset. He saw, through a belt of trees, that there was a small building shining white amongst the stand of thick, dark-leaved mango trees. He could no longer bear to wait. He decided to walk to the white building and see what it was – it might be a place where he could bring Zeena so that they could talk together in peace.

The building turned out to be a small marble pavilion, half in ruins, perhaps built by one of the Mogul emperors. There was a sprawling bush of white jasmine growing close against one side, the white starry flowers spilling their blossoms on the cracked marble tiles. Their scent, always strong at night, filled the air around the slender pillars that still supported the domed roof. A perfect place to bring her – they could talk here, hidden from everyone.

There was a marble bench, quite unspoiled. He imagined

Zeena lying on it – he did not want to talk. He wanted to kiss her until she answered his kisses with her own. He wanted to make love to her at last, and discover her true feelings for him. Would she really be prepared to leave her way of life and come half across the world with him? Did she know anything about love, a man's love for his woman, or was she still imagining that love was what they had shared together so far – speaking glances, short, hurried embraces, words and sighs? He really had no idea of her feelings. He was sure – burningly sure of his own. He would discover Zeena's feelings this evening. There had already been so many impediments in their path that he wondered if she could have changed towards him. If she had – he felt as if a dark abyss of loneliness had opened before him at the very thought. Oh where was Zeena now, what was she doing behind those shuttered windows? It seemed to him that she was always hidden from him, either behind walls, or behind veils.

It was growing dark – he could bear this waiting no longer. He would go and find her now, break into the Zenana if he had to, and bring her out. He turned to leave the pavilion and saw her coming towards him across the lawn, hurrying, her silks blowing about her, a veil across her face.

While Alan had been impatiently waiting, Zeena, behind the shutters that annoyed him so, had been clutching at her own patience, while Sushi and Gulrukh had been starting the long involved business of bathing and dressing, as Gulrukh felt she should be dressed to go out and meet her future lord. Gulrukh was spinning it out as long as she could, longing to tell her side of the days that had passed, and longing to hear Zeena's story. Sushi did her best to hurry. Now at last, the bath, hair washing and drying, combing and arranging was over. Jewelled chains were twisted into the thick, shining coils of Zeena's hair. Earrings were chosen, discarded, and chosen again. Zeena stood naked before the mirrored walls of the dressing room, entirely surrounded by discarded chiffons and silks, brocaded coats, and jewellery boxes spilling their precious contents on the floor at her feet. Gulrukh had found nothing that she thought suitable.

"Oh, Gulrukh, please just dress me in anything and let me go. You said your father had only allowed me half an hour to dress. Alan is waiting outside, I know, and I think an hour has passed already."

Zeena's pleading was ignored. Gulrukh was determined. "He must see you at your best, let him wait – they will call us, do not be so worried. You think he will not wait? Eh, what shame to run after a man who will not wait! Of course he must wait. Now, Sushi, where are the sticks of colour for the eyes? Give them to me. Zeena, hold your breath and keep steady while I outline your eyes. There – you are a moon of beauty, he will see you for the first time as you should look and he will die of desire. Sushi, give me the red *sari* with the gold border."

"I cannot," said Sushi, almost as impatient as Zeena herself, "that *sari* is locked in a cupboard in your dressing room, Gulrukh Begum. You know that."

It seemed to Zeena that Alan was more likely to die of impatience, than desire, after waiting out in the garden for a bride who did not come. She sent Sushi a pleading look, and Sushi said, "Gulrukh Begum, if you wish to dress her in the red *sari*, what of the emeralds and pearls I have dressed her hair with?"

"Tst, of course they are wrong, stupid girl. Take them out

at once while I go and get the rubies and the red *sari*. It must be red for a bride, for luck."

Gulrukh whisked out of the room just as Sushi, with an adroit kick, pushed the red *sari* further under the bed, snatched up an embroidered grey silk robe and veil and helped Zeena put it on. "A moon of beauty, indeed, Khanum. Now go in joy – be quick, my mistress is coming."

Indeed, Zeena could hear the clack of Gulrukh's heeled slippers along the passage. She opened the unguarded garden door, and ran out barefoot.

The grass was soft under her feet. The evening was soft with the autumn's fading warmth. She stood for a moment to look about her. There was no sign of Alan. Across the lawn she could see the little pavilion glimmering in the last of the light. She was sure that Alan would have gone there to wait – if he had waited at all. Well, if he had not waited, she was afraid that it meant that his love was cooling – and who would wonder at that? He was an Angreze, and Englishman – and they were not known for patience. But was he truly English? Did he not come from the far north of that distant unknown island. Perhaps the northerners were different. If not, and he had not waited, what was left for her? The shadows of uncertainty came back to cloud over the happiness she had felt. She half turned to go back into the palace, then heard Gulrukh's angry voice speaking to Sushi. No. She could not face another hour of dressing and being ornamented, and perhaps no reason for it all in the end. She turned back and ran across the lawn, where Alan stood waiting for her. He watched her come, remembering their first early morning meeting, when it had seemed to him that she was a being from another world, coming towards him blown on some planetary wind. Now again, it seemed that she was unearthly. Silver and misty clouds surrounded her, the moon was her home. Had he really imagined her lying on the marble bench in the pavilion? He was afraid to touch her. He stood in silence and watched her drift over the grass towards him.

Zeena was so pleased to see him that for a minute she could not speak. He *had* waited – therefore he did love her. When they did finally find words they both spoke at the same time.

Zeena said, "I thought that you grew impatient and did not wait for me—"

Alan said, "I thought you were not coming – I was coming to break in the doors of the Zenana and bring you out." Then the sense of what she was saying came to him. "Of course I waited – but I was afraid that they would not let you come. Oh Zeena, you are still veiled? Do I have to wait for some ceremony before I can see you unveiled?" She looked up at him, thinking of how her marriage ceremony would have been, the gold and the glitter, the watching eyes of countless distant relatives – and felt no regrets.

"The bridegroom must lift the veil, to see his wife clearly for the first time."

Alan waited, unsure of her meaning. The rising breeze that came with sunset stirred the folds of the veil, lifted it a little, and he thought he saw her smile. He put out his hand and raised the veil and bent to kiss her. She said something which he did not hear. He heard her the second time, or thought he did, but could not be sure. "What did you say?"

There was a thread of laughter running through her words. "I said that the bride was very often in bed for the lifting of the veil."

Katharine Gordon

The sound of soft laughter, of a man's rejoicing voice –
these things had been heard in the little pavilion before – and
the silence of delight that followed. Then only the evening
breeze whispered, while the moon rose and turned the garden
to silver, unremarked by anyone.